NOTHING
BUT
SKY

NOTHING
BUT
SKY

AMY TRUEBLOOD

Mendota Heights, Minnesota

First Edition
First Printing, 2018

Book design by Jake Nordby
Cover design by Jake Nordby
Cover images by Nadya Korobkova/Shutterstock; Alhovik/Shutterstock; Gorbash Varvara/Shutterstock

Flux, an imprint of North Star Editions, Inc.

Library of Congress Cataloging-in-Publication Data (Pending)
978-1-63583-016-3

Flux
North Star Editions, Inc.
2297 Waters Drive
Mendota Heights, MN 55120
www.fluxnow.com

Printed in the United States of America

For David, Olivia, and Ryan
My heart. My soul. My everything.

And for little girls everywhere . . . no matter what
people say, never be afraid to chase your dreams.

"You can do anything you decide to do. You can act to change and control your life; and the procedure, the process is its own reward."—Amelia Earhart

1
The Rough Hands of Gravity

Lincoln, Nebraska
July 9, 1922
65 days until World Aviation Expo

Blue sky, perfect day to fly.

Uncle Warren's favorite phrase ran through my head as I trudged behind Daniel across the field. His thick wall of a body parted the growing crowd like a sharp wind bent back trees. With a brown fedora clutched between his calloused fingers, he collected our fee. His voice boomed across the acres of wide-open farmland: "Twenty-five cents to watch the best flying circus in all the Midwest!"

He shouldered through the bustling crowd of dapper-dressed men and ladies decked out in their church finery. Silver and copper coins plinked across the wide brim of the hat before sliding down inside the crown. I picked up my pace, trying to keep up with his long strides. The pointed stares and gasps of surprise when people recognized me were all part of the routine now.

When Daniel finally came to a stop at the edge of the old farm road, I peered around his tree-trunk arms and into the hat. Five, maybe six dollars in change. As Sundays went, it wasn't a bad take for a show where I could fall to my death at any moment.

Once the coins were firmly settled in Daniel's pockets, the slight *clink* of change filling the air as we walked, he nodded to the line of spectators gathered near a long row of fence ten feet away.

Their bodies were pressed together in a tight huddle. Their heads tilted towards a cloudless afternoon sky. I should have been down the road waiting at my mark, but I loved the chaos of the growing crowd and their lively shouts.

"Looks like folks are itchin' for a show, Grace. You sure about this trick? Road looks mighty rough. I count at least five potholes from here."

He shaded his dark brown eyes from the sun. Worry lines pinched around his mouth as he surveyed the long stretch of dirt that ran alongside Farmer Grant's property. Nothing but dust, cows, and green Nebraska farmland as far as the eye could see. The air tinged with the familiar scent of manure. The countryside awash in yellow as late-blooming black-eyed susans sprang up in haphazard patches along a mile of battered wood fence.

"It's fine," I swatted away his worries like the flies buzzing near my head. "This is the only stretch of property where the roadster can pick up enough speed." I stood on my toes to pat his wide shoulder in reassurance. "It's time to dazzle the hometown crowd before we take it to other cities."

Daniel's eyes narrowed into that look that warned he was worried, but smart enough not to say any more. "You listen to Nathan and don't fool around. You know how he can be about these new tricks."

"I can't listen to his griping about angles and wind speed for another minute. We've been practicing this for six weeks. It's time to put it to work."

A few young boys in corduroy knickers and newsboy caps raced past us. Once they reached the fence, they elbowed their way to the front.

"Don't go gettin' too big for your britches. None of these folks expect anything but you shuffling across the wings of that plane. You'd do well to remember that." He turned on his heel, and headed back in the direction of the hangar.

Daniel could choose to be a black cloud on an otherwise sunny day, but I wanted to revel in being back home in Lincoln. Traveling all over Oklahoma and Texas these last weeks had turned tiresome. While our earnings from shows in Stillwater and Amarillo kept our heads above water, it was nice to sleep in my soft bed rather than roll around on hard-packed ground with nothing but a raggedy, old patchwork quilt for comfort.

With Daniel gone, I skirted around the crowd now scattering onto the road. Children sat atop their father's shoulders, the late afternoon sun melting the ice cream in their hands. Red-cheeked ladies adjusted wide-brimmed hats and fanned themselves, praying for any kind of breeze.

Stepping over discarded handbills that touted, "The Soaring Eagles: Nebraska's Greatest Flying Circus," I found an open path and raced down the dirt, dodging cow patties and those ankle-deep potholes Daniel had spied. When I reached my mark at the end of the fence, I closed my eyes and waited for a familiar buzz to fill the air. A moment later a low rumble shook the ground. I opened my eyes and a scarlet-red biplane soared overhead, its propeller slicing through the wind. It did a quick barrel roll, the body spinning in a circular motion, before it made a wide turn. Seconds later a roadster broke away from the masses and stopped only inches from where I stood.

"Well, what are you waiting for, Grace? We're burning daylight here." Nathan, our team's second in command, frantically waved me forward.

I dashed toward the car, pulling my goggles over my eyes. With the Model T's top down, the wind would snarl my dark curls in seconds.

Once I settled in the seat, Nathan put the car in gear and sped forward. "This'll be tricky with the wind picking up." He fought to control the car as we raced down the bumpy road. "If you can't reach the ladder on the first pass, don't risk it. I can always bring you around again. When it gets close, you grab that bottom rung with both hands. No funny business, you hear. And if you see any of Rowland's planes, stay put. This is not the time for a mid-air dogfight."

Leave it to him to ruin the moment with one little name.

He glanced over his shoulder, his warning look telling me I better listen. We both knew what was at stake, but unless I promised to be smart, Nathan wouldn't steer the car toward our mark.

"Got it." I pointed to a red scarf tied to the fence a hundred feet away. "Now focus on why we're here. We got money to earn."

The swelling crowd surged toward us to get a closer look. We sped down the road and the weathered wooden fence flew by in a blur. Dairy cows skittered back across the field, spooked by the grinding engine of the old roadster.

"Starting the count," Nathan called.

I stood and pressed my boots against the seat. My feet shifted and rotting, yellow upholstery poked out in several spots. Nathan's arm popped in the air, his black hair flying in the wind. A rooster-tail of dust swirled behind us. Anticipation burned in my chest as his hand splayed open, and his fingers counted down from five.

The roar of the plane's prop echoed behind me as it approached. A loud *whoosh* rattled in my ears. My body shook with the force of the wind. There was no time to think. No time to be afraid. The rope ladder appeared above my head. I waited a beat and anticipated the signal. Nathan's last finger disappeared, and I jumped as the car hit a pothole. Momentum slammed me forward. I grasped the bottom rung with one hand before rocketing into the air. With a collective gasp, the crowd raced toward the road.

Dangling ten feet above the car, I swung about like a marionette with one snapped string. The rope spun in a circle, doing its best to buck me off.

"Let go!" Nathan's wide eyes darted between me and the plane dragging me through the sky.

My slick fingers slid down the rung. The ground below was a churning cloud of dust, reminding me of tornados that swept across the plains. Landing on the hard soil would surely break a leg and most likely both my arms. Not a pretty sight for my home-town crowd.

"Grace, drop now!" Nathan's ragged voice tore through the haze clouding my mind.

Shaking my head, I focused on my only chance: steadying the ladder. I held on and stilled my body, trying to calm the force of the wind. With a deep breath, I closed my eyes and allowed nature to take over. People were counting on me and we needed the extra money this trick would bring.

With the ladder still spinning like a whirlwind, I swung my legs back. My hand slid farther down the rung. The air current pulled me back then shot me forward. I caught the bar just as my other hand slipped away. Hanging by one arm again, I gasped for my last bit of strength. Thick, black exhaust flooded my lungs. I shoved down the fear filling my chest, not wanting to think about what would happen if I couldn't hold on.

The nose of the plane tipped up and jetted me back into the lower rung. My body twisted through the sky, but at least now I was holding on with both hands.

My uncle had warned me about this trick many times.

If you can only grasp the bottom rung, you're in trouble. Your body weight will spin the ladder, and it'll be impossible to climb against the force of the wind. If you don't steady the line, you'll drag for a few moments before your sweaty hands slip from the rung or the power of the wind snaps the tether, sending you to a fast and painful death.

His haunting voice filled my ears. I tuned out his words and let the whistle of the wind calm me. My mind emptied. The air urged my body forward. I was like a lone swing on the playground, and I rocked with the movement. Back and forth. Back and forth, attempting to steady the line. With a final push, my body weight catapulted me up. I swung one leg over the lowest rung. The braided rope of the ladder pressed against my face and started to unravel in my hands.

Martin had two jobs as our mechanic: keep the planes running and the equipment in good condition. Obviously, he'd forgotten about number two, which now might send me plunging to the ground.

Climb, I commanded myself.

Bit by bit the rope came apart in my fingers. My heart jackhammered against my ribcage as I scrambled up the rungs until my feet were firmly on the wing. Tattered pieces of what remained of the ladder scattered in the wind like pollen in late spring.

Oh, Martin and I would definitely have words after I landed.

Once I had a tight hold on the outer strut, a wooden pole supporting the upper and lower wings, I hoisted myself up. Every inch of me pulsed with adrenaline. The rope burns etched into my skin throbbed. I should have been afraid, but I'd never felt more alive.

I moved hand-over-hand past the flying and landing wires, which stretched from the upper wings down across the lower wings in an x-shaped pattern. These mechanisms kept the wings from twisting, especially during difficult mid-air maneuvers. For me, they were a secure way to move across the plane's frame without a bobble.

The wind picked up and pressed against my goggles. Some pilots carried a rabbit's foot or religious talisman for luck, but I had my trusty specs. They'd been a gift from my uncle for my fourteenth birthday. Through downpours and dust storms they'd protected me from the elements, and I refused to perform without them.

The plane banked left and headed back in the direction of the crowd. With a secure grip on an outside flying wire, I blew kisses to the sea of waiting bodies. Each of their heads tilted toward the heavens. Toward me. Their cheers were swallowed by a rush of wind, but the tangle of raised arms and smiling faces told me they were eager for more.

Uncle Warren brought us around again. The fields raced by in a sea of mossy greens and muddy browns. A slow count passed my lips. The oily scent of gas and exhaust flooded my nose. When the wind filled with a sharp twist of warm and cold air, I kicked into a headstand. The top of my aviator cap pressed against the wooden frame, while my feet were secured by two leather straps above me. I held the pose while we buzzed past the masses, making sure the crowd got a good view. The plane leveled off and I eased back down.

We soared through white streaks of mist. Once off the wing and belted into the training seat, I shot a fist in the air, giving the "all clear" signal. We moved into a loop, turning upside down while the sky and ground switched places for one blissful moment. The rough hands of gravity pinned me to the seat. A brief feeling of weightlessness filled me with a comfort I could never find on the ground. My only wish was to be back on the wing with the wind in my face and nothing but sky for company.

The plane's tires bumped along dirt and grass. We raced forward, the tail skid dragging behind us until we slowed down. Once the propeller stopped, I released my seatbelt. Before I could climb out, a meaty hand slammed down over my arm.

"What were you thinking, girlie?" Uncle Warren's thick cheeks tightened into a scowl. "You nearly got us killed."

Over the last six months, I'd pushed my tricks to the edge. Dangled by one leg off the bottom skid. Hung by a single hand while the wind batted at my body—all without a parachute. Every trick had been a success. Our crowds grew at each show, and so did the money lining our pockets, but that didn't stop the lectures. The problem was Uncle Warren still saw me as the skinny thirteen-year old girl who showed up one late fall day with a note claiming he was my last living kin.

He swore I'd get myself killed one of these days, but if we didn't take risks, we didn't eat. Ever since the war ended, barnstorming teams were popping up across the country. If the crowds weren't thrilled, we didn't have a show.

"I'm fine," I said, hoping to convince him the bobble was only a slight hiccup in the show. "The farm road was a bit rough in places, but Nathan and I managed." I slid my hands into my pockets, doing my best to hide their ragged state.

Wrinkles pinched the corner of his eyes. Having a young girl dumped in your lap did that to a man. I'd tried to make the best of our lives over the last five years. Much to his unhappiness, I'd taught myself how to balance on the wing. Do a handstand between the struts. I even climbed down to the lower skid, a u-shaped brace protecting the plane's frame from the ground, and did a single-leg hang. Sure, it wasn't traditional women's work, but it kept us together and that was all that mattered.

"Hooey! I saw you swinging like a monkey on that rope. If your hand had slipped, you'd be good as dead now. I should have never let you finish school early to join the team full time." His voice wobbled as he mumbled something about me, the plane, and how my father would've murdered him if he was still alive.

"I've been in trouble before, and I always figure a way out." I climbed down onto the lower wing and jumped to the ground.

Uncle Warren's oversized belly jiggled as his feet touched the dirt beside me. He pulled a cigar from his pocket, bit off the end, and spit it to the ground. He inched closer and put his hands on my shoulders. "You think you've got nine lives, but one of these days you're going to push a trick too far. Don't give Alistair Rowland that satisfaction, my dear."

Just the sound of Rowland's name made my skin crawl. His barnstorming team had popped up in our part of Nebraska last year, and ever since he'd been attempting to push us out. Constantly trying to outdo us with his shiny planes and fancy costumes. That's why today's trick was important. Why Nathan and I had practiced it for weeks. Nobody on Rowland's team had the guts to do a car-to-plane transfer. His men were all too big and slow to pull it off.

"The crowd loved it and you know it. In fact, I'd guess we made enough to cover expenses for this week and maybe a bit more." I said the words hoping to soothe him, but the deep caverns in his forehead warned he wasn't budging.

"That's not the point. Your risks are . . . well, risky!" He ripped off his aviator cap, rubbing the few strands of gray hair he had left.

It was the same lecture every flight.

Don't go too far out on the wing.

Careful of the struts when we bank.

Barnstorming is a dangerous business.

What he didn't understand was the plane was part of me. Over time I'd learned her strengths and weaknesses. Where to put my hand for the steadiest grip. Which foothold kept me secure against the strongest wind. To most people the Curtiss JN-4, a Jenny, was just surplus left over from the Great War, but to me she was a trusted friend. She helped keep my family together and was one of the few things I counted on in this world.

"It turned out fine, but I thought you said Martin was getting a new ladder. Ours is, well . . ." There was no cause to finish the sentence unless I wanted to make the frown lines around his mouth grow deeper.

"I had to let Martin go."

"Why? That's our third mechanic in a year."

"Caught him drinking again. If the feds caught one whiff, they'd shut us down. I can't let that happen. Not when there's so much at risk." His words lingered in the air between us. I caught his meaning, but didn't say a word. When he got this worked up there was no point in arguing.

I only got a few steps away from my uncle before Nathan intercepted me. Dirt covered his hair and skin in a fine, brown layer. He was tall and wiry thin with a thick, black beard. Most gals thought he was a real catch, but to me he looked a little too much like Abe Lincoln.

"I warned you about that stunt. Why don't you ever listen?" Just like my uncle, when it came to our performances Nathan never held back.

"Can you imagine what that crowd would've done if you'd taken a nosedive?" I shrugged. It was better to let him get it all out at once. "They would've screamed in horror and then asked for all their dough back, making today worthless." He kicked at a rock in frustration, sending it tumbling across the runway.

"Nathan, do you see where I'm standing? Two feet on solid ground." I nodded down to my body. "And look at that, all in one piece, too," I joked.

No matter how many times I tried to tell him I was okay after a trick, he still wasn't convinced. While I appreciated his concern, his big-brother hovering wore on me after a while. Like Uncle Warren, he still saw me as a little girl. Sooner or later he was going to have to open his eyes and see I'd grown up.

He slapped his hands over his pants, a puff of dust billowing up into the air. "Grace, why are you always causing a ruckus?" A smile ticked at the corner of his mouth. He could never stay angry at me for too long.

I yanked my goggles down and rubbed the layer of dirt from my lips, doing my best not to wince at the scrape against my raw hands. "Aw, Nathan, stop being a wet blanket. Without me life would be too predictable."

"I like predictable," he muttered. He tried to stand firm, but for all his protests he had to admit what we'd pulled off today was amazing.

"I don't know why I bother, Grace. You're just as thick-skulled as him." He jabbed a finger in the direction of my uncle, who called for his help to guide the Jenny from the landing strip. Like a finely tuned dance, Nathan waved to the left, helping him turn around and head in the correct direction.

With both of them occupied, I dashed inside the hangar, hoping for a little peace. Instead of silence, I was greeted by Daniel's heavy footsteps thundering in front of the workbenches. His mitt-sized hands opened and closed frantically. His body, wide and thick as an old oak tree, tensed as he turned to face at me. When spectators got sight of him moving through the crowd to collect our fee, they never thought about stiffing us. Funny thing was, Daniel was as soft as they came. His gentle Georgia accent and easy demeanor made him more of a sweet dog than a growling wolf.

He took two steps toward me and stopped. He raked a hand through his deep copper hair. "Grace, darlin," he took a deep gulp, "I warned you about that road."

I moved closer and matched my whisper to his. "I'd never do anything to risk our future, Daniel. We're a team. If one of us goes down, we all go, right?"

This wasn't the first time he'd questioned one of my mid-air decisions. In Sioux Falls, he had been madder than a poked hornet when I put my foot through the fabric covering one of the wings. After a show in Topeka, there'd been no calming him after I nearly plummeted off the lower skid during a surprise thunderstorm. As part of our act, he and Nathan did their own aerobatic routine only minutes before, but nobody questioned *them* about the danger. If I fell, or one of our planes went down, we'd all be sunk. We'd seen it happen to the Crazy Conroys from Coeur d'Alene and a handful of other teams over the last year. One crash, one death, and a barnstorming future was over.

It wasn't that I didn't understand or care about my team's worries, but we needed four hundred dollars to get to the World Aviation Exposition in Chicago. The event was a little over two months away and we were still one hundred and forty eight dollars from getting there. The Expo was more than another barnstorming show. It was a chance to perform on the national stage. Compete against other performers for a shot at a Hollywood contract that promised steady pay. While other outfits were either dying or quitting, securing a deal like that meant my team, my family, could stay together.

"All I'm asking is you think long and hard about what you're doing in the air. One of these days . . ." His voice lifted above his regular whisper and it stopped me cold. Daniel was a lot of things but he wasn't a shouter unless you gave him good reason. "Well, you're going to get hurt." He snapped his mouth shut and walked straight out of the hangar. The look of fear and disappointment in his eyes sent an icy shot right through my heart, but I couldn't let it change my mind. Ever since I'd read about the contest in the local paper, I'd plotted how we would get to Chicago, and I couldn't let the team's worries keep us from that dream.

2
A Little Trouble

A tiny brass bell chimed above my head as I walked into the Skylight Diner. The scent of bacon and fried eggs filled the air. Waitresses in blue gingham dresses rushed coffee cups and plates overflowing with food to waiting customers. At the center counter, farmers clad in dirt-covered overalls sat shoulder-to-shoulder with businessmen in stiff wool suits. Each man barked louder than the other, discussing the Great Railroad Strike and Babe Ruth's latest suspension.

Ignoring the stares from the men at the counter, I found a vacant booth in the back corner. Every bone in my body protested as I inched across the black leather bench. The new trick pushed each of my muscles to the limit. My fingers throbbed beneath my white cotton gloves. The skin on my palms was an ugly map of blisters and rope burns. It was much too hot to wear the gloves inside, but if my uncle and the boys saw the brutal state of my hands, they'd make every excuse to keep me out of the air.

"Oh, Grace. You look a mess." My friend Ethel moved toward me. Her roommate and best friend, Mary raced to her side. Together they gasped as their gaze landed on my torn clothes.

I swept back a hair that had been plastered to my forehead with sweat and dirt. The girls stayed rooted to the floor, staring at the tear below the collar of my work blouse and the widening hole near the ankle of my worn pants.

"Lunchtime crowd is getting bigger. Tips must be good." I focused on the chalkboard menu hanging over the center counter and hoped they'd forget about my battered body. Ethel motioned for me to move across the seat. Mary slid onto the bench across from us.

Over the last two years Mary and Ethel had gone from being acquaintances to true friends. They'd travelled to Lincoln from Gering, near the Wyoming border, where'd they'd been lifelong chums. Ethel was the oldest of eight and spent most of her childhood raising her younger siblings after her Ma died giving birth to baby number nine. Mary's father was a mean drunk who'd promised her hand to the boy next door, hoping his wealthy father would join their two farms together. Mary tried to be a dutiful daughter until the boy backhanded her for asking a question during a nickleodeon. According to Ethel, she and Mary ran off under a moonless sky two days later and never looked back.

I admired them both for taking a chance. For coming to Lincoln to search for independence and freedom. They'd taught me to live each day like it was an adventure, even if for them adventure meant serving hash and eggs to dirty farmers and oily businessmen until they could earn enough to take the train to Hollywood, where they dreamed of being starlets on the silver screen.

Ethel nudged me across the booth. "Aren't you going to get in trouble if you sit with me?"

She turned over a spoon to look at her reflection, fluffing her blonde hair she'd pinned up short to look like her favorite screen actress, Mary Pickford. "We're fine here for a minute. Archie, that rat, hasn't given us a break since the breakfast shift."

Mary, who was so tiny her feet didn't touch the floor when she sat, took a deep swallow and pushed her curly, brown hair out of her eyes. Her thin, pink lips trembled as she glanced slowly around the room. It was one of her little quirks. If she saw a certain type of man—tall, thin, and dark-haired—her eyes went blank as if lost in her own world. Ethel would try to shake her out of it, but she'd stay focused for a minute before she'd come back to life.

Ethel leaned forward and snapped her fingers. Mary blanched, her stare landing on their boss as he paced behind the counter. "Ethel, maybe we shouldn't sit . . ."

"It's all right, Mary," Ethel's soothing voice tried to reassure her. "He and the customers can wait a minute." Ethel turned and put her hands on my shoulders. The weight of her touch made me wince. "Honey, what did you do now?" She tensed as she looked me over. "Did you fall? Are you hurt? Your uncle needs to stop making you do all those crazy stunts."

"He's not *making* me do anything," I said, maneuvering away from her touch. "The car-to-plane stunt was just a little trouble today."

"What kind of trouble?" Mary's voice rattled in a terrified whisper.

I shrugged and looked around the room, not wanting to meet her gaze. "The rope ladder may have unraveled in my hands."

"What?" Ethel shrieked, causing more than a few stares from a group of businessmen seated at a nearby table. "You could have fallen to your death!" She shook her head in disgust. "I hope your uncle gave that Martin a stern lecture."

"He'd already fired him," I said. My hands felt like they'd been doused in gasoline and set ablaze. "Now we're without a mechanic, again, which isn't helping our plan to get to Chicago."

Ethel groaned and gave me her patented "you've lost your mind" look. She and Mary had only seen me perform once. For days after, they tried to convince me to take a job here at the diner or as a sales girl at the local mercantile. While I appreciated their concern, I wasn't the kind of girl who'd be satisfied to wait tables or stand around all day selling needless goods over at the department store on O Street.

"Grace," Ethel started in, her fingers twirling nervously around a wisp of hair. "We've been friends since you sat in that corner two years ago. She pointed to a small, wooden table in the back of the crowded room. "Back then you were just a little bit of a thing, sitting with your uncle and quietly ordering a glass of lemonade. The two of you shared a chopped ham sandwich like you always do on Mondays. But look at you now, a wing-walking star." She stopped short and smoothed down the tattered hem of her uniform. "You've proved to everyone how brave you are. Don't you think it's time you start considering what comes next? Perhaps settle down. Find a handsome man. Start a family."

When men looked at me they only saw one of two things: a woman who didn't know her place or a shot at some sort of fame. I didn't have much experience, but it wasn't hard to figure out that the last thing I needed in my life was a man.

"Listen girls, I'm not changing my job *or* my mind. Now what's good on the menu today? My uncle ordered me to eat something hearty, but we're still short on funds for Chicago so how's about something small?" Ethel wiped crumbs from the edge of the table. "The chipped beef sandwich is fifteen cents and edible, but don't order the pea soup. I wouldn't feed it to my dog."

"Your landlady wouldn't let you have a dog anyway."

"Well, if I did," she said, tapping a finger to her bright red lips, "I wouldn't feed it that slop."

Mary continued to give me a motherly stare and reached across the table. When she pressed a menu into my hands a yelp escaped my lips. Before I could pull away, she clasped my wrists and pulled back the edge of my gloves. Her tiny fingers trembled as she stared at the angry, red welts and oozing blisters etched into my skin.

"Oh, Grace," she gasped. A young couple in the booth next to us stopped talking and looked in our direction. After yanking my hands from her grasp, I concentrated on the menu. I'd dealt with enough stares today.

Ethel bounced up from the booth. "Mary, go into the kitchen and put in an order for a chipped beef sandwich for Grace. We had a new fifty-pound block of ice delivered today. I'll go and break off a few pieces for those burns."

"Thank you," I mouthed to Ethel as she guided Mary's tiny frame back to the counter.

With the girls focused on their new tasks, I eased back a corner of my right glove and was greeted by a patch of angry slashes and burns. As I peeked at the raw skin, a strong sensation sent a prickle down my back. I looked up to find bright green eyes staring at me from a booth across the room. Once I locked eyes with the young man, a strange heat filled my cheeks.

After taking a few calming breaths, I glanced up, preparing to stare down those eyes. What I found instead was the gray, steely glare of Alistair Rowland. His snake-like smile showed off a set of straight, white teeth only people with money could afford. Louis, who was a strange combination of both chauffeur and bodyguard, hovered behind him.

"What did I hear about ice and burns?" He *tsk*ed and slid onto the bench across from me. "You know that wouldn't happen if you joined my team. We'd purchase leather gloves. Custom-made to protect those precious hands of yours." He smoothed down the edges of his crisp, white collar and stared at me like a prize at the penny arcade. "I've got my eye on a chap training over at the Lincoln Airplane School by the name of Charlie Lindbergh. People say he's quickly becoming the best pilot in the nation. Put the two of you together and nothing would stop The Skyhawks."

He slid the black fedora off his head and placed it on the table. The umbrella he always carried like a cane clattered down onto the floor beside him. I never could figure out why he carried that thing. We hadn't seen rain in weeks, much to the local farmers' dismay.

With a swipe of his hand, he smoothed back his straw-colored hair so not a single strand was out of place. Rumors were he came from a long line of dukes or earls. Other whispers said his money came from his father, who was a racketeer wanted by Scotland Yard. Girls may swoon over his thick English accent, but all it reminded me of was his haughty ways. He had a wad of dough and elegant clothes, but that didn't buy him class, tact, *or* manners.

"I don't care about some new flier. And a true gentleman would ask before presuming to sit down with a lady."

Louis moved in, his thick, wide face twisting into a sneer. "Things are under control here, go grab a bite," Rowland ordered. Louis found a table a few feet away. His watchful eyes only moved away for a moment to look at a menu. "Let's not start off on the wrong foot, Miss Lafferty."

It was hard not to laugh in his face. Our conversations had been the same dull go-around since his barnstorming outfit arrived in town six months ago. As owner and manager of The Skyhawks, he offered me a job every time we crossed paths. Insisted I'd be happier with the fancy costumes and mediocre stunts his team performed. In each instance, I turned him down before he could get through his entire pitch.

"There's something to be said for a fresh start," he continued. "You can't say my persistence doesn't intrigue you."

I played with my napkin, too tired and sore to play this game with him. At a past show I'd overheard an organizer turn him down for top billing, telling Rowland his act didn't have enough shine to attract a crowd. It explained why he'd stepped up his recent pursuit of me. Without a girl performer, his team was like every other all-male outfit clogging up the skies.

"Isn't there some other gal you could go and pester, Mr. Rowland? There's got to be at least a dozen women who would love to be part of your flying circus."

He cracked a smile, flashing those bright teeth at me again. "As I've said many times before, you may call me Alistair, and none of those women are you. Let's be honest, I'm only concerned for your welfare. The sky can be treacherous. Terrible accidents can happen, especially when you do not have the means to keep your equipment in tip-top shape. Why, only a few weeks ago in Coeur d'Alene, a pilot's engine stalled, sending both he and his wing walker to an awful death."

"Yes, I know. We were supposed to perform after them. The explosion and height of the flames is something I'll never forget."

"Amateurs." Rowland said carelessly, brushing lint from the top of his perfectly tailored coat. "They should have never been in the sky."

What did he know about performing? Had he ever been 500 feet in the sky with nothing but the wind propping you up?

"Did you even see their act?" I snapped.

"Well, no. But—"

"They were very good," I interrupted. "I first met Arnold Conroy and his son, Michael, at a show outside Boise. Michael taught me how to create a leather loop so I could hang off the lower skid. We didn't see each other as competition but as fellow fliers, which is a lesson you and your team could learn."

Uncle Warren begged me to act like a lady, at least when I was in public, but when it came to Rowland something unraveled inside me. "Instead of passing judgment, your time would be better spent working on your own team. Last I heard they were having trouble with the car-to-plane transfer. We're performing it again tomorrow at one p.m. Maybe you should stop by and see how it's done."

Okay, perhaps not too ladylike, but I couldn't help it. My mouth was quicker than my mind when it came to Rowland.

The false smile died on his lips. His expensive, gold pocket watch clicked against the table as he leaned menacingly close. "Do not get uppity, Miss Lafferty. All it takes is one slip for a team to go down." His words were a blatant nod to my bobble today. Of course he'd been at the show. Since his team started crowding our skies, he'd made a point of watching me at every opportunity.

"Everything all right here, Miss?"

The young fella with the bright green eyes appeared at the

table, leaning at an angle that favored his right leg. He swapped a dark glance with Rowland, and neither flinched.

"We were having a private conversation, sir." Rowland focused back on me, ignoring Bright Eyes's sneer. Louis hopped up from his seat and stalked toward us. His fists curled at his side, begging for a fight.

An angry flicker moved across Bright Eyes's face. "I wasn't talking to you."

"Thank you for your concern," I said, locking eyes with the young man. "But Mr. Rowland was just leaving."

Rowland's hands grasped the edge of the table, his fingertips turning white. He didn't take kindly to being dismissed by a woman, but with an audience growing around us he had no choice but to retreat.

He shooed Louis back and moved to the end of the booth. "Until we meet again, Miss Lafferty." With a quick flick of his wrist, he popped the fedora on his head, grabbed his umbrella, and turned for the door. Louis shot a dark look at Bright Eyes before following Rowland out.

Once they were gone, Mary and Ethel reappeared with a large bowl of ice water. Their eyes went wide as they took a long look at Bright Eyes. Ethel slipped around him and set the bowl in front of me. "I think this will help, honey."

When I didn't reply, she pulled Mary back to the kitchen, their giggling whispers filling the room.

Bright Eyes looked at the bowl and arched an eyebrow. "Ice water from a bowl? You must be thirsty."

"It's not to drink, it's for . . ." I stopped. Explaining my injuries only led to more questions, none of which I wanted to answer, especially with a man I didn't know.

"It's for what?" He gave no hint he was going to move, sliding his fingers over a thick scar that cut into the bottom of his chin.

"Thank you for coming to my aid, but I'm fine now." I pulled a napkin into my lap and waited for him to take my cue and return to his table.

"A dame like you shouldn't sit alone. It brings unwanted attention." He made a point of staring at the spot where Rowland sat only moments ago.

Heat moved up my neck. Who was he to tell me how to behave? "I did not ask for your opinion, sir," I huffed, turning my attention back to the icy water. The chipped pieces began to melt and crack, and my hands itched to feel their cool relief.

He bent down and pulled a familiar-looking scrap of yellowed paper from the ground. Turning it over in his hands, he unfolded the worn edges. The once-black ink that seeped through the thin parchment was now a dusty shade of gray.

"Palm Coast Studios announces aerobatic contest to be held at Chicago's World Aviation Expo," he read aloud. "Winning team receives multi-year Hollywood contract, including room and board and a chance to perform before major film screenings."

I swiped the aging paper from his hand. "That's mine. It must have slipped out of my pocket."

He paused for a minute before shoving his hand in my direction.

"What are you doing?"

"Introducing myself. I'm Henry Patton." His hand hung over the bowl for a few seconds until he realized I had no intention of shaking it.

He could be a gangster or a grifter. He certainly looked the part in his white linen shirt with the sleeves rolled to the elbows. His five-button serge vest hid the tail of a blue tie that reminded me of the sky I had flown through only hours ago. Uncle Warren's words of caution about men like him rang in my head, especially about the ones who seemed to have a quick temper.

"Mr. Patton, as I mentioned before, I do not need your assistance." I righted my shoulders and stared him down so he knew

I meant business. "Besides, I'm sure you want to get back to your table before someone takes it."

"Before I go, I believe you owe me a thank you for getting that stiff suit outta your hair."

The heat that once burned in my chest shot straight to my mouth. "I'm not saying thanks for something I didn't ask for. Heavens, are you always this brutish with strangers?"

"Oh, never mind. Good day to you, Miss." He turned on his heel and stalked back to his table. Once he was seated, he grabbed a menu and pretended to read.

It took a few minutes for my racing heart to return to a normal beat. Why couldn't he just be a normal gentleman and leave when asked? He had some nerve thinking he deserved a thank you for sticking his nose in my business.

When I finally caught my breath, I looked down at my hands. With the slightest movement my raw skin peeled back from the white cotton. Removing my gloves would make my already throbbing palms yowl in pain, but it had to be done.

I slid my fingers under a cotton edge. Quick and fast. It was the only way to do it. I closed my eyes and counted down from three. Before I'd finished, the table shifted and the seat across from me squeaked.

Without hesitating, Henry plunked my hands into the bowl, covering both the table and me in a spray of water.

"What are you doing?" I sputtered.

"Helping. The moisture will loosen the fabric's hold on your skin."

He tossed a napkin in my direction. "Sorry about the mess," he said, pressing my hands farther down into the bowl. Once the fabric was soaked through, he slid each glove away from my skin.

"How'd you know to do that?" I bit my lip as the water seeped through the fabric, cooling my burns and turning the ache into a numb sensation that went from pain to pleasure in seconds.

"In the trenches it was easy to get cut up. Medics would bandage us quickly to prevent infection, and warned that if the wrapping came loose before it was healed it'd tear the fresh skin away."

He pulled the soaked gloves from the bowl and placed them on a nearby napkin. His fingers returned to the water and pushed my hands down deeper into the icy mix.

"So, what's *your* name?" he said, like it was an order rather than a question.

"Grace. Grace Lafferty." My choked voice sounded nothing like my own.

"Mind if I ask how your hands got all torn up, Grace?"

More questions I didn't want to answer. "It's a long story, Mr. Patton."

"It's Henry. And I like long stories," he huffed.

I shook my head, trying to ignore the way his hands slid across my skin. "If I answer your question, will you promise to leave?"

"If that's what you want." His face stayed a tense mask while he continued pouring water over my cuts and burns.

"Ever heard of a flying circus?" I winced as ice slid over a jagged cut.

"Sure. Pilots use old training planes to do tricks and such." He reached for another napkin and laid it flat on the table. With care, he pulled my hands out of the water and patted them dry. It was strange how his body was wound tighter than a pocket watch, his mouth set in a concrete frown, but his touch beyond feather light.

"Uh," I mumbled, trying not to hiss at the pain. "My team uses those planes to do aerobatics, wing walking, and parachute tricks at fairs and special events."

"You're telling me a young thing like you dangles off the edge of a plane? That's ridiculous and, well, plain stupid."

He leaned forward and examined the blisters covering my palms as if oblivious to the insult he'd flung in my direction. At shows I'd heard the whispers. Felt the stares of men who disapproved of my time in the sky. But Mr. Patton was the first person to openly display his disgust to my face.

I sat up straighter and yanked my hands away. "I'm eighteen, I'll have you know. And what I do is *not* ridiculous."

The edges of his lips twitched as if holding back another insult. He had small lines around his eyes, but the smooth skin on his face said he wasn't more than a few years older than me. Who was he to judge what I did with my life?

"And your battered hands? That comes from holding on to the wing too tight?" He shifted back, crossing his arms over his chest as if I owed him some sort of explanation. Typical of the men I encountered. Expecting that if he paid attention to me, he should be rewarded with an element of conversation.

"Well?" he pressed.

"These came from a new trick we just started performing." I dropped my hands into my lap and tried not to shudder from the pain.

"A trick that involves rope burns?" He gave me a look I'd seen many times before. The slight tilt of the head. The arched eyebrow. All of which said he thought I was out of my mind. "Guess that explains why you're carrying around that paper. You planning to enter that contest?"

"I've kept my promise and answered your questions. Now it's time for you to leave, sir." I focused back on the bowl, ignoring his penetrating gaze.

"That's probably best." He hesitated for a minute, his eyes darting between me and his table. "In the future, you should think twice before sitting alone, Miss Lafferty."

"I'll be fine, Mr. Patton," I rolled back my shoulders. "I always am."

He slid to the end of the bench with his leg dragging behind. He held my gaze as if daring me to comment on the way his body compensated for his injury. I quickly looked away. With men returning from war with all kinds of injuries, Uncle Warren said it was best not to stare.

Once steady on both feet, he turned and bumped into the waitress at the booth behind us. A tray of dirty dishes spun in the air before careening straight to the floor. The sound of shattering glass and plates quieted the frantic room.

The color drained from Henry's face. He grabbed the edge of the booth like it was the only thing keeping him upright. "No! Stop!" he shouted. His entire body shook. Curses flew from his mouth before his body twitched again, his angry words turning into what sounded like a prayer. Quick puffs of breath left his mouth as he whispered something that sounded like, "It's not real."

A businessman from a nearby table tapped his shoulder. "Fella, you okay?"

My hand hung in the air. Should I touch him? Shake him? Do anything to create a commotion so people would stop staring? I hated the staring. That sick feeling like you were a bug being examined before someone was brave enough to put a boot to you.

Henry blinked twice and swiveled his head back and forth as if he couldn't recall how he'd gotten here. The room stayed silent, breathless, waiting on his next move. He turned to me, his face the color of chalk. The flare of brilliant green in his eyes was now a muted black, as if all the light was snuffed out of him.

"Do you need help, Mr. Patton?" I asked quietly.

His eyes widened as he took in the pitying stares and the pin-drop silence of the hushed room.

"No. Please excuse me." He shouldered through the crowd. His footsteps crushed shattered plates and shards of glass into tiny bits. He slammed through the front door, the once-sweet chime of the bell becoming a toneless thud.

Ethel appeared at the table and placed the chipped beef sandwich in front of me. The steam from the plate filled my nose with a rich gravy aroma. She placed her hands firmly on her hips. "He rushed out of here in a hurry. What did you say to him?"

"I didn't say a thing! The plates crashed and he raced out of here."

Mary appeared with a glass of lemonade and tucked an extra napkin under my plate. "That was strange. Do you think he had some sorta episode?"

I couldn't help but glance at the door. Mr. Patton was strange. An irritation. But I still wondered where he'd go and if he'd be all right.

"Well, no matter. He sure was handsome." A pink blush bloomed across Mary's cheeks.

"I know," Ethel said. "He was a real looker with those full lips and broad shoulders."

I couldn't help but groan at their single-track minds. "You're both wrong. A man like that amounts to nothing but trouble."

Mary continued to fill my glass, her petite fingers barely fitting around the handle of the pitcher. "I can't afford the lemonade," I said.

She swiveled around and when she didn't see her boss she smiled. "It's on the house."

Mary patted my shoulder and shuffled toward a table packed with businessmen. Ethel pretended to clean the edges of my booth in an attempt to look busy.

"I worry about you, Grace. You can't get through this world alone. One of these days you're going to have to open your heart to someone."

I shook my head and focused on my meal. Earning enough money for Chicago and winning that Hollywood contract was the only thing that mattered. My heart and everything else would have to wait.

3
The Dos and Don'ts of Flying

July 10, 1922
64 days until the World Aviation Expo

Uncle Warren gave two long toots on the horn of his motorcar. It was my regular warning that I had to be out of bed and ready for work in five minutes. I stumbled around my small bedroom, gathering up what I hoped was a clean pair of linen pants and a blouse with only a few grease stains on the sleeves.

I rushed out the door, yanking on one boot and then the other, doing my best to ignore the dull throb in my hands. When I landed in the passenger seat, Uncle Warren offered his regular early-morning grumble before heading in the direction of town.

When I first arrived in Lincoln on the morning train after my parents died, I stayed with Uncle Warren in his little apartment overlooking the mercantile. But after two men, soused to the gills, brawled in the hallway in front of our door, he used his vaudeville money to buy a small farmhouse on the edge of town.

It took a while for the little place with the bright white eaves and yellow paint to feel like home, especially since Uncle Warren had no idea how to cook or take care of me. He'd tried one time to be domestic, insisting we fill the empty coop outside with chickens, but that idea died quickly when I admitted eggs made me sick. Wide-eyed, Uncle Warren chuckled under his breath, confessing he didn't like them either. Guess we had more things in common than just our wide, ice-blue eyes.

The car chugged along until we hit the edge of Lincoln. There was something magical about the town waking up for the day. Shopkeepers frantically cleaned the sidewalks in front of their stores, swirls of brown dust flying off their brooms. Ice and milk trucks rumbled down Main Street, stopping at the butcher shop and local hotels to make their deliveries. The signs of the city coming to life got under my skin and quickened my pulse.

When we reached the hangar a mile outside the city limits, I jumped out of the car and rolled back the rust-colored steel door. The heady scent of gasoline, grease, and oil hit me as the dry wheels squeaked in protest. Inside, Nathan and Uncle Warren's Jennys sat wing-to-wing. In the far corner, a small room acted as Uncle Warren's office. Across from the office were two makeshift workbenches. Hammers, pliers, and various screwdrivers covered the low, wooden tables.

Uncle Warren made his way to his office. I'd seen the state of his desk. He'd be knee-deep in paperwork for hours.

Perfect.

It took several trips but I managed to pull mats from a dirty corner next to the office and drag them under the wings of Uncle Warren's plane. Once they were settled in the right positions, I pulled a wire spool from the pocket of my pants. The early morning light reflected off the stiff, silver cable. I'd coined my new trick the "Showstopper," and it would be our ticket to winning the aviation contest. No performer, man or woman, had ever dangled from a plane only by their teeth. I planned to be the first if I could determine the right cable strength to bear my weight.

Once up on the wing of Uncle Warren's Jenny, I released the new rope ladder until it pooled down onto the ground like a coiled snake ready to strike. With a single leap, I hit the ground and stretched out the rungs until they were flat against the cement.

The spool of wire tightened in my still-raw hand. A nervous energy pulsed through my veins. I pulled out the rubber and metal mouthpiece I'd fashioned out of spare parts and placed it in my mouth. It was a secure fit, but would it be strong enough to hold my weight? Would the wind shear make it impossible to hold on? All questions I'd better figure out before I flung myself off the edge of the Jenny with only a thin piece of wire, and a strong jaw, to keep me from plummeting to my death.

I stared at the new ladder for a few minutes more before securing it back under the body of the plane. The boys and Uncle Warren could not know about the trick until I was convinced it would work. If they caught a whiff of what I had planned, they'd make every excuse to keep me on the ground.

After stretching out on the mat, I moved into a headstand and focused on balancing my weight. My body was a taut wire, my aching hands the foundation that steadied me. I relaxed into position and a yawn pulled at my lips. I swallowed it back down. Even a slow release of air could throw off my center of gravity. If I fell here I would crash against the mat, but one mistake in the air could mean death.

Keeping my body upright, I closed my eyes and imagined being out on the wing, hundreds of feet above the Nebraska countryside. My body remained still.

"Doesn't all the blood rush to your head if you stay like that too long?"

Bright green eyes flashed through my mind. My balance shifted and my back slammed into the mat. I gasped, desperate for a breath, but the air wouldn't come. My head swam and silver spots colored my vision.

The man stepped onto the mat. A newsboy cap sat low over his face, but I'd recognize those eyes anywhere. "Take a deep breath," he whispered. "Imagine your lungs filling with air."

I tried to breathe but nothing happened. A bead of sweat rolled down my forehead. Small bits of relief slowly returned to my lungs and glorious air poked my insides like sharp needles.

"What are you doing here, Mr. Patton?" I finally gasped.

The better question is what are *you* doing here, Miss Lafferty?"

"I," the air struggled to fill my lungs. "I work here." When I finally stood, the world tipped sideways. The edges of my vision went wobbly like when Uncle Warren flew us upside down for too long.

"Maybe you should sit." He offered his hand, but I ignored it and sunk down onto the mat.

"You didn't tell me why you're here." I rubbed at the painful throb beginning at the back of my neck.

He shifted on his feet and looked away. I followed his line of sight as he focused on the tool benches and then the Jennys parked a few feet away.

"Well, are you going to answer?"

He searched the hangar as if looking for something and mumbled under his breath.

"You need to speak up."

"I forgot my hat and coat at the diner yesterday," he said slightly louder. "Your skittish friend with the dark hair, I think her name was Mary, asked why I was in town. When I mentioned I was on my last dollar and looking for work as a mechanic she gave me this address." He hesitated, pulling his cap down and curling the brim around his fingers. "Your blonde friend practically pushed me out the door and in this direction."

Mary and Ethel. Those two were like a dog with a bone. They meant well, but sending a stranger to my hangar was not only wrong, but dangerous.

"I'm sorry my friends sent you here for no reason, Mr. Patton." Slowly I climbed to my feet again. This time I braced myself for the room to swirl but thankfully everything stayed in its place.

"Again, it's Henry. And don't you need a mechanic?"

"Yes we do, but I'm not about to allow you near my planes. I hardly know you, and well, after yesterday."

"You don't like me. I get that a lot." He slid the cap off his head and scratched a hand through his nest of light-brown hair. "It's obvious I'm not good with people, but engines and I get along fine. Here, let me show you." He sidestepped me and approached my uncle's Jenny.

"Wait." I chased after him as he hobbled toward my uncle's plane.

He reached up and ran a hand over a landing wire near the edge of the wing. "The tension is off here, and this turnbuckle needs to be replaced."

"That may be true, but . . ."

He spun around and slowly bent down to examine the landing gear. "One tire looks low, too." He pushed up his sleeves, the lines around his eyes tightening into a squint.

I inched down and stared at the tires. The right one sank lower than the left. "Okay," I huffed, "so you know a few things about planes."

He moved to the front of the Jenny and examined the propeller. "My Pa was an aviation enthusiast and amateur pilot. He had a friend who let him fly and work on his Wright Model HS. When I got older he let me tinker with her. Even took me up for a few lessons."

His eyes lit up as he talked about his family, and my head began to spin again.

What I would give to have shared the sky with my father.

"That's all interesting, but it doesn't make you a qualified mechanic."

He turned toward the workbenches. His mouth twisted in displeasure. "Are those your tools?"

"They belong to the team."

"You need to have more respect for them. Having your wrenches and pliers scattered about exposes them to heat, moisture, and rust. They should go back in the kit immediately after use." He moved to the wooden tables, examining each tool before straightening them out in a perfect row.

"That's how we've always done things, and those tools work just fine for us."

Who did he think he was? It didn't matter if he was more handsome than a film star, he couldn't waltz into the hangar and pass judgment on how we took care of our equipment. He'd never been out in the field trying to repair a flat tire. Or stuck in the mud, rain pouring from the sky, while we replaced a guide wire to keep the upper and lower wings secure. "Again, Mr. Patton, I'll ask you to leave."

Ignoring me, he removed his thin, linen jacket and hung it over the open cockpit of Nathan's Jenny. He shoved back the cowl and looked at the engine. I circled to the back and climbed onto the wing. I hovered only inches away as he poked his hand around the fuel and oil lines, adding to my increased irritation.

"Did you not hear a word I said?"

He leaned in eyeing a single spot. "Oh, I heard you, *Grace*."

When he found what he was looking for, he rolled up his sleeves. "There's a hairline crack in the oil line. It can be fixed in minutes if you have the right parts."

I sat back on the edge of the wing and crossed my arms over my chest. "Shows what you know, *Henry*. I already replaced that line twice and there's still a leak."

The line of his jaw tightened. "You've worked on this engine?"

I tipped my chin up. "Of course. If I'm scrambling around on the wings, I should know what's keeping me aloft."

"Well, maybe you didn't replace it right," he insisted, following me around the side of the plane. "Even more reason I should take a closer look."

"You will do no such thing." I jumped off the wing and blocked his path back to the engine. "Make one more move and I'll have you tossed out on your ear." My hands curled at my sides. I stepped closer, hoping he'd wilt under my threat.

"I see the hands are feeling better." He nodded to my fists and inched in. "Tell me, Grace. Who's in charge around here?"

He was so close I could smell the soap on his skin. See the uneven edges of the scar on his chin. "What makes you think it's not me?"

"I can't see some girl—"

"Some girl what? Go on. I'm curious to hear what idiotic thing you'll say today. You seem to have a talent for rubbing people the wrong way."

He chewed on the inside of his cheek as if considering what to do next. I wasn't "some girl" to be trifled with. This hangar was my home, and no man was going to tell me what I could do here.

Before I could order him to leave again the office door swung open. Uncle Warren hovered in the doorway. "Grace, who is this? And why is he in my hangar?"

"Uncle Warren, this is Mr. Patton. He wants to speak to you about the mechanic position."

Henry blanched. "Uncle?"

"Yes, Warren Ferguson is my uncle and owner of this hangar. But everyone calls him Warren. Guess Mary and Ethel left out that detail."

Let's see how he liked being the one off-kilter now.

"Yes, they did." He shoved his hands in his pockets but held my stare. "No matter. I'm still here to apply for the job."

Nathan and Daniel appeared at the hangar entrance. When they noticed Henry, Nathan made a beeline for the wing of his Jenny, his long legs pounding against the concrete. "I don't know who you are, but if you know what's good for you you'll step away from my plane."

Henry stumbled back, his leg dragging behind him. "I'm not

here to cause trouble. All I wanted to know is if you're hiring a new mechanic. I need the work."

"Have any experience?" Uncle Warren barked, examining the way Henry's body tilted to the right.

"Yes. As I told Grace, my father was familiar with an older Wright model. I helped him work on it until I entered the military."

"Old Wrights aren't Jennys." Nathan scrubbed at his black beard in irritation. Daniel moved around the side of the plane, surveying every inch of Henry.

"No, they're not," Henry replied, not flinching as Daniel's massive form moved closer to him. "But, I did have a chance to work on a few planes during the war when my division wasn't in the field. I'm also a quick study and a whiz with engines. I'm saving up to own a garage one day so I can fix all kinds of machines."

"How old are you? Where were you stationed? France? England?" Nathan fired at him.

"I'm twenty-four and I was in France." Henry's face tensed as if each answer tore open an old wound. "Grace mentioned you have oil pressure issues. I had a chance to take a look and I think I know what's causing the problem."

"She let you touch the planes?" Nathan shot me a heated look that could have melted the paint off the plane.

"I watched the whole time," I snapped. "And I told him I already fixed the line."

"It could be more complicated than just replacing one part," Henry volleyed back.

"Really?" Uncle Warren's face went from pinched to curious in seconds. "We've been trying to correct the problem for weeks. What would you suggest?"

Henry motioned to the plane and Uncle Warren followed. As soon as they disappeared behind the tail, Nathan was on me.

"What are you doing, Grace?" His spit the words out with so much anger I took a step back. "You know we have rules. This isn't a playground. Unless you're a part of the team, you don't set a toe inside this hangar. Running props can take off an arm or even a head." He used his height to loom over me. It was a trick he often used to get me to back down.

"I didn't bring him here, so don't start, Nathan. I know the dos and don'ts of flying."

"How did he find out about the job? Warren hasn't had a moment to tell anyone about it," he pressed.

"I told Mary and Ethel at the diner yesterday. Henry was there and left his coat behind. They told him when he went back to retrieve it."

He went to his plane, checking the oil lines that Henry had touched. "This smells like Rowland. I don't like it."

I would have thought the same thing except I'd seen their tense exchange at the diner. "Stop your bellyaching. Uncle Warren will see in seconds he's not qualified and Mr. Patton will be gone."

Daniel leaned in to listen to Henry and Uncle Warren's conversation. "I'm not sure about that. He knows an awful lot about engines, and with Nathan's plane out of commission it's hard to compete with The Skyhawks. At our last show Rowland's team took in as much money as we did, and I know how you love keeping track of our funds." His mouth twisted up and his bright red freckles folded around his teasing smile.

"The four of us are doing just fine," Nathan grumbled. "Who's to say this one will hang around anyway? Grace always seems to chase them away."

"That's not true," I argued.

Nathan stifled a laugh. "Really? The first guy, what was his name?"

"Otis," Daniel chimed in.

"Yes, Otis. You threw a wrench at his head because he had the nerve to tell you where to walk on the frame. And the second gent,

Frank, he left us high and dry in El Paso after you kicked him in the shins, not to mention a few other unmentionable parts."

I swallowed back the words I wanted to hurl in his direction. They didn't know the real reason I acted that way. How Otis put his hands on me when they weren't looking. Or the times he slid coins from the fedora into his pockets between shows. The numerous times Frank "accidentally" slipped booze into my drinks, swearing he thought the cup was his. And Martin was the worst. It wasn't just his drinking or his preference for gambling rather than maintaining the planes. I'd also caught him trying to tell other teams about what new stunts we were working on. If it meant a dollar in his pocket, he was willing to spill our secrets to any buyer, and that wasn't something I'd ever tolerate.

The boys tried to protect me like big brothers, and it was easier to let them think I was the root of the problem then allow them to unleash their fury on those men, even if they deserved it.

Henry and Uncle Warren continued to talk. They stopped next to Uncle Warren's propeller, and I followed to hear their conversation. Henry swept a hand over one of the blades and leaned in to examine where the bolts connected to the nose. He asked my uncle about flight time and maintenance logs, things none of the past mechanics ever questioned.

Uncle Warren pointed to the landing gear and Henry took his time bending down.

I moved back toward the boys, who still watched Henry's every move. "Hate to admit it, but we do need help. The last time I was up on the wing of your plane, Nathan, hot oil burned my cheeks. And we still haven't replaced all your guide wires." I sighed. "Daniel's right. If we're going to compete with The Skyhawks we do need a mechanic. Preferably one who works more, talk less, and doesn't cost as much as Martin." I glanced to where Henry and Uncle Warren hovered near the landing gear.

"Whoever we hire, it better be quick," Daniel said. "The contest is ten weeks away and we don't have enough money to get us to Chicago."

"One hundred and thirty-five dollars short, to be accurate," I said.

Nathan grumbled under his breath as Henry struggled to climb up on the wing. His leg dangled along the edge before he stiff-armed himself into a steady position. "Well, I hope Warren knows what he's doing. Whether it's this gent or someone else, they have to be qualified because one mistake could send any one of us straight to the grave."

4
A Rough Life

July 15, 1922
59 days until World Aviation Expo

Uncle Warren hired Henry after he promised he could fix the oil problem without spending too much dough. Over the last several days he'd worked nonstop, not only repairing the line, but adjusting the landing gear on Nathan's plane and repairing a few wobbly turnbuckles. I expected Henry's presence to be an irritation, like the mechanics before him, but he kept to himself, working quietly and not speaking more than a few sentences to me.

I slid under the body of Uncle Warren's plane and tightened a loose nut near the fuselage. On the last turn, the pliers slipped from my hand and clattered to the ground. I reached for them but the tip slid through my greasy fingers and bounced across the floor. A loud clank echoed through the hangar.

Heavy footsteps paced back and forth. Henry's low voice filtered down to me, a mixture of curses and a quiet prayer. The pliers slipped through my fingers again. Before I could pick them up, his boots thumped across the floor toward me.

"If you can't hold onto the tool properly, you have no business being in this hangar." His words were more a growl than a sentence as he bent down to face me. While a cool breeze swept into the hangar, sweat beaded his forehead and his skin was the color of ash. His gaze flitted back and forth between me and the plane. He closed his eyes, muttering under his breath like he'd done in the diner.

"Spit it out if you have something to say."

His eyes snapped open, his pupils wide. "Did you check that bolt properly?"

"It looked fine," I said, finally getting a tight hold on the pliers.

"Fine?" he gritted out in any icy tone. "Fine means there's a chance of making a full loop revolution and losing one of your wheels mid-air. Or hitting your landing while your axel snaps beneath you because you haven't checked the bolts properly."

Each word that slipped from his mouth had more venom than the next. He'd been fine up to this point, working on his projects and leaving me in peace. What suddenly made him turn into such a heated louse?

He shimmied across the ground on his back until he knocked my shoulder, pushing me out of the way. His eyes went dark as he ran a finger around the bolt's rough edge. He reached into the pocket of his blue coveralls, pulled out a wrench and started to loosen the nut.

"Stop! What are you doing? I just put that in place."

"Never use pliers on bolts. It weakens and disfigures them." He worked the bolt until the nut came free. Once it fell into his hand, he shoved the thin, circular metal inches from my face. "This should be tightened firmly but not with all your strength. It's one of the basics of mechanics."

With the bolt grasped in his hand he raised it to his eye. The vein in his neck throbbed while he examined it from all sides. "How long have you been working on these planes?"

"Since I was thirteen."

He closed his eyes like my answer was too much to bear. "It's a wonder they're still flying."

Now that he was talking to me, I remembered why I preferred his silence.

He slid out from under the body of the plane. I quickly followed. There was no way I'd allow him to speak to me in that tone. Not in my hangar.

"What's wrong, Mr. Patton? Are you threatened by a woman doing a man's job?"

He stopped only feet from his tool kit and spun around. "No, I take this job seriously. I've watched planes go down all over France from malfunction and poor maintenance." His hands shook at his sides and his voice was as tight as one of the landing wires. "Some of those needless deaths came from people touching planes when they weren't properly trained."

Before I could reply he marched toward me. "All bolts have to be examined before being placed. This one has rust around the edges and almost no grease. Also, it's too big for that spot under the fuselage. If the plane shook for any reason, it would work its way free and split the wood, bringing the whole plane down." He dragged in a deep breath and lowered his voice, rubbing a hand behind his neck like it was taking every ounce of his strength not to scream. "Not to mention the fact, Miss Lafferty, that you placed it wrong. All bolts need to be put in top-down, front to back, from the outside in. When placed correctly, even if the nut comes off mid-flight, the bolt will remain in place thanks to the pull of gravity and pressure from the air stream. Following that small rule may be the difference between life and death. Your death."

I opened my mouth but no words came out. All those years I'd worked with our mechanics, I'd never heard that rule. I tried not to wince as I thought of the horrible outcome he described. Perhaps he knew more about planes than I gave him credit for. I was so used to having to check after the imbeciles who worked for us before that I didn't know how to step back and let a real mechanic do his job.

"I told your uncle if this arrangement was going to work you needed to stay away from my planes." He limped back to the tool bench. A loud *thunk* shot through the hangar as he tossed his wrench back into the tool kit.

The sound of blood rushed through my ears. Heat sprang to

my cheeks and I stalked in his direction. "*Your* planes? The Jennys are more my responsibility than yours. Who do you think stands out on the wing at 500 feet battling the elements? Not you."

"Is that right?" His eyes narrowed into thin slits. "When was the last time the wings were aligned? How many hours have the planes been in the air before you've given them a thorough inspection? You say you know these planes, but at the end of the day I'm responsible for making sure they're in the best shape possible. Every adjustment ensures your entire team stays alive. Or don't you care about that?"

His words were like a slap in the face. How dare he accuse me of not caring about my team. Every risk I took was so we could earn enough money to stay together. Each stunt. Each show got us closer to the World Aviation Expo and that Hollywood contract.

Nathan and Daniel came scurrying around the side of the Jenny as our argument escalated.

"What's going on?" Daniel asked, leaning a thick arm on the frame of Nathan's plane.

I jabbed a sharp finger in Henry's direction. "He thinks I don't care about our safety."

"Did you say that?" Nathan pounced on him as if waiting for the chance to argue.

"Warren hired me to do a job, but I can't do that job if I'm following her around all day to make sure things don't fall apart mid-air."

I'd never struck anyone, but Henry's arrogance was pushing me to the edge. "For the last five years I've spent close to every waking moment in this hangar. Since then I've touched, disassembled, and reassembled every part on these Jennys. I might not have had training like you, but I know these planes."

Daniel grimaced. "He has a point, Grace." He nudged Nathan's shoulder, encouraging him to agree.

"Guess, it's all about how quickly you want to get in the air,"

Nathan grumbled. "Although I haven't seen all his work yet, so I'm reserving judgement."

"I'm tired of this," I spit out. "Since we started working together, I've had to fight to do the simplest of tricks. Now I have to argue with him," I stabbed a finger in Henry's direction, "over when and where I can touch the planes?" My voice trembled, but I refused to give in. "Let me remind you I am also a member of The Soaring Eagles."

'We know that, Grace," Daniel said in a hushed voice, trying to calm me.

They could protest all they wanted, but I wouldn't stop working on the planes. It comforted me to know how the spark plugs ignited the engine. How the fuel lines gave the plane her power. For me, knowing the inner workings of the plane was like understanding human nature. If you knew what made someone angry, it was easy to avoid their wrath. Agreeing to not touch the planes was like saying I wouldn't take a breath.

"Grace!" Uncle Warren's voice boomed through the hangar. He approached, the stubby brown cigar bobbing between his lips. With a snap of his head to the right, he ordered the boys away. Once they were out of earshot, he leaned an arm against the wing. "What's all the shouting about? I can hear your screech straight through the office walls."

"What did you promise Mr. Patton?" I demanded.

Uncle Warren glanced over his shoulder at Henry and gave him a firm nod. A growing sense of dread glued my feet to the floor.

Noticing the staredown I had going on with Henry, Uncle Warren reached for my sleeve and pulled me to the hangar entrance.

"I hired a qualified mechanic. He needs to be able to do his job without you pestering him every two seconds."

"These planes are as much my responsibility as his. I can work alongside Henry, that way we can save more money for Chicago. We still have over a hundred dollars to earn."

"Grace," he groaned. "All those other mechanics were hacks, but Henry knows what he's doing." He dragged a hand across his forehead. His eyes flicked to my tangled hair and oil-covered clothes. "Young women shouldn't be climbing all over the ground, getting grease on their cheeks. It's not proper." He rested a hand on my shoulders, his eyes glassy. "Your mother, God rest her soul, would have my head if she could see you right now."

I pulled away from his touch. He always used my dead parents as an excuse when he wanted to guilt me into doing a task or listening to his commands. Most days I gave in, but not today.

"No one cares what I look like down on the ground. My one and only job is to look presentable when I perform. Every other day I should be allowed to act and dress as I see fit."

"Please listen, Grace. I know how terribly you want to get to that Expo, but without a good mechanic we're sunk. If you keep aggravating Henry, he'll quit like the others. Do you want that?"

Yes, I wanted that smug rat face gone.

"No," I grumbled. As much as I hated it, he did have a point.

"I worry about you." His shoulders sagged. "This is a rough life and I need you to be safe. It might take a bit longer to earn the money we need, but it's worth it to keep the planes flying properly."

"But he's . . . He's . . ." I lowered my voice as Henry's eyes darted in our direction. "He's not right. He gets angry for no reason."

"He gets angry because you're a fly in his lemonade. It wouldn't be a problem if you'd let the man do his job."

"It's more than that." Uncle Warren hadn't seen the vacant look in his eyes—now, or before, in the diner.

"That young man may have his quirks, but there's not a fella who comes home from war without some issues. Let it be."

I tapped my foot against the ground. The boys had scattered across the hangar. While Daniel was busy double-checking his parachute, Nathan examined his oil line again. Maybe I was being too hard on Henry. In the end we all wanted the same thing—to get to Chicago. And if it was going to happen, having him along might be our only shot to keep the planes going.

"I've given my word to Henry that you'll stay out of his way and that's the end of it. Obey my rules, or the only time you'll set foot in this hangar is before a show." Uncle Warren chomped down on his cigar and marched back in the direction of his office, mumbling something that sounded like "behaving like children."

"A month and a half," I muttered under my breath. That's all we needed to keep the planes in good shape before Chicago. I could keep my head down. Leave Henry alone. I'd come to the hangar in the early morning and late at night to work on the Showstopper. I was close to getting the mouthpiece to fit perfectly. I only needed to confirm the wire would hold my weight so I wouldn't plummet 500 feet to my death.

Oh yes, I could figure ways to work around Uncle Warren's rule, and no one, including Henry Patton, would stop me.

5
Hang Him by His Thumbs

Springfield, Missouri
July 22, 1922
52 days until World Aviation Expo

Despite the growing tension in the hangar, we headed out the following week for a series of performances. In the closer cities, we usually flew straight into town, did our bit, and returned home. For this round of shows, Daniel and Henry rode ahead of us on the train and set up camp at each location, while Uncle Warren, Nathan, and I flew in hours later. It meant borrowing a roadster for the car-to-plane transfer, but with Henry now on board he could check the car over twice before letting Nathan drive. Much to my surprise, my pulse had dulled to a thorough hum with Henry around. Even though he marched around the hangar like he owned it, I knew one of the tires wasn't going to fall off the roadster as we bulleted down the road at fifty miles per hour.

Audiences arrived in droves as we visited towns along the northern edge of Colorado before moving to the small cities dotting the Iowa and Missouri borders. Each crowd was more raucous than the last. Men, women, children, even grandparents were packed side by side in the grandstands as we performed loops, barrel rolls, and whip stalls that shot us into the dreamy, blue sky before gravity shoved us back to the ground.

Today's show was at a fairground outside of Springfield, Missouri. Red, yellow, and black biplanes dotted the grassy parcel of land behind the grandstands. The scent of popcorn and roasting hot dogs tinged the warm summer air. Performers in caps and flying goggles chased after their mechanics as they performed last-minute inspections.

Dodger Phelps, head of the McKinley Flying Circus, stepped on an apple crate only feet from the stands. The edges of his cream-colored suit fluttered in the breeze as he bellowed through a large, yellow megaphone.

"Welcome to today's spectacle, folks. Sit tight and hold on to your hats, ladies and gents, because what you are about to see will knock the breath out of ya. These pilots and their performers are about to show you death-defying stunts that only the bravest souls in the world would attempt. Show them your approval by shouts and claps. And if you're brave enough, stick around after the show for a chance to take your own ride in the sky!"

Whispers rose to a fever-pitch in the rickety, wooden bleachers that swayed with the slightest puff of wind. Mothers clutched their children's hands as famous performers like Lillian Boyer, Mabel Cody, and Bugs McGowan tore across the sky. Their barrel rolls and loop-the-loops were the closest things to poetry in motion I'd ever seen. The *ooohs* and *ahhhs* emanating from the crowd were a symphony to my ears.

"Miss Lafferty."

In his light-gray suit and matching fedora, Rowland was dressed more for a dinner dance than a barnstorming show set up in the middle of a dirt field.

"Nice day for a show, wouldn't you say?"

The man was like a rodent. Always popping up where he wasn't wanted.

"A few too many clouds for my liking, but it'll do," I managed to say without too much venom.

He arched a hand over his eyes. "Did you see Miss Boyer's plane? Her name written in bright white type along the side? You could have that too if you joined The Skyhawks." He swung his hand across the sky in a dramatic flourish. "Picture it. Your name in bold script along with a picture of your face. A showman like ol' Dodger would love it. With a plane like that you'd never be the last name on the bill again."

I chuckled under my breath. His offers kept getting more ridiculous. "No one wants to see my mug painted on the side of a plane, least of all me."

He scrubbed a hand over his chin in thought. "All right then. What will it take to get you to agree to join my team? Name your price."

"There's nothing you have that could sway me. Go find another gal who'll swallow your promises of fame and packs of lies."

He yanked the edge of his fedora over his snow-white brows. "You may not appreciate my approach, but you'll always get the truth from me, Miss Lafferty." His gaze darted to where my team scrambled around the Jennys. "Can you say the same about the people you claim to trust?"

It was hard not to laugh directly in his face over his desperation. "Thank you once again, Mr. Rowland, for reminding me why I continue to take risks. Every trick I perform, every dollar we earn, is a moment closer to wiping your team from the sky."

Before he could say another word, I marched toward our planes. He thought he could get me to doubt my team, but his words had the opposite effect. Now more than ever I wanted to show him—and the rest of the world—what The Soaring Eagles were capable of.

After Henry confirmed our planes were ready, Nathan and Daniel took off. They performed a series of rolls, spinning the entire plane in a clockwise motion across the sky. When they leveled out, Nathan maneuvered the body of his plane upside down, traveling in an s-shape. Once upright, he swooped the belly just feet above the ground before returning the plane to its original position. He finished with an inverted whip stall, shooting the nose of the plane straight into the air until it lost altitude. The plane tumbled into a circular spin, heading tail-first toward the ground. Gasps rippled through the crowd as the plane hurdled down. The quiet murmurs exploded into excited roars when he regained control and shot back across the sky.

As a final part of their routine, Daniel climbed out onto the wing. After doing a series of single-leg dangles, he let go and tumbled through the air. The crowd held their breath as his body twisted and turned in a succession of backward rolls. I still don't know how he got his huge body into such a small, tight ball. Cries of terror morphed into sighs of relief once his parachute opened and he sailed into an easy landing.

With Daniel safely on the ground, I dashed toward Uncle Warren's plane. As soon as my safety belt was secure across my lap and my lucky goggles in place, we barreled down the dirt runway. My stomach took its familiar tumble as the wheels lifted off the ground. Speeding across the bright blue sky, I reveled in the thrum of the plane below my body.

Once we were at the right altitude, Uncle Warren called my name. I turned in the seat and he gave me the regular signal: two quick taps to his head, urging me to "be smart" during the performance. When I nodded my reply, we moved into a sharp dive, circling toward the ground. Adrenaline pulsed through my veins and black exhaust flooded all my senses, burning my eyes and throat. I held on until he swooped down low across the ground. We shot straight back into the sky, and after a few barrel rolls, I adjusted my flying goggles and climbed out of the seat.

Today's routine would be simple. A single-leg dangle, followed by a two-arm hang. Then I'd scramble to the top wing and finish with a crowd pleaser I'd dubbed the "Shiny Nose."

Even with everything going on with the team, and Henry's annoying presence, these were the moments I lived for. Amongst the clouds and the heat of the sun, the pressure in my chest disappeared. People said I was crazy for choosing this job, but they were wrong. Barnstorming filled me with an unexplainable joy; and getting to Chicago, earning that Hollywood contract, was the only way to ensure I could do this for the rest of my days.

I continued through my routine and once I was done I clambered up to the top wing. With my arm wound tightly around the wooden strut connecting the top and bottom wings, Uncle Warren took us down low. As we buzzed past the crowd, I pulled out a silver compact and powdered my cheeks. Whistles and boisterous applause filled my ears as we shot back up toward the sky. Once I slipped the compact back into my pocket, I inched across the Jenny's frame to the opposite side of the plane. When I reached the edge of the wing, a deafening grind from the engine rattled in my ears, and we dropped at an accelerated rate.

"Grace!" Uncle Warren screamed.

A teeth-rattling roar shook my body. At first I thought it was our own engine over-throttling, until I saw the belly of another plane, midnight black, just feet above my head. The Skyhawks' logo sneered at me from the tail. The plane sped over us, and its downdraft shoved me to the edge of the wing. I held on to the flying wires stretched across the wing, praying the force didn't rip me from the plane. My shoulders ached as I used all my upper body strength to hold on. Wind screamed in my ears while the draft acted like an invisible hand trying to tear me off the wing. A scream of terror escaped my mouth as the rough edges of the flying wire sawed into my hands.

I bent down and curled into a tight ball. My mind spun in several directions as I tried to figure out the best way to stay on the wing. The engine continued to buzz above me and fury replaced the terror humming through me.

Rowland's stunt wasn't going to be the end of me. I tightened my grip. The steel wires gnawed deeper into my palms and a heady, copper scent rushed over me as blood trickled down my wrists and dripped onto the fabric of the wings.

The roar of the engine faded. As quickly as the plane appeared, it vanished, as if the whole incident was a figment of my imagination. The only thing that proved it was real was the searing pain in my hands and the lingering black exhaust scalding my throat.

Once I was sure it was safe to move, I climbed down into the seat, leaving a trail of bloody handprints in my wake.

We hit the ground with a jarring slam, the tires barely compensating for our weight. Once the propeller stilled, Uncle Warren hopped out of the cockpit and moved across the wing toward me. Nathan and Daniel sped toward us. Henry limped as quickly as he could behind them.

"Are you hurt?" Uncle Warren asked in sharp, quick breaths.

"I'm fine." I forced a smile to my lips even though every inch of my body was screaming. This was not a moment to overreact. If I did, Uncle Warren or the boys would cause a scene, driving the spectators—and our money—away. We'd earned over thirty dollars with the last set of shows and were a hundred away from Chicago.

"Grace," Nathan's mouth tightened into a thin line. "Don't lie."

Trying not to flinch, I undid my seatbelt and climbed onto the wing. When my feet hit the ground, I slid my hands into my pockets and spun in a circle. "See. All in one piece."

I swept past them and toward the grandstands. The crowd jumped to their feet. Their deafening applause told me they thought The Skyhawks' stunt was all part of the show. Uncle Warren tipped his hat to the crowd like a true showman. He barked at the boys who took their own bows.

I made my own exaggerated curtsy. When I glanced up, my gaze moved through the grandstands until I landed on the familiar gray fedora. Sitting front and center was Rowland, Louis at his side.

He tipped his hat in my direction, a self-satisfied smirk dancing over his lips. This was his game to prove he could control me. Force me to think about his new offer. My pulse pumped with a complicated mix of rage and fear, but he'd never see it. Instead of buckling to his whim, I took another step forward, tore my lucky goggles from my neck, and shook them in the air in victory. The grandstands rumbled with applause as I whipped the crowd into a thrilled frenzy.

After we gave the spectators a final wave, Uncle Warren offered dollar rides to anyone interested. As soon as the words were out of his mouth, men, women and children rushed down the steps toward us. Photographers and local journalists added to the sudden crush.

"Take them in Nathan's plane," I said to Uncle Warren.

"What? Why? Don't you think we should talk about what happened?"

"Later," I insisted. "For now, collect as much money as you can."

Before he could protest, I moved back from the growing mob. The last thing I wanted to do was shake hands.

Henry raced behind me. "Where are you going?"

"That's none of your business."

Seeing a small break in the crowd, I moved along the side of the grandstands. Even though his limp seemed to be getting worse, Henry stayed on my heels.

Once we were free from the masses, I rushed toward an area shaded by a dozen oak trees and sunk down onto the grass. The reality of what occurred finally hit me. My entire body shook like a loose landing wire. I rolled my palms toward my stomach and took in two full breaths, hoping to calm my racing heart.

Henry searched the length of me and stopped at my hands. "What are you hiding?"

"Nothing. I need a break. Clear my head before the next show. Why don't you go find my uncle? Or better yet, find some needless work to do so you can earn more money for your precious garage."

I hoped the sharp edge of my words would send him away. With him hovering, I couldn't examine the damage.

He started to pace, although it was more of a painful hobble. "This is crazy. Why would you do this when there are so many other jobs out there for women?"

"There's absolutely nothing crazy about what I do."

"You could have been killed!" His voice cracked on the final word.

"Don't you think I know that?" My hands throbbed. I wanted to scream from the pain, but I needed to stay calm if Henry was ever going to leave. "Death is a possibility every single day with barnstorming."

He opened his mouth to say more but I continued. "Have you ever been to the circus?" His eyes widened like I was indeed mad. "Have you?" I repeated.

"Once, when I was young." He sighed and sunk down onto the grass next to me.

I realized my mistake. He took the question as an invitation to sit, and I had to bite the inside of my lip to keep my body from trembling. Even though I hated the thought, if he was going to stay a member of The Soaring Eagles he had to understand I wasn't some foolish girl playing a deadly game.

"Uncle Warren took me to see Barnum and Bailey's circus when I was fourteen. He won the tickets in a card game and insisted we see the show."

'What does that have to do with—?"

"Let me finish," I bit out.

His mouth tightened but he motioned for me to continue.

"The scariest and most fascinating part of the show was the tightrope walker. Her name was Bird Millman. She was so popular they shut down two of the rings and focused the spotlight on her. When she appeared above us, at least twenty-five feet in the air, with only a small parasol for balance, I felt like my heart stopped.

The entire tent went quiet when she moved along the wire as if she were taking a leisurely stroll. Not once did she hesitate or bobble."

Henry nodded. "I saw her, too."

"Do you think she set a toe out on that wire without thinking about the risk? Of course not. What separates her from the ne'er-do-wells is her understanding of the job and hours upon hours of practice. That's what divides the professionals from the amateurs. And the amateurs almost always get hurt." His forehead creased as I went on. "Do you want to know how I stayed on that wing instead of getting swept out into the sky?" He gave a slow nod again. "When I grabbed onto a wire, I knew to curl my body in and make myself small. It's difficult for air pressure to suck you off a wing if it doesn't have any purchase. If I'd let myself get rattled, forgotten what it takes to stay safe, the wind would have surely carried me to my death."

The image of being torn out into the clouds unsettled me but I wouldn't let him see it. "There's no room for fear in this job, Mr. Patton. I've spent hours practicing for that moment and today it served me well." He opened his mouth to speak, but I stopped him. "When you look at me what do you see?"

He let out a long breath and shook his head. "I see a young girl who hasn't had enough life experience to understand what she's risking."

I held back a rough laugh. It was a typical response from a man who knew nothing about me. "Well, that's where you're wrong. I've seen enough of the world to understand that every day I perform is a risk. Of course barnstorming is my choice, but it's no different than any woman who works in an office or delivers food in a restaurant. We all have the same goal: to survive and take care of our loved ones. My work just happens to be on top of an airplane rather than behind a desk."

I shoved my hands into my pockets and winced as my raw skin scraped against the fabric.

"Let me see your hands." Instead of his regular barking tone his voice bordered on tender.

I locked eyes with him. "I'm fine. Go back to the planes."

"I can tell you're hurt." He scooted in closer, his leg brushing mine. Like that day in the diner he reached for my hands, pulling them from my pockets. He turned them over and sucked in a breath. I waited for a lecture, a look of disappointment, but instead he reached for the cloth he always kept in the back pocket of his coveralls and pressed it to my bloody skin.

"Why didn't you say anything? You need medical attention."

I dug my fingertips into his wrist. "You can't say a word. If Uncle Warren knows about my hands he won't let me back in the air." We had our differences, but I hoped he would listen. "Please, Henry, I need to perform."

"The boys told me how you count every single dime the team makes. How important it is to get to that event in Chicago. Is that why you carry around that paper in your pocket? Glance at it several times a day when you think no one's looking?"

A chill shot through my aching bones. I thought I'd been secretive about the paper weighing heavy in my pocket. Reminding me what was at stake for me and my family.

"It's important we get to the Expo. Without a shot at the Hollywood contract, I don't know how long The Soaring Eagles can stay together. Every day there are more planes in the sky and fewer performances to go around."

I hated confessing the truth, but I needed him to keep my secret. To understand why this life meant so much to me. He worked his jaw, his eyes darting between me and the planes moving across the runway.

"You may know mechanics, but I need you to accept that this is all a part of barnstorming." I pointed to the grandstands. "That crowd is the biggest we've seen in weeks. When we move on to the next town there's a chance no one will show up. That's a wasted day, not to mention fuel and wear on parts. It also means we don't eat, and some abandoned field is our only place to sleep." I tried to steady my voice. "Every nickel we bring in means we have a shot at staying together. I can't allow injuries to my hands, or any other obstacle, to stand in the way of what this team needs." Although they throbbed, my fingers continued to clench his wrists, hoping my plea stirred some compassionate part of him.

After a long, agonizing minute, he peeled my fingers from his wrist. "Wait here. I'll be back in a moment." He limped past the grandstands and disappeared into the massive red-and-white performers' tent.

I tightened the cloth around my hands. Blood continued to seep through the fabric, turning the dusky, white material a light shade of pink.

What was I going to do? I had to go back in the air in less than an hour and my hands were slashed to a bloody pulp. In their current condition, it would be impossible to grip the guide wires and struts.

Henry reappeared at the tent opening a few minutes later and he wasn't alone. Rowland's goon, Louis, was at his side. At first, they stood close like they were having an easy conversation. A minute later Henry's shoulders tensed. A flailing of hands and finger jabs to the chest followed. After a few more angry stares, they parted ways.

Henry stomped back in my direction without bothering to look at me. Once seated on the grass, he closed his eyes and did that odd whisper thing again. I wanted to ask him what it meant. Why a wrench hitting the floor or the sharp slam of a car door made his body tremble. But the ache in my hands reminded me we all had things we were desperate to hide.

He remained quiet while he pulled a handful of items from his pocket. A canteen of water, a tube of ointment, and a few strips of white cloth. Each breath passing between us was tenser than the next.

"What did Louis want?"

With a deft hand, Henry loosened the bloody cloth. Again, he refused to meet my gaze. A low hiss left his mouth. He dabbed at the pooling blood before turning over the canteen, using the water to rinse the deepest cuts.

"He asked if I knew where you'd gone to after the performance. I guess Rowland wanted a word."

Once my skin stopped oozing, he slathered both my hands with the sticky, yellow ointment. Even though his fingertips were calloused, his touch was gentle.

"And what did you say?"

He paused for a minute, dabbing at my hand again. "I told him," he shook his head and pressed at the skin with a little more force. "I told him it would be a cold day in hell before Rowland got near you again." He gnashed his teeth together. "He said you should be grateful. He had the nerve to tell me the flyover was supposed to help your act, make it look more perilous to the crowd. He actually thought Rowland was helping. He even . . ." his words broke off.

"Even what?" I asked.

"Forget it," he said. A darkness swept across his eyes and stopped me from pushing for more of an answer. The ointment stung my ravaged skin but I stayed still and let him work.

"Doctor and mechanic," I said, grateful he wasn't running off to tell my uncle about my injuries.

"No, not quite, but with all the dangerous equipment on the farm you have to be ready for anything." His voice went soft as he bandaged my wounds, finally looking at me. "That's the best I can do considering the circumstances. I'm not sure how you're going to hide it from your uncle."

"That's why pockets are important." I slid my hands away, trying not to meet his intense gaze.

"You need to rethink that plan. Those bandages could come undone at any time."

"It's my choice. I've been through worse."

Gathering the items, he shoved them back into the pockets of his coveralls. "You've made me a co-conspirator now. If your uncle finds out I hid this from him, he'll sack me for sure."

I'd dreamed of him being fired in a variety of ways, but he'd helped me in a time of need. "I promise, I'd never rat on you."

"Maybe not, but I still feel guilty." He eased his hands back and looked to the spot he'd stood only minutes ago with Louis. "Tell me one thing. Why would Rowland act so reckless?"

A white plane belonging to The Flying Finellis banked around and came toward us, doing a tight barrel roll as it soared over our heads. Even from here, I could smell the heady combination of gasoline and burning oil.

"I'm the last one to ask why The Skyhawks do anything. The flyover could have killed me, and if both planes spun out . . ." It was hard not to shudder at the thought. "Well, it could have killed a lot of people on the ground, too."

His eyes searched my body, taking in my worn blouse and grease-covered pants before returning to my hands. His shoulders eased down and he shook his head slowly. "I know things have been tense between us, and we have differing views about the planes, but if you could teach me more about barnstorming, perhaps I wouldn't be such a burr in your side."

"You're much more than a burr," I grumbled.

His chuckle was low and deep, and it set off an odd warmth in my belly I'd never felt before. What was going on here? Were we coming to some sort of truce?

I stared up at the bright blue sky and contemplated how much I wanted to tell him.

"When The Soaring Eagles started out, Uncle Warren didn't want me to be a part of the team. At least not at the beginning,"

I admitted. "But I didn't really give him a choice. Every day after school, I'd show up at the hangar. Beg him to take me up. After a few flights, I climbed out onto the wing. It felt like home and I never wanted to leave. He swears if my parents knew what I was doing, they'd hang him up by his thumbs."

"Where are your folks? I've never heard you mention them. Do they live in Nebraska?"

After what happened this afternoon, the last thing I wanted to talk about was my parents. I reached for a small rock on the ground and hurled it into the distance. It bounced twice before disappearing into a patch of tall grass.

"They're dead," I said quietly. "Nothing more to say."

The lines between his brows furrowed. "My folks are gone too. My ma passed right after my seventh birthday. Her heart was never strong. Pa died while I was fighting in France. Tractor accident." His body crunched forward like the words caused him physical pain. "Now it's only me and my sister."

The thought of my own sister sent a sharp pain through me. The last time I'd seen Anna, her once-rosy cheeks had been white and lifeless.

"You have a sister? What's her name?" I asked, choking on the slow-forming knot in my throat.

"Caroline. You remind me a lot of her. Feisty. Headstrong."

His steady gaze made that warmth in my belly move up into my chest. Needing a distraction, I yanked a dandelion from the dirt, wincing as the stem poked my palm. "I love these."

The corner of his mouth twitched as he watched me examine the spindly petals. "You do know that's a weed, right?"

"No it's not. It's magic."

"Magic?" he chuckled. "How?"

With a deep breath, I blew on the wispy fluff. "Every time you blow off the petals you make a secret wish and the wind carries it away. It's akin to blowing out the candles on a birthday cake. Dandelions are like secret wish granters."

"And what did you wish for?"

"If I told you, the wish wouldn't come true."

He pulled his own dandelion out of the dirt and closed his eyes. A breeze whistled around us. After all the noise and excitement of the day, I welcomed the silence—and surprisingly, the comfort—of Henry's company.

While I tried to ignore the pain in my hands, they continued to throb under the tight cloths. "Maybe I do need gloves." I shook them out as if it might dull the pain.

"I still can't believe Rowland had his team pull such a dangerous stunt. Can't you report him?"

"No. The last thing we need is the feds nosing around. There's talk the government is starting to police the skies, especially after the incident in Boise. If they find problems, they could confiscate our planes and shut us down. That would be the end of the flying circuses. For now, every barnstormer needs to be careful—which doesn't seem to be a priority to Rowland or any members of his team."

"What happened in Boise?"

"A father and son team had engine trouble. Plane went into the ground nose down not too far from the grandstands. The smell of burning metal, charred skin—it was awful." I looked up at the sky, not wanting him to see my fear.

"I can't make you many promises," he rubbed at his injured leg, "but I will do everything in my power to keep The Soaring Eagles' planes safe. Contrary to your belief, I'm not just here to earn money for my own dream. I'd like to help you all achieve yours by getting to Chicago."

He chewed on his lower lip and pulled another dandelion from the ground. Of all the words I'd expected him to say, offering to help us get to Chicago was not one of them. Unlike the other mechanics we'd hired who sought fortune, fame, or a touch they didn't deserve, Henry genuinely wanted to keep us safe. For the first time my hopes of traveling to Chicago didn't seem like my dandelion wish, but a reality that might come true. His honesty, and the way he took care of me today, had made it very hard to dislike Henry Patton.

"Earlier you told Warren to use Nathan's plane for rides. Why?"

"When a customer forfeits their hard-earned dollar for a chance to soar in the sky, the last thing they want to see is bloody handprints on the wing." I quickly twisted my palms out in front of me. "Makes for a very uneasy ride."

"I could see why that might cause a problem."

"Could you imagine the screams from some of those women if they looked down and saw my blood smeared everywhere?" It was a horrible thought, but I couldn't help but laugh.

Henry tried to keep his face serious, but his shoulders began to bob up and down. Seconds later, he let out a loud chuckle. He was handsome when his face wasn't twisted into its regular scowl.

"We should not be laughing about this," I insisted in between my own giggles. "Because it's very serious."

"True," he said, a raucous laugh now escaping his lips. "Very serious."

"Yes, it's terrible. Especially when I think about you scrubbing all that fabric on the wing. It's going to be quite the job."

My laughs turned into a full-blown fit, and my stomach started to ache. Maybe this was what people meant when they said you had to laugh so you wouldn't cry. All I knew was being able to joke about today was like letting steam off a too-full tea kettle. I hated to admit it, but without Henry to distract me I might have gone in search of Rowland, which never turned out well.

"Grace!" Uncle Warren stalked across the field toward us. "Glad to see the two of you are having such a grand time," he snapped. "Henry, do you think you could pull yourself away from my niece long enough to look over the Jennys? We do have another show in an hour."

"Yes, sir." Henry pushed himself up off the ground but wobbled to the right.

I reached out to help him but the look he shot me was icy enough to freeze the sun. "I don't need your help," he muttered. "I can stand just fine on my own two feet."

So maybe there wasn't a truce between us.

Once he was steady, Henry limped toward Uncle Warren. He glanced back in my direction before leaning in to whisper in his ear. Uncle Warren nodded, focusing on the lower part of my body.

No. He wouldn't tell him about my hands. He couldn't, not after he promised to keep quiet. Not after I explained how important it was that I perform again today.

"I'll take care of it," Uncle Warren replied in a flat voice. He flailed a hand in the direction of the grandstands, ordering Henry back to work.

I stood and only got two steps towards him before he blocked my path. "Henry says you're tired. How about you let the boys go up first again for this next show? Give you a minute to catch your breath."

All the air squeezed from my chest. He'd kept his promise.

"Although if I had my way," he grimaced. "We'd be done for the day."

"No! Our contract with Dodger states we only get our money if we complete two shows. If we don't perform it's a wasted day, and Alistair Rowland gets what he wants. I will not let him win."

Uncle Warren clenched his aviator cap in his hand and shook it in my direction. "This is about safety. Don't you see that?" His voice rattled, and his arms moved out like he wanted to embrace me, but then they fell to his sides. "Your folks trusted me to take care of you. I won't let them down."

"You're doing a fine job, and this isn't about safety. It's about who can stay the strongest—who can take a hit and continue to fly. When we go back up today, we'll be showing The Skyhawks we're the best team in the sky."

"I saw Rowland staring you down." He jabbed a finger in the direction of the stands. "The man is waiting for something bad to happen." His entire body trembled as he pulled a cigar from his pocket and shoved it between his teeth.

"Rowland may think he's got the upper hand, but The Soaring Eagles are smarter and stronger than any stunt he can pull," I said.

"Maybe you're right," he grumbled. "But still, we need to be even more cautious now."

We walked back to the landing strip and Uncle Warren broke off to find Nathan and Daniel. I approached our Jenny and my line of sight landed on the blood splatter along the wing. Rowland may think he'd won with that idiotic stunt, but nothing he did could keep me from the sky. Nothing.

6
Itching for a Fight

Lincoln, Nebraska
July 24, 1922
50 days until the World Aviation Expo

When I walked into the hangar two days later Uncle Warren's office door was closed, but I could hear his low grumble inside. He'd left before I was out of bed this morning, which was unusual.

After pacing for five minutes in front of his office, I went in search of Henry. He'd kept his word after the flyover and I felt the need to thank him for his discretion. I called his name, but instead of finding Henry under the fuselage of one of the planes, I discovered Nathan and Daniel talking in a corner. Daniel placed a hand on Nathan's shoulder which he promptly knocked away.

"What's going on?"

"Why don't you ask that sap Warren hired?" Nathan grumbled. His eyes darted back and forth between me and the tail of his plane. When I moved in that direction Daniel reached out a hand to stop me.

"Grace, darlin', you need to talk to your uncle." His lips pinched together, warning something was wrong.

I dodged around him. An old work tarp was stretched out behind Nathan's Jenny. Nuts, bolts, and wires covered the length of tattered cloth. Next to the pieces sat a propeller blade. A breath caught in my chest. Scrambling to the other side of the hangar, I came to a jarring stop. Both wheels were off Uncle Warren's plane. One was completely deflated while the other looked like it was losing air quickly. A faint hiss filled the air.

"What in the blazes is going on?" My shout echoed off the four walls.

The office door banged open and rapid footsteps raced in my direction. Uncle Warren appeared and rushed toward me wild-eyed. "Grace, come into my office. We have some issues to discuss."

"Yes we do!" I waved to the floor. "Why is Nathan's propeller on the ground? And why are the tires off your Jenny?"

"Calm down. I promised Henry when we returned home he could do a thorough inspection of the planes."

"Without my permission?" Nathan interrupted.

Uncle Warren pointed a finger at him. "You need to clam up! Last time I looked, I still ran this outfit."

They stood in a stalemate until Nathan retreated behind his plane.

Uncle Warren took in a long, deep breath, clenching the brown stub between his teeth. "Unfortunately, during his inspection Henry discovered problems with both Jennys yesterday."

"What problems? The planes need to be ready to go. We have two shows in Kansas City tomorrow. We need that money for Chicago."

Uncle Warren shifted back and forth on his feet. His eyes moved around the hangar in search of something or someone.

"Henry," I called out.

He walked out of the office and focused on the floor. His limp was more pronounced than the days before.

"Do you have something you want to tell me?" He shuffled to the other side of the room like he was avoiding me. "This is a small hangar. You can't hide."

I moved to follow him when Uncle Warren's thick fingers circled my wrists. His touch scratched over my palms and I tried not to hiss. I'd managed to keep my injured hands a secret and I wasn't about to confess now that they were healing. "Grace, we're grounded. No flights for at least a week until we can replace Nathan's propeller blade and repair the tires on my plane."

I wrenched away from his hold and stomped toward Henry who hovered near the oil-stained tarp.

"Not two days ago, you promised you'd help us get to Chicago, but that won't happen now that our planes are in pieces. Will you please tell me what's happening?"

When he finally turned to face me, my head went light and I stumbled into the wing. A dark-blue bruise colored his left eye. Dried blood covered the split in his lip and the deep scratch across his right cheek.

"Who did this to you?" I asked. He stared straight past me and didn't say a word. "Why aren't you speaking?"

Daniel and Nathan stepped forward, eyes wide, as they took in Henry's torn shirt, covered in blood stains.

"Goodness gracious," Daniel whispered. Nathan stayed uncharacteristically quiet, unable to look away from the deep gash over Henry's eye.

"Last night, Henry was here late trying to scrub blood off the wings." Uncle Warren looked down at my hands and huffed. "He also wanted to check over some issues with the planes. After taking a few pieces apart, he headed home to get some rest. On the way to his boarding house, Rowland's thug jumped him. His landlady found him this morning in the street and he insisted she bring him here."

The argument in front of the tent flickered through my mind. "We have to go the police," I insisted.

"No. There aren't any witnesses. It's my word against Rowland's man."

I walked to where Henry now sat. Even with the cuts and bruises, his bright green eyes were still beautiful. He tried to sit up and look at me but winced at the small movement.

"Why would Rowland's goon do this?"

"He didn't say much." It was painful to watch him try and get out the few words. "Except if I valued my life I wouldn't fix your planes anymore." Pain etched into his eyes as he gasped. "When you and your uncle took that hard landing after the flyover it damaged the tires. And I ran ink over your propeller, Nathan. If you bend down and look, you'll see a hairline crack." He tried to stand and wobbled on his feet. "Here, let me show you."

Nathan trod slowly behind as if shell-shocked by this revelation. After examining the prop, Nathan sat back on his heels and shook his head. "That could have been a disaster in the air." He reached forward and gripped Henry's hand. "Thank you."

Henry swayed and Daniel caught him before he hit the ground. My stomach tumbled as I helped guide him back to the workbench.

"Henry, this all happened because of me. I'm sorry."

"My injuries aren't your fault." He spoke slowly, rubbing his side. "That man was doing Rowland's bidding."

"You don't have to say any more. I'm going to stop this."

My footsteps echoed across the concrete as I ran for the hangar door. I was done playing this game. First it was the constant hounding. Then the flyover stunt. Now Henry was attacked. It couldn't continue. Alistair Rowland and I were going to come to an understanding. If he wanted to play dirty, I could play dirty, too. A few misplaced spark plugs could disable his entire fleet.

Anger bubbled in my veins as I crossed the landing strip. Before I could move onto the dirt road leading back into town, Daniel caught up to me.

"Where do you think you're going, darlin'?"

I sped up my footsteps. Uncle Warren had sent him to stop me, but a herd of wild bulls couldn't hold me back. Before the day was over, Alistair Rowland and I were going to have it out. His man could work me over too if he wanted, but one way or another his antics were going to end.

I only got five more steps before Daniel stepped in front of me.

"Get out of my way."

"No. You're all worked up and that's not a right state to be in if you're going to face Rowland. Times like these call for cool heads. And right now, I'd say yours was on fire."

"I said move, Daniel."

He crossed his thick arms over his barrel chest and widened his stance. "You're itching for a fight and I won't let you go."

I dodged to his left. Like he knew what I was planning, he shot out an arm and stopped my forward motion. Once he had hold of me, he tossed me over his shoulder like a sack of flour.

With solid steps, he walked to the hangar while I kicked and screamed until I was hoarse. When he finally set me down, tears burned at my lashes. Henry could barely see out of his right eye and it was hard to listen to his labored breaths.

How could I apologize for that? No matter how many "I'm sorries" I uttered, it would never make things right.

7

Dark Streets and Unsavory Characters

July 28, 1922
46 days until the World Aviation Expo

The noise inside the diner was louder than a propeller spinning at full speed. I sat at a stool near the counter and gazed up at the specials on the chalkboard. I didn't want to be here, but Uncle Warren forced me out of the hangar after he caught me needling Henry again about our Jenny's carburetor. For days, he'd warned me to leave Henry alone so he could work, but the pull to help proved to be too much, especially since Henry winced and gasped every few minutes.

After realizing I couldn't afford anything but a small glass of lemonade, I spun around, trying to locate Mary and Ethel. I found Ethel first in the back corner, chatting up two men in army uniforms. Mary was on the opposite side of the room, her dark curls plastered to her forehead as she cleared coffee cups and plates from a table.

"What will it be, doll?" An older waitress stood across the counter, a pencil shoved into her tight gray bun.

"She likes lemonade." Mary moved toward the counter, her tiny body struggling with a tray full of dirty plates. "This is my friend, Grace." She heaved the mound of dishes, cutlery, and coffee cups onto the counter and a shy smile lit her heart-shaped face. "I can take it from here."

"This isn't your section," the waitress snapped. Mary shuffled back. Her hands shook and her eyes took on that glassy, vacant look again.

Ethel moved in front of Mary like a protective shield. "It is now, Gloria."

The waitress must have already had a tumble or two with Ethel because she huffed and stomped away.

"Grace, we're so glad you're here. Aren't we, Mary?"

Mary slowly bobbed her head and slid back onto a stool next to the counter. Her chest heaved up and down. Ethel watched closely as Mary's breathing slowed and a pinch of color returned to her drawn face.

"A reporter stopped in for lunch yesterday," Ethel went on patting Mary's hand. "He mentioned seeing one of your shows and said it was only a matter of time before Hollywood snaps you up."

"Hollywood," Mary said, blooming slowly back to life like a flower waking in the morning sun. "Wouldn't that be a dream, Grace?

"The movie magazines say Mary Pickford lives there. Maybe you could rub elbows with her." Ethel sighed. "And that Rudolph Valentino," she cooed. "He's the most gorgeous man on the planet."

Ethel looked me up and down, tapping her chin. "Of course you'd have to do something with your hair and clothes. But I could see you being a starlet in no time."

Mary bobbed her head in agreement. "You're sure pretty enough."

It was hard not to glance down at my worn clothes and laugh. It would take much more than a new dress and a haircut to make me fit into that glamorous world. "Being a star has never been my goal," I admitted. "Yes, I want to win that contract and get to Hollywood, but that dream isn't about being famous. The whole point of the contest is to get regular work for The Soaring Eagles. To earn enough so we don't have to sleep in fields after a late show or eat pork and beans from a can several days in a row."

"But don't you want more, Grace?" Ethel asked. "One day you won't be eighteen anymore and you'll need to do something else. Isn't Hollywood a logical choice for a performer like you?"

"As long as there are planes, I can work. And thanks to you two, Henry is turning out to be a great mechanic. We'll win that contract and our security. A steady paycheck. It also means my uncle will stop pestering me about finding a more suitable line of work."

A curious look moved across Ethel's face. She started to say something when Archie screamed at her to help a customer at the counter. Ethel ignored him as she and Mary went back to chattering about Hollywood and the latest news they'd read in one of their movie magazines. Their conversation veered onto picture shows and how they wanted to catch the new feature playing nearby.

"Our shift ends in ten minutes. Come with us, Grace." Mary pleaded.

"Yes, come along," Ethel urged.

Going back to the farmhouse to sit in uncomfortable silence with Uncle Warren was not my idea of a good time, but I wasn't sure listening to the girls gab about their Hollywood dreams and the handsome new dishwasher was any better.

"We're paying for your ticket," Ethel insisted. "And you cannot wear that drab outfit."

She pointed to my wrinkled ensemble. Her finger moved down the length of me and stopped at my scuffed boots.

"Sorry, girls. This is all I've got."

Ethel's bright blue eyes lit up. "Wait. I was supposed to go on a date yesterday, but that cad stood me up." She rushed back into the kitchen. When she reappeared, a wine-colored silk dress dangled from her hands. "I left this in the back, but I won't be needing it now."

"In that outfit, you'll be beautiful," Mary gushed.

"You're gonna look gorgeous." Ethel rushed forward, pressing the material against my body.

"Putting on fancy rags, or rouging my cheeks, is not going to make me a different person." I waved the dress away. "This," I pointed to my wrinkled pants and dirty boots, "is who I am. Famous or not." The girls didn't bother to argue. They'd known me long enough to understand that once I set my mind to something I wasn't going to change.

Summer heat prickled against the back of my neck as I rushed down the street behind Mary and Ethel, who were still grumbling about me not wearing the dress. Touring cars and coupes bounced along the road, their horns blaring at each intersection when traffic came to a stop.

We hurried past the drug store and hardware store, our foot-steps clicking along until the twinkling lights of the Piccadilly Theater appeared. We paid our seven cents at the glass ticket booth and headed through the giant oak doors. Once inside, we rushed past wood-framed advertisements for *Sherlock Holmes* starring John Barrymore. Mary stopped and gasped at a floor-to-ceiling color image of Gloria Swanson's latest film, *Beyond the Rocks.*

With the lobby clock chiming the time, we rushed toward the circular, oak staircase, taking the stairs two at a time. We chose seats near the center balcony and slid into the hardback chairs to wait for the velvet curtains to pull back.

Mary looked over her shoulder and gripped the edges of the chair.

"What's wrong?" I asked.

She blinked her long lashes twice and shuddered.

"Mary, look at me." Ethel reached across my lap and took her hand.

Slowly Mary peeled her eyes open and took another glance over her shoulder. She shook her head and took in a long, dragging

breath "It's nothing," she whispered. "I thought I saw a man I recognized from home but I was wrong."

"No one knows where we are, honey. It's been two years." Ethel
patted her hand. "Why don't we go to the ladies room? Freshen
up a bit?"

Ethel stood and cocked her head to the end of the aisle. "Grace,
you coming?"

"No. You two go ahead."

Mary stood and smoothed down the edges of her lace dress.
My heart ached watching her thin, wobbly legs trail behind Ethel.
Mary going rigid in public wasn't something new. At least a half
dozen times since I'd known the girls, Mary had stopped cold in
the middle of the sidewalk, or halfway through taking an order,
convinced she recognized a face from the town they'd so desper-
ately escaped. She might be a grown woman, but she was terrified
of being dragged back to Gering and a life she didn't want.

The house lights went dark. A spotlight hit the front row. The
pianist scurried across the stage and found his way to the right of
the screen. The crowd tapped their toes to the snappy overture
until a haunting melody eased through the air.

At the end of the row an older couple looked in my direction
and whispered. Perhaps I should have followed Mary and Ethel,
but I was tired of people judging how I should behave.

A group of men chattered behind me, urging each other to be
bold and sit next to me. I turned to offer a quick "no," but before
I could get the words out a body settled into the seat next to me.

"Sitting alone again? Didn't that cause a bit of trouble a while
back?"

"What are you doing here, Henry?" I whispered, ignoring his
jab.

"The truth?"

I nodded but kept my eyes fixed on the screen. "I'm still waiting
on that final part to come in, so I can't do any work at the hangar.

And Nathan and Daniel may not complain, but my room at the boarding house is no bigger than a shoebox. I couldn't look at the four walls anymore. Even though my ribs are still aching, I decided to take a walk. As I was rounding my building, I saw you and your friends rushing down the street, so I followed you."

He stared at me until I finally met his eyes. The bruise under his eye had faded to a yellowish-green, and his lip was almost healed. "I'm not a cad, I promise. I only wanted to make sure you got here safely. You know, dark streets and unsavory characters." He didn't say the words but his meaning was clear—he was worried about Rowland's goon making another appearance.

We sat in silence, the words filling the screen, nothing but the steady movement of our breath for sound. Out of the corner of my eye, I watched him. He was wearing what looked like a new suit that was a shade lighter than charcoal. A shadow of whiskers covered his chin. His full mouth moved up and down as he read the dialogue. Every once in a while he noticed me looking, and the deep dimple in his right cheek appeared. I caught him staring a few times, too.

The lights flickered and "*The End*" appeared on screen. We stayed in our seats while the audience filed out. Once the final musical note faded away, I glanced over my shoulder.

"Those men left about half way through the picture, probably to go bother some other nice gal whose friends deserted her."

"They didn't desert me," I said too quickly. "I bet they were embarrassed to come back in after the show started. They're out in the lobby waiting. I'm sure of it."

"If you say so." He grabbed the armrests and took a moment to stand. His hands shook. Dark blue veins bulged under his skin. On instinct, I reached out to help him.

"Stop!" His tight mouth twitched. "I don't need your help."

"You don't need to snipe at me," I huffed. "It's not a sin to accept help even if it is from a woman."

His shoulders softened and he shook his head. "I understand you're trying to be kind, but I can't have you looking at me like I'm some broken toy you're keen on fixing. This is how I am, plain and simple. I may wobble a bit, but I'm perfectly capable of standing on my own."

A sad smile slid over his lips. He turned on his heel and walked to the end of the aisle.

8
Not My Idea of Fun

Thick maroon tapestries covered the lobby walls, making the room hotter than a henhouse at midday. Women readjusted their cloche hats, trying not to wilt under the heat, while men fished cigarettes out of their suit pockets.

I batted away the gray swirls filling the room, intent on finding Mary and Ethel in the crowd. Henry remained at my side while I moved across the heavy carpet. It took every ounce of strength not to tell him to leave after he'd snapped at me for trying to help.

"Grace!" Ethel raced toward me, towing Mary behind her. They were followed by the two men I'd seen earlier in the diner. The flush of happiness in the girls' cheeks made me bite back the angry words forming in my throat. After what they put up with at the diner, they deserved to have a good time.

"We're sorry we missed the movie. Our new friends, Earl and Frank, walked by and we got to talking," Ethel explained.

"Yes, we're sorry," Mary repeated. Her voice was barely audible above the din of the crowd. She shifted farther behind Ethel, her gaze darting curiously in the direction of the man with bright blond hair that Ethel called Frank.

Ethel reached out her hand to Henry. "Well, hello again," she cooed.

Henry removed his hat and shoved it under his arm. He gulped and pulled the tab collar from his throat before shaking her hand. "Nice to see you again."

"Gals, how about that party?" The men cocked their heads toward the door.

"Oh yes, Grace, come with us. Frank and Earl are going to a party uptown with a jazz band," Ethel gushed. "And of course, Henry, you're invited, too," A shy smile slid across her lips.

"Can't," I said abruptly. "Need to be at the hangar early tomorrow."

Henry's brows shot up at my lie. The truth was I knew how the girls operated. They'd continue to badger me until I gave in, and tonight I didn't have the patience for it. "Go on and have a good time. You two deserve it."

Ethel and Mary couldn't hide their disappointed frowns. They'd spent countless hours trying to get me to let loose and experience the growing nightlife in Lincoln. I'd heard stories about the wild jazz parties in private speakeasies, and racing to hide from the police after they were raided. Getting thrown in jail with a bunch of soused hooligans was not my idea of a good time.

"Fine," Ethel huffed. "But please make sure our girl gets home safe."

Henry gave her a sharp nod. "I'll see to it."

The men guided the girls to the door. I gave Henry a half-hearted smile when Mary and Ethel's shadows disappeared into the night.

"You don't need to walk me home. I'm sure you have other plans."

"I have no other plans. Plus, your uncle would have my hide if I didn't see you home."

I couldn't help but glance down at his leg. "It's over a mile."

He followed my gaze. "Again, I'm a lot sturdier than I look."

Once outside the theater, a blast of slick humidity swept across my cheeks. As we walked along the busy road, Henry's profile in the moonlight was striking. The sharp angles of his cheeks. The strong line of his jaw. I was still curious about that small scar on his chin. Did he get it in the war while he was buried deep in a trench?

Our steps echoed across the wide street. He hooked his arm

through mine and inched me to his side so I wouldn't step into a gaping hole in the middle of the walkway.

"Thank you," I said, pulling away quickly.

His brows knitted together. "I know you don't believe this considering what's passed between us, but I *am* a gentleman."

My lips pursed in response. He could say the words, but it didn't mean I believed them.

A smirk lifted the corner of his mouth. "My sister does the same thing when she's holding back what she really wants to say. The only things missing are the clenched fists."

"Oh, I'd do that, too, but my hands are still a bit sore."

We continued toward P. Street, the sounds of the city filling the silence. A low, mournful melody floated from an open window at a nearby restaurant. Next to it, raucous laughter spilled from the entrance of the Central Hotel as a group of people not much older than us headed out for the evening. Sequins and pearls covered the women's knee-skimming dresses, while shiny black top hats adorned the heads of the men.

"Do you miss her? I mean your sister." My voice caught on the word.

"Yes," he sighed, pulling down the brim of his hat. "She's fiercely independent like you. Her husband's name may be on the deed to the farm but she's an equal partner."

"Do you miss it? Your farm?"

"Can't say I do. I always knew I'd work with machines one day in a big city."

I pointed to the opposite side of the street. "We need to cross here." When we were only steps off the corner, a loud boom echoed through the air, nearly knocking me off my feet.

"Sam, get down!" Henry's hand slammed against my shoulder. I winced from his vise-like grip as he forced me behind a parked car.

"Get your hands off me!" I shrieked.

He swiveled his head left and right. The whites of his eyes went wide. He reached along his waistband, his fingers fumbling for something that wasn't there.

"My gun! Where's my gun?" he shouted. His body trembled. Sharp breaths burst from his mouth before his head swung back in the direction of the noise.

What was happening to him? It was like he'd forgotten where we were.

"Henry," I whispered not wanting to startle him. When he didn't move, I said, "Henry, we're in Lincoln. It's okay." His shoulders continued to twitch. "You're safe." He faced me and dug his fingers into my arms. His eyes were vacant, like his body was here but his mind was in a completely different place.

A Model T filled with men rumbled down the street. Their catcalls at the women along the sidewalk filled the night air. Henry blinked twice as if trying to figure out where he was. His fingers tightened against the thin edges of my shirt before he looked into my eyes.

"Oh my god, Grace. I'm sorry." He snatched his fingers away and crawled to the curb.

My nerve endings continued to snap with adrenaline. When my heart stopped galloping like a wild horse, I moved to sit next to him. The city hummed around us. Pedestrians moved on the sidewalks. The trumpet of a car horn floated through the air. It was like the last few seconds never happened.

"Funny how a car backfiring can sound like a gunshot," I said.

He fingers slid down his face. "You must think I'm out of my mind."

"No, I don't think that at all." My hand settled on his back to comfort him. It might not have been the proper thing to do, but I couldn't bear to see his body shake.

"My reaction. It was instinct. From the war." His clipped sentences were sharp and filled with what sounded like regret.

"In the diner when we first met, you acted frightened. And just now it was the same thing, except this time you called me Sam. Was that a friend of yours?"

The veins in his neck pulsed wildly. His hands opened and closed into clenched fists. It was a quick, frantic movement made over and over like he was trying to ground himself in the moment.

"I didn't mean to scare you," he said without answering my question. I nodded and tried to hide my shaking hands in the pockets of my pants.

He turned, his hands hovering inches away as if he was afraid to touch me. "Did I hurt you?"

"No, I'm fine. Tougher than I look."

The set of defeat in his shoulders set me on edge. I'd been in the same spot once. Helpless and afraid of circumstances beyond my control. After my family died, I pretended their deaths didn't mean anything. That I could go on with my life and not think about them. All I'd wanted was to push away the fear and anger so I could be normal again.

But for months after I first arrived in Lincoln I would wake to Uncle Warren shaking my shoulders as I cried out for my parents and sister.

"Do you want to talk about it? The war?" I asked.

"No. I don't like thinking about it, much less speaking about it."

I understood what he meant. You could fool yourself into believing you had a normal life if you never thought or talked about your past. It was easier to put those feelings away in some small box locked deep inside your heart rather than face it every day.

He pushed up off the curb, favoring his leg until he could get his balance. I knew better than to reach out this time. Once he was steady, he took my hand. "Let me honor my promise to see you home."

"Are you sure? It's really not that far."

As he slid his fingers through mine, heat zapped across my skin.

I'd never held hands with a man. He gave me a reassuring smile as if he could hear the frantic thrum of my heart.

We only got a few steps when he stopped abruptly. "I know I have no right to ask this considering what's passed between us, but I beg you not to tell anyone about my, uh, episode. I really enjoy working with the boys and Mr. Warren." He twisted his neck as if trying to work out a kink. "And, well, you too, of course." He bowed his head as if surprised by the confession. "I need this job if I ever want to own my own garage. If you forget tonight, I will do everything in my power to ensure The Soaring Eagles are a success."

I chewed the inside of my cheek as he watched me. "You did keep my secret after the flyover. I suppose I can show you the same courtesy."

"You won't regret this decision. I promise I will help you . . . I mean the team . . . win that contract."

"Fine. As teammates, we agree."

A wide smile crossed his lips. "Let's make it teammates *and* friends." He nodded down the street and led the way home.

9
Silent Agreement

Jasper, Arkansas
August 5, 1922
38 days until World Aviation Expo

On certain summer days the sky was so blue it was like we were flying through a watercolor painting I once saw at the Lancaster County Fair. Dark sapphire overlapping azure on top of a cornflower blue you only saw in the wild.

Uncle Warren leveled out the plane. When I turned in my seat to face him he gave his head two sharp taps. A welcome rush of electricity snapped through my body. After eleven long days, we were finally back in the air.

With quick hands, I unlatched my safety belt and climbed onto the wing, my hair whipping behind me like a dark, tangled sheet. A fierce wind forced us to the east and the air pressure made it difficult to stand. The Jenny throttled forward over the top of wide, white fields bursting with acres of cotton. With a sharp bank to the right, we soared over the roof of a weathered barn. A rooster-shaped weather vane guided us to the west and back in the direction of town.

My leather saddlebag bumped against my hip as I hoisted my body onto the lower wing. I only had one shot to do this right.

We buzzed down over cows and other livestock, the scent of manure filling my nose. In the distance, the buildings of the town reflected the early morning sun. Uncle Warren's hand rose above his head in a closed fist. With that signal I edged farther out onto the wing. Once my feet were secure, I opened the flap on the bag.

We nosed down to 500 feet and soared over the shops and restaurants, alerting the citizens to our early morning arrival.

This was the first time we'd been to Arkansas. Uncle Warren picked this place because of the acres of open fields that surrounded the small town. The county fair in Little Rock was also at least three months off and a two-hour drive away, so he guessed the residents would be clamoring for any kind of entertainment.

While not a big city performance, this small barnstorming stop provided two things The Soaring Eagles needed: practice and money. The contest was only five weeks away. After being grounded for over a week, and with expenses piling up, we were a hundred and ten dollars away from that dream. I was still working on the Showstopper whenever I was alone in the hangar. Over the last week, I'd discovered that the wire I'd picked was too thin to bear my weight when I jumped from the lower skid, and the rudimentary mouthpiece still cut my mouth open in certain places. It needed more work before I could convince my uncle to let me jump from the plane with only a wire clenched between my teeth to keep me from certain death.

We eased down over the farthest end of town. The roar of the prop ricocheted off the brick buildings like a bullet shot inside a tin barrel. This was the first pass to rattle the windows and stir the townspeople. On pass two, we shifted our wings left and right as we made another low buzz over the rooftops. To gain interest in our show, we had to make every moment count. On the third flyover, when the streets were crowded with gawkers, I dropped the handbills. The thin pieces of paper cascaded down like burnt-orange leaves in the fall. Black ink covered every square inch, advertising:

The Soaring Eagles Spectacle: An aerobatic show with death-defying tricks, parachute acrobatics, and barnstorming not seen this side of the Mississippi.

With the handbills littering the streets, we did another circular pass. Now it was time for the real show. I slid the satchel off my hip and knotted it around a strut. Uncle Warren kept us level above the buildings. He flew in one large circle, and then turned around for another approach. We weren't low enough. I scooted in on the wing and banged the side of the body to get Uncle Warren's attention. Once I caught his eye, I pointed down. Up this high the shopkeepers could barely see me. But if we went lower, until our wheels almost skimmed the tops of the buildings, the townspeople would get a taste of what our real show would be like later today.

The Jenny continued on its forward path. I motioned down again. We glided down until the wheels almost grazed the roofs. I swung out with one hand, clasping a wood strut and spinning around the edge of the wing. The crowd's eyes never wavered as we sped back around and I moved into a headstand. The wind snapped against my goggles and it was hard to keep the smile from my lips. Thirteen days without battling the elements felt like a lifetime. My body craved the taste of the wind. Mist on my cheeks. I was finally home.

The wind from the east batted at my body, and I held steady, focusing on the next trick. While I'd had my fair share of battling the elements, Mother Nature did her best to beat me back. We'd fought before at higher altitudes, and my iron will always seemed to bend hers.

We flew down past the town one more time before heading toward the farm where Uncle Warren had paid to set up camp. The two-story, weathered barn with its chipped red paint would act as our hangar until the first show this afternoon. Ignoring my arguments, Uncle Warren had paid extra to move the livestock to their outside pens, claiming the stench inside was too much.

Once we were back over the vast fields of cotton, I climbed back into my seat. When the engine reached all its sixty-five horses, the nose of the plane edged up into the clouds. The inverted loop shot all the blood to my head. The edges of my vision became a hazy blur. My body rose off the seat for half a breath before gravity slammed me back down. This was my life and I never wanted to give it up.

~

Ten minutes. That's how long we had to wait before horses, wagons, trucks, and Model Ts bounced across the open field toward us.

Before we could jump down from the wings, we were swarmed by a group of men who peppered us with a dozen questions about flight. Uncle Warren told them for a dollar he'd give them each their own ride. A thick wad of bills weighed down his pockets before he could answer the first question.

While Uncle Warren busied himself with the townspeople, Nathan pulled me to the side.

"People are whispering something about you buzzing over the mercantile in town?"

"We had to get low enough to create a commotion. Pull people out in the street."

"Did you think about what could have happened if you'd clipped a wing and went down with all those people around?"

I peeled his hands off my arm. "What's gotten into you? This is how we perform. How we get people to our shows."

He straightened out his shirt and huffed. "I'm just worried about your safety. I've seen enough to know what can happen if you take too many risks."

He spun around and marched back to where Daniel entertained a few young boys by hoisting them up onto the wings of Nathan's Jenny.

After a few minutes they lost interest and encouraged Nathan and Daniel to join them in a pick-up baseball game in a nearby field.

Good, that would keep Nathan out of my hair for a while.

A band of women nearby watched me with curious eyes like I was a sideshow performer—not sure if they should approach.

Some days I wanted to hold up my hands and promise not to bite. I let them stew for a few minutes before I found the smallest girl in the crowd and asked if she wanted to try on my lucky goggles. Stiff shoulders soon relaxed and the children clamored to touch my leather jacket. The women grew bolder too, asking how I got the knots out of my hair and what it was like to wear pants.

The chatter rose and children started chasing each other in circles, trying to keep the goggles to themselves. Henry leaned back against the barn door to watch the scene. After what happened in the street, we'd relaxed into a tentative friendship. Without my knowledge, he'd spoken to my uncle about allowing me to service certain parts of the plane under his supervision. Over the last week we had worked side by side, aligning the wings, fixing turnbuckles, and double-checking the tension in the landing wires, all without a single grumble from him.

With the late summer weather holding up, Henry spent most of the time outside with the planes. The skin on his arms was a warm shade of bronze. The ends of his hair, once a light brown, were now woven with gold.

He cocked his head and waved me toward the barn. When I reached him, he pointed to a landing wire on my uncle's Jenny. "Place your hand at the top." I climbed onto the wing and reached for the wire. As he directed, I slid my hand down the steel.

"Feel anything?" he asked.

"It's secure at the top, but lower down it has some give."

His bright smile turned his eyes greener than the late summer grass. He reached for a shiny wrench and a brand-new pair of pliers that were settled amongst the tools lined up in a perfect row along the Jenny's frame.

"Where did those come from?"

"My sister Caroline sent them to me. In my last letter, I told her mine were getting worn out."

"That was kind of her."

He gave me a brief nod and pointed to the wire again. "That's a good catch. An experienced mechanic can tell by the feel of the wire if it's tensioned properly."

He moved in closer, showing me how to correct the tension on the turnbuckle. The heady scent of oil and soap on his skin filled my nose as I worked the wire. The heat of his breath tickled the hairs on the back of my neck and shot goosebumps over my skin.

We're just friends and teammates, I reminded both my head and heart.

"Do you see that?" He pointed to a little girl on the edge of the field.

"What about her?"

He climbed down and offered up a hand to help me to the ground. His touch sent a familiar warmth through my stomach. "She's been watching you from the moment you landed."

The girl clung to her mama's long skirt but her eyes never moved from me. I took a step to the left and her head moved with me. Testing her, I jumped back to the right and her warm, brown eyes followed.

"Her ma hasn't paid a lick of attention to her. The other children tried to coax her into a game of tag, but she's never moved from that spot, from watching you."

"Watching me? Why? Do I have something stuck in my hair?" I felt around the top of my head for a loose branch or leaf.

"No," he chuckled. "Can't you see the adoration and wonder in her eyes? Go talk to her, Grace. She's entranced by you."

"I . . . I wouldn't know what to say."

Giving the children my goggles was one thing, but speaking to this girl was out of the question. When we interacted with the townsfolk I was always cordial, but I did my best to stay away from the younger girls. They reminded me too much of my little sister, Anna. The ache of looking at them made my heart so heavy it was hard to breathe. She would have celebrated her fifteenth birthday this year. While I didn't do it intentionally, I found myself searching out girls in the crowd who might look like her. Would she have looked more like Ma or Pa at this age? Her coloring was similar to mine: coal-black hair and arctic-blue eyes. We both favored Pa, but while I was on the shorter side, Anna was long and thin like our Ma.

"Don't you want to talk to her?" he asked.

"No. She looks shy. I'd scare her away."

I walked further into the barn past the empty pig pens and horse stalls. Even though the animals were outside, the stench of manure burned my eyes and nose.

Henry limped up beside me. "Don't you know what a swell gal you are? You're braver than half the men I met in France." He glanced over my shoulder to the little girl. "You're a proud barn-stormer. Go out and show her what being in the sky means to you. Your words may inspire her to walk among the clouds one day, too. Don't deny her that privilege."

I blanched at his words, not sure I'd heard him right. The kind tone in his voice still took some getting used to, and I couldn't help but wonder if this was all an act so I'd keep his secret.

As if he could hear my thoughts, he stepped in closer so there were only inches between us. "These past weeks I've been unfair to you. I see the joy you bring people when you perform. For those few minutes, you mesmerize them, make them forget their troubles. I may be stubborn, and somewhat set in my ways, but I'm not blind to how your work affects the crowd."

The girl continued to stare in our direction. Her coloring wasn't the same as Anna's, but the light in her eyes made me think of her.

"All right, I'll go, but only if you come with me." He waved me forward and I followed him across the dirt field we'd used as a landing strip.

Every time I took a step closer the girl skittered farther behind her mother. I stopped ten feet away. Her tiny, brown shoes were the only visible part of her. "Hello, little one," I said, trying to coax her out, but she stayed hidden behind the bulk of her mother's skirt.

Before I could backtrack, Henry limped forward. "Ma'am, what's your daughter's name?"

The woman reached behind her and pulled the girl forward. "This here's Ruby."

The little girl blinked rapidly. Her chest pulsed in and out with quick breaths.

"Ruby, I'm Henry." He reached his hand toward me, wiggling his long, thin fingers. "And this is Grace."

His hand was like a lifeline and I held onto it as he pulled me toward the small girl with tight, brown curls. She stared at me for a long moment. With small measured steps, she approached. Once her warm palm melted into mine, I released an unsteady breath. I looked to Henry for help. He motioned for me to kneel so we were eye-to-eye.

"Was that you up in the plane, miss?" Her voice was soft as the wind chime that hung outside my farmhouse—both lyrical and haunting. My mouth went dry and all I could manage was a nod. "You looked like an angel up in the clouds."

The smile that had once lit her face faded. "My pa went to heaven before I was born. Ma said he died in the war keeping me and other children safe. Do you think that's true?" she asked the question more to Henry than me.

"It's absolutely true," he answered.

Her mouth puckered for a moment as she studied him. "You were in the war too. I can tell."

"By my limp?" he asked, attempting to stand straighter.

She shook her head. "No sir. You've got marks around your eyes. My pa's friends who came back from the war have the same ones."

Henry's brow furrowed. "Marks?"

"Yes. Marks like you're holding back all the sadness in your eyes."

Henry's shoulders tensed at her words. I eased Ruby away to give him a moment. "Want to see the plane? Maybe stand on the wing?"

Her head bobbed up and down. The edges of her sweet curls brushed against her rose-pink cheeks. With her hand still clenched in mine, I steered her toward the prop. Once we reached the front of Nathan's plane, I hoisted her up and encouraged her to touch the blade. She hesitated.

"Go on. It's only polished wood. It won't hurt you." She cringed back into my shoulder. The velvet softness of her hair settled into my collarbone. My heart thrummed in my chest as she clung to me. Trusting me to keep her safe. Safe in a way I could never keep my sister.

I held her tighter and somehow managed to find my voice. "How about we do it together?"

With her hand perched in mine, she glided her fingers along the wood. Her body relaxed as we walked around, skimming over the scarlet-colored body and touching all the other parts of the plane. She even let out a high-pitched giggle when Henry plucked her out of my arms and deposited her in the training seat.

His conversation with her was easy and it was hard not to smile at the tender way he held her hand. Ruby squealed when he placed her on the edge of the wing. In a flash, I saw my sister as a child. If she were still alive, would she say I was out of my mind for wing walking? Or would she be scrambling to join me?

Ruby's laughter filled the air as Henry placed her atop his shoulders. He balanced before leaning forward so she could touch the top wing.

As we returned Ruby to her mother, the little girl took Henry's hand and pulled him down toward her. She cupped her hand over her mouth and whispered in his ear. When she finished she looked him directly in the eye as if urging him to swear a solemn oath. A wide smile covered his lips in silent agreement. She waved a quick goodbye to us both and raced toward her family's waiting truck.

"What was that all about?"

"Oh, Ruby gave me a little bit of advice."

I laughed. "You're taking guidance from a five-year-old now?"

"Yes," he said confidently. "Because I believe that little girl has more smarts than the two of us put together."

"Really?" Ruby's old truck lumbered across the field, and I couldn't help but be curious about what she'd said to bring such a bright smile to Henry's face.

10
Taking Matters into Your Own Hands

Barbecued beans, fried chicken, and collard greens lined each of the tables in the open field. After two shows, one frightened cow that broke through a fence, and a dog who decided to use Daniel's favorite coat to have puppies, it had been quite a day.

"We'll get a free dinner and more tips," I said, urging Uncle Warren to accept the farmer's invitation to stay.

As the moon started to rise, men huddled in one corner whispering about President Harding's latest radio address, the Babe's new contract with the Yankees, and the government's latest shootout with bootleggers. The crowd only went quiet when one of the men pulled out a worn banjo. He began to strum a slow, sweet melody. Men and women glided away from the tables and into each other's arms. Their bodies swayed in perfect time with the music. Nathan and Daniel didn't hesitate to pull young women from the benches. Even Uncle Warren managed to make his way into the crowd with a dark-haired lady on his arm.

Henry sat at a nearby table. His back was rigid. His eyes fixed on something in the distance. Nathan appeared at my side and pulled me into the fray. He twirled me while the music grew louder. The crowd clapped and sang along to the old country song. The tight lines around Nathan's eyes softened. Maybe he was finally going to loosen up.

"Dancing in the middle of a corn field," I said. "Think I've seen it all now."

"I certainly wasn't expecting it from this crowd. You have to give them credit though, they know how to turn an empty field into a party." He bobbed up and down as if his mile-long legs took a minute to adjust to the song's rhythm.

"I saw you and Henry leave this afternoon with one of the farmers," I said. "Where did you go?"

He spun me in another circle. "Henry needed some extra bolts. I told him I'd go into town with him."

"Did you get what you needed?"

"Sure did." He danced in a circle around me. "I didn't trust him in those first days, but after he caught the crack in my propeller I realized he was a good hire." It took Nathan a while to trust anyone, and if he was praising Henry it meant he'd earned it.

Over the last weeks we'd grown into a solid team. As soon as each show ended, Henry was quick to assess the planes and make the necessary adjustments. If our performances kept up, and the crowds continued to grow at each stop, by my calculations we'd have just enough money to compete at the Expo.

The melody picked up pace and couples continued to filter out onto the field. Children scurried out from behind their parents, chasing each other in circles in time to the music. The women's skirts swished above the ground as their partners spun them. The men stomped their dirty boots and raised their voices to sing along. The banjo's twang echoed across the field and seemed to hang among the stars that dotted the clear summer night.

As the song wound to a close, Daniel appeared and tapped Nathan on the shoulder. "It appears the farmer's daughter doesn't have a partner." Daniel nodded in the direction of a young woman in a light-pink dress sitting at a nearby table. A matching pink flower adorned her fair hair. "What better way to say thank you for his generosity than by having one of our lead pilots take her for a twirl?" Daniel was laying it on thick, but Nathan was a sucker for compliments, especially when a woman was involved.

"All right." Nathan released me and walked in the direction of the girl. Her bright blue eyes lit up when he pulled her out into the growing crowd.

Daniel spun me around, but my attention stayed on Henry's table.

"Take matters into your hands and ask him to dance," Daniel said while we swayed back into the melody. The light from a nearby campfire made his red hair glow as bright as the dancing flames.

I shook my head. "What if Henry doesn't dance because of his leg?"

He narrowed his deep-brown eyes. "I never said anything about Henry."

Heat filled my cheeks. It was impossible to hide anything from him. "We're only friends. Besides, I couldn't ask him to dance. It wouldn't be proper."

We moved in a circle while I made every effort not to stomp on his toes. I may be able to glide across the wings of a plane, but on the ground I bumble over my own two feet.

"Darlin', when have you ever done anything proper in your life? You should do what's right for you."

Daniel always chose his words carefully. If he felt strongly enough to have this talk with me, then his words were something I needed to consider. We were out in the middle of a field in a small town, dancing to a single banjo. Perhaps proper didn't matter.

"Grace, listen." His voice turned surprisingly stern. "There's a reason I sent Nathan away." I pulled back and was surprised to find his gentle smile gone. "You spend too much time at the hangar planning your next trick or taking care of us and your uncle. That's not fair to you. You're a young girl who needs to have a life outside of barnstorming." I tried to move away, but he caged me in between his massive arms. "Sure, when we look at you, both Nathan and I see the fifteen-year-old girl we met when we joined The Soaring Eagles. But over these years, you've grown into a capable young woman. A woman who sneaks a pillow onto her uncle's chair so his back will stop aching. Fixes a broken zipper on Nathan's flight jacket without a word. Triple checks my parachute before a show." He twirled me out and spun me back in again. "And don't quirk up your eyebrows like you don't know what I'm talking about." His mouth turned into a grim line. "We may not always be around. You need to think about the future."

What did he mean they might not always be around? We were a team. We'd always be together.

He stopped dancing and gave me a determined look like he wasn't going to let me go until I agreed. "Go find Henry. Dance. Have a little fun. Be eighteen, for heaven's sake!"

How did he always get inside my head? Force me to see things in a different light? On days when the crowds were too much, or a performance hadn't gone as planned, Daniel's lopsided grin always made my heart light. He carried his own pain from the war, but he never let it show. Nathan told me that during a fierce ground battle Daniel had saved the lives of several soldiers. When he returned home he was awarded the Distinguished Service Cross, but hid it away. He always thought of others before himself and never expected praise. He was just my sweet, somewhat irritating Daniel.

After giving me one last spin, he nudged me in the direction of Henry's table. The deep strum of the banjo continued to fill the air. Couples swirled around each other, the firelight giving their faces a perfect, yellow glow. I dodged around them and reached Henry's table only to find his seat was empty. I swiveled around and searched the area, but he was nowhere in sight. The farmers at his table were caught up in a conversation about wheat prices and how the Yankees were sure to win the pennant.

"Excuse me. Did you see where Henry went?" They stared at me with puzzled eyes. "Our mechanic? About six foot, light-brown hair," I added. "Did you see him leave?"

They ignored me and went back to discussing whether or not

Ty Cobb was washed up as a ball player. When I turned away, a man with a long, white beard and kind brown eyes grabbed my hand. He pointed a knobby finger in the direction of the barn.

"Young fella went that way. Might want to hurry on if you want to catch him." He gave me a wink before turning back to the conversation.

The stench in the barn was a foul combination of hay and manure all wrapped in wet mud.

"Hello? Henry, you here?"

When only the crickets answered, I edged toward Nathan's plane. The barn was lit with only a few oil lanterns, casting long, ominous shadows along the wood walls. If Henry was here, he'd be under a plane checking the wheels or on the wing fixing a wire. He took his work seriously. Uncle Warren told me on more than one occasion he had to drag him out of the hangar long after the sun had gone down.

When I didn't find him, I walked out of the barn and right into Uncle Warren.

"Been looking for you. We need to talk."

He grabbed my arm and pulled me to the side of the barn. "You see that gent with the brown fedora?"

I squinted at one of the benches illuminated by the bonfire in the middle of the field. A thick man with wide-set shoulders leaned toward two ladies who were knee-deep in a story about chasing three loose pigs.

"What about him?"

"He's from Little Rock. Drove up here this afternoon. What to know why?"

I shrugged. "He likes airplanes?"

The lines around his eyes went tight. "You could say that. He works for the government. Apparently, someone in town was not too keen on our little flyover today."

Stepping back into the shadows, I looked at Uncle Warren, who even in the faint light was a deep shade of red.

"Are we in trouble?"

He shoved his hands into his pockets. "There's a new aviation division that's been created to protect the public. Those crashes in Oklahoma, Illinois, and Boise have the government worried about what we're doing in the sky." He pulled an unlit cigar from his mouth and twirled it nervously between his fingers. "They've assigned him to this part of the country to monitor all the barnstorming teams. With the complaint against us, we'll be forced to provide an itinerary for all our shows. And there'll be spot inspections."

"Inspections? Why?" I practically shouted.

"Keep your voice down." He glanced around to make sure no one was listening, but the crowd was too busy singing and dancing to care about what we said. "They'll be checking our landing gear. Maintenance on the engines. Wear-and-tear on the struts and skids." He narrowed his eyes. "If he detects any issues, we'll be grounded until they can be fixed, which will be tough considering we already have a hard time keeping up with new parts." He ground his jaw in irritation. "We're also required to carry two parachutes in case of emergency."

"Fine. We'll follow whatever the government says from now on," I said.

He spit out a harsh laugh and popped the brown roll back into his mouth. "Fat load of good that does us when . . ." He stopped mid-sentence. The government man strode in our direction, a notepad clutched in his hand. Uncle Warren plastered a welcoming smile to his lips. "Mr. Sorenson! This is my niece, Grace Lafferty."

The man towered over Uncle Warren, his fedora casting a shadow over his eyes. He shook my hand and tipped his hat back to reveal a round face with cheeks so thick he resembled a squirrel hording nuts for the winter.

"You've told her why I'm here?" He pursed his lips, looking me over. A sneer tugged at his mouth when he landed on my pants and muddy boots. I knew that look—it said I should be running around with a swollen belly rather than hanging off a plane 500 feet in the air.

"Yes," Uncle Warren replied.

Mr. Sorenson murmured as he flipped through his notebook. "Miss Lafferty, the government thinks your chosen profession is quite dangerous. Because of that, I'll be making regular visits to your shows. We need to make sure you don't hurt yourself or anyone else."

I curled my toes inside my boots, trying to stay calm. My fingers wanted to rip the notebook from his hands. What did those notes say anyway? That we were a nuisance to the public? That we were taking too many risks? None of that mattered. The government needed outfits like us. Without barnstormers, they'd have dozens of retired war planes on their hands and mounting debt.

"What's that supposed to mean? We take great care to be safe in the sky."

He snapped through a few more pages in his notebook. "We received word this morning that a plane flew dangerously low over the center of town. According to the report, the tires were only inches from the rooftops. Is that true?"

I crossed my arms over my chest. "Did the witness see us first hand?"

"That's not the point," he barked. He shoved the pad back into his coat pocket. "You endangered the lives of everyone in the town. We now have a record of your antics. If you or any of your *team*"—he spit out the word like it was dirty—"try anything like that again, the government will ground you for good."

The situation stunk of Alistair Rowland. He had eyes everywhere. I was sure he'd had someone report us as soon as we flew over town. How dare he, considering what his team did to me in

Springfield? I should have never let Daniel stop me from going to see him.

"Listen here—"

Uncle Warren stiff-armed me across the chest, warning me not to say another word. "We hear you, Mr. Sorenson. We'll maintain a safe distance above the crowd from now on as long as you government boys keep a close watch on the other teams as well. We've also seen some antics the government would not appreciate."

"You worry about your own outfit," Sorenson huffed. "The government will keep an eye on everyone else." He yanked his hat down over his eyes and headed for a black Packard sitting at the edge of the field.

"He won't be able to follow us everywhere," I said as the car disappeared into the night.

"Will you never learn, Grace?" Uncle Warren yanked the cigar from his mouth and threw it at the ground. "Boise was just the beginning. The government is closing in. If we want to stay afloat, we need to follow the rules. One more toe out of line and there'll be no Chicago."

"We're not doing anything different than the other teams," I protested. "You know this is Rowland's doing anyway. The man won't stop until we are grounded and he takes our part of the sky."

"There's no proof Rowland is involved. Anyone in town could have reported us." He gave a disappointed shake of his head and walked back toward the bonfire.

Uncle Warren could hide from the truth, but I refused. The only way to be rid of Rowland was to get to Chicago and win that contract. Without it, our days in the sky were numbered.

11
A Dance Can Save Your Life

The full moon lit my way as I stalked across the field. Sorenson's warnings filled my head. The government would not shut us down. There *would* be new tricks; we'd just have to be more careful about how and where we performed them.

I sunk down and pulled a piece of dry grass out of the ground. Twirling it between my fingers, I listened to the frogs begin their toneless hum. The cicadas joined in with their own night music. I closed my eyes and let the summer breeze dance over my body.

"Grace, you okay?" I popped open my eyes to find Henry standing at the edge of a corn row a few feet away.

It was only a matter of time before Uncle Warren told the boys about the government's sudden interest in The Soaring Eagles. For now I wanted peace, so I forced a smile to my lips. "I'm swell. Just enjoying the night."

He limped toward me and pointed at the ground. "May I?"

"Of course." I shifted across the dirt as he eased himself down next to me. "Nathan said you two bought bolts in town today. It was nice of you to ask him to go along."

His brows furrowed for a minute before he tilted back his head and pointed to a gathering of stars. "Did you know that group is called the Big Dipper?"

"The big what?"

"An army pal of mine liked astronomy. One night when the battlefield was quiet, he showed me this gathering of stars called the Big Dipper. It's really a cluster of seven stars that help make up the constellation Ursa Major."

I followed his finger. The pattern began to form against the sky's black canvas. He traced the image over and over until I could see the handle and the four stars forming the cup.

He placed his hands behind him, wincing as he stretched out his long legs. "Why aren't you dancing?"

"Dancing is not my forte. And considering my name, that's very embarrassing."

He chuckled. "I get it, *Grace*." The shy smile that danced across his mouth vanished as suddenly as it appeared. "I miss dancing," he said, slowly rubbing the back of his calf.

My breath hitched. How could I have been so thoughtless?

"The summer I turned fourteen, Caroline dragged me out into the barn every evening after dinner. She'd laid out hay bales in a perfect square. Once she had me in place, she'd sing an Al Jolson tune and convince me to waltz with her. I whined about it but I secretly enjoyed those moments."

He stretched his leg up and down, his breath hitching with each movement. "One night we were dancing around the outside of a hay bale and I tripped right over a shovel. The dang thing reared back and I got this." He tapped at the scar I'd been curious about below his full lower lip. "But all those hours of sweeping back hay and twirling my sister around eventually paid off. My ability to spin a dame helped me get quite a few dates." His throaty laugh made it impossible not to smile.

"In fact, dancing saved my life one night in France."

His hands twisted in his lap. He hadn't talked about the war since the night on the street. I stayed quiet as the mice in the field, hoping he'd tell me more.

"We were in a small town just outside the Argonne Forest. It was late and we thought the entire town was asleep. My squad and I found an abandoned building and decided to settle in for the night. We were a sight. Fifteen motley men in soiled uniforms piled into a small, burned-out cottage. After twenty days in the trenches, the lot of us stank worse than any pig pen I'd ever mucked out." His eyes, once bright and alive, were now lifeless. "What we didn't know was the cottage was a spot for the Germans to bring the local French girls for secret trysts. We were all asleep when a man and woman wandered into the building. I woke when I heard them kissing and swaying in a drunken dance.

"*Tu as les deux pieds dans la même chaussure*," he said quietly.

"What does that mean?"

"It doesn't translate well, but the woman told the man he danced with two left feet. He wasn't happy, but I couldn't hold back my laugh." His body went rigid as he shifted his legs again. "When the man spotted me he pulled a gun. He pointed it at my chest and then at the bodies of my fellow soldiers."

My body tensed in anticipation of his next words. Maybe this was how he was wounded.

"*Veux-tu apprendre á danser?*" he said, looking back up at the sky.

I stared at him, entranced by the French rolling off his tongue even though I didn't understand a word.

"I asked if he wanted to learn how to dance." He let out a rough sigh and shook his head like the memory pained him. "The soldier stood his ground, looking between me and my buddies. It was fifteen against one. He could've put a few bullets in us before anyone had a chance to react. I had to get him outside."

He rubbed at his legs again, wincing as his hands made contact. "The couple argued for a minute, switching between French and German, making it impossible to follow the conversation. At that time, my German was limited to the words *gun* and *surrender*." His voice cracked and he took a deep breath. "When the man finally calmed down, he pointed to the small stone courtyard and I followed. With a gun pointed directly at my head, I moved around the dirt and rubble teaching him the steps for a waltz."

The lines around his mouth twitched. "When I was done, he moved into the arms of his girl. She was thrilled. After a slow dance and a few kisses, the woman convinced him to leave. When I returned to the abandoned house I silently thanked Caroline for her months of lessons."

Since soldiers began returning from the war several years ago, I'd heard only tales of epic battles like Gallipoli and Verdun. Of men racing across fields, valiantly shooting their weapons and doing their best to capture the enemy. Henry's story forced me to think of those faceless men who'd quietly risked their lives every day. The ones who weren't heralded in the papers but still shielded their pals from gunfire, and did small things like teaching the enemy to dance so their friends could live.

"You were so brave," I said. "I'm not sure I would have been able to move, much less teach someone to dance."

"Who knew a waltz could save a few lives?" His face drained of color like that night on the street. The line of his shoulders went tight and he slipped away to that dark place again.

"Henry," I said reaching for his shoulder. "Stay with me, okay?" He blinked twice, his body tensing under my hand. "You're safe. I'm right here," I whispered. He shifted to face me and his eyes went wide.

"Gracie, I'm sorry." He placed a trembling hand over the spot where I gripped his shoulder.

"Don't be. We're in a field enjoying the night. I just need you to come back and show me those stars again." His head dropped in defeat and he looked away. "Come on, show me again," I encouraged him.

When he looked up he searched my face. I wasn't sure what he was looking for but I gave him my widest smile. This is what friends did for each other. They worked together. Comforted one another when times turned rough. His pupils grew wider as he focused on my lips. My heart fluttered. My throat suddenly dry.

"The stars," I managed to mumble.

He blinked twice and then pointed to a twinkling cluster directly over my head.

"The Big Dipper is there."

He continued speaking about the other constellations. His breathing slowed and the tension in his mouth relaxed.

"I'm glad we have this time," he said, breaking the silence after a few minutes. "Ever since the diner, I've wanted to apologize for acting so out of control." He hesitated. "And just now . . . I didn't mean to scare you. Small things, like a sharp sound or a memory, remind me of the war."

"You don't have to explain. I understand how memories can shake your soul. And we're friends now. We can talk about our lives." A quicker flicker of what looked like regret passed over his face before he focused back on the night sky.

A new melody weaved its way across the field. Henry closed his eyes, his shoulders swaying to the music.

"Isn't that a gorgeous tune, Gracie?" When I didn't respond, he opened his eyes and met my gaze. "Why are you staring at me like that?"

"Gracie?" I said. "No one calls me that."

He released a laugh filled with joy and something more, as if a heavy burden he'd been carrying had suddenly vanished like the moon slipping behind a patch of clouds.

"You're too serious. Always talking about business, performances, how the team can earn its next nickel. You could use a playful name. It fits you when you smile, which I think is not entirely enough."

He tilted his head toward mine and leaned in. A strange ache filled my chest. All I had to do was inch in a bit more, and I would feel the smooth skin of his lips. Taste my first kiss. My heart sped up as I looked into his deep-green eyes. Was his pulse racing as fast as mine, or had he done this numerous times before?

The wind rustled the corn stalks behind us and snapped me back to reality. What was I thinking? He didn't want to kiss me. He was only being kind because I'd kept his secret. I scrambled to my feet before I did anything ridiculous.

"Think I should go. We've got an early day tomorrow."

He blinked twice in surprise. "Please stay. I don't want to be out here alone. This place reminds me too much of France. Will you sit with me a little while longer?"

The twang of the banjo reached a heightened pitch and muffled laughter filled the air. If I went back to the party now, I'd only get sour glares from Uncle Warren or curious glances from Daniel—neither of which was appealing.

I sank down a safe distance away, intent on not making a fool of myself. He looked directly at the wide space between us. When I didn't move, he pointed to another patch of stars and explained how to find the Little Dipper.

12
Only Pinpricks on a Map

Lincoln, Nebraska
August 24, 1922
19 days until World Aviation Expo

After whirlwind performances in Pine Bluff, Omaha, Dakota City, and Lexington, we returned home for the annual state fair. Uncle Warren negotiated five shows for us, which was a good thing because we were only thirty dollars away from getting to Chicago. We'd had our setbacks, but it was difficult to contain my excitement knowing we were close to having the funds for the contest.

I dashed toward the hangar, hoping to get an early start. The sun was just stretching its golden rays above the horizon. Birds squawked in the nearby oak trees, their song welcoming the morning. It wasn't quite September, but a cool breeze raced across my skin promising fall wasn't far off.

I planted my dirty boots in front of the hangar and took a deep breath. Today would be the day. The right strength of cable settled in my left pocket. My sturdy mouthpiece pressed into my right. I'd finally found the courage to tell my uncle about the Showstopper, and no matter his arguments, I wouldn't take no for an answer.

Rolling up my oil-stained sleeves, I pushed back the oversized door. But only two steps inside I skittered to a stop. Whispers echoed off the walls. The scent of stale cigar smoke and oil tinged the air. Why was my uncle here this early?

"Maybe we should give it a day before we tell her," my uncle grumbled.

"No. You can't wait." The defeated tone in Henry's voice sent a chill across my skin.

"Grace needs to grow up and listen to reason for once. It's as simple as that," Nathan said.

"That girl is going to be angrier than a bullfrog without a tongue if you don't show her the telegram today," Daniel huffed.

"What telegram?" I said.

They each leapt nearly five feet in the air as I moved around the tail of Nathan's Jenny. They stayed tight-lipped even as I walked toward my uncle and yanked the telegram from his fingertips.

"All participants in Chicago Aviation Expo expected to pay a daily fifteen-dollar hangar charge," I read out loud. "Additional fee will be expected with final contest payment by September 1. No exceptions will be allowed. Sincerely, R.O. Knickerbocker, owner, Palm Coast Studios."

Uncle Warren stood with his shoulders rigid, his hands buried deep into his pockets. Daniel tried to stay small in the corner, which was impossible considering he was practically the size of a bear. The only one who bothered to look me in the eye was Henry, whose repentant stare seemed more suited for church than the hangar.

"Why are we just hearing about this now?" I glanced down at the telegram. "This was sent almost a week ago."

"That's my fault," Henry said. "It came while you were all out flying. I shoved it into my coveralls and I just remembered it this morning."

Uncle Warren shifted back and forth on his feet and concentrated on the ground. When he finally looked up the dark caverns under his eyes made me take a step back.

"I've been over the numbers, Grace. The eleven days we were grounded set us behind. The entry fee is due in a week. Add to that lodging and food, as well as the new fee, and well, we can't afford it."

I crumpled the telegram between my fingers. "We'll park the planes outside."

Uncle Warren chomped on the end of his cigar. "No. The rules clearly state that every plane must be housed inside."

"Fine. We'll raise our ride fees. Add a few more shows over the next several days. We'll get that extra money."

Uncle Warren's gray hair shifted down across his tense brows. "There's no time, Grace. Even if you worked around the clock, even if we all did, it wouldn't cover our expenses. It's best we accept it and move on," Uncle Warren said. "We have to focus on our next set of shows."

"That's it?" I cried. "You're giving up on everything we've worked for over these past months?"

"Grace, let it go. We're not headed to Chicago!" Nathan stared me down, willing me to give in, but I refused to let this dream go.

"We can't put ourselves into a hole, darlin'." Daniel said. "Our priority needs to be our upcoming shows. If a part breaks, or a tire goes bad, we need to have money. By using all our funds for Chicago, we'd be putting ourselves in an awful position." He stepped forward and opened his thick arms, as if an embrace would help heal the ache in my heart.

I inched away. I didn't want his comfort. "I can't believe the lot of you! Giving up without thinking about all the other ways we can make this work."

"And what are those ways?" Nathan's voice shot up an octave.

"We could charge extra for autographs and pictures. Something. Anything to help."

"This conversation is over," Uncle Warren snapped. "We are *not* going. Our job is to focus on these next five shows. We wow the crowd and earn enough so we can keep this team together."

"But that's why we need this contest!" I insisted.

"No more, Grace." Uncle Warren placed his hands on his hips. "I'm done looking at all of you. Hangar is closed for the day. Get out of here. Go to the fair. Have some fun. Come back tomorrow morning at dawn and we'll get the Jennys ready for the next shows." He reached into his pocket and pulled out a new cigar. "You heard me," he growled around the brown stump crowding his mouth, "Out!"

Nathan and Daniel moved across the floor, leaning in to whisper to each other. Henry dropped his tools onto a nearby bench. He caught my eye and cocked his head toward the door like he wanted to talk, but I wasn't in the mood.

I walked toward Uncle Warren. With everyone else gone, I could work my magic. Talk him into finding some other way to get the money we needed.

Before I could say a word, he held up a hand to stop me. "Don't think you can sweet talk me. You know I'd do anything to make this happen for you, but we don't have the money." He reached an arm around my shoulder. "If we want to keep The Soaring Eagles going, we need to perfect our routines and keep doing shows." After giving me a squeeze, he turned on his heel and walked back to the office.

"Gracie." Henry's voice moved through the hangar as if he was a ghost. The sound of pity and sadness was too much to take. I raced out the doors, unable to face the truth.

Our landing strip stretched for a quarter mile to the east, heading back toward town. It had once been part of Old Man Murdock's farm, but he gave up on the property after discovering the soil was too dry and rocky to grow anything but weeds. Once Uncle Warren paid for the parcel, he cleared the land and built a small hangar. Most teams parked their planes outside, but my uncle was insistent about protecting the Jennys from the elements. It explained why he took the new contest fee so seriously.

When we weren't in the air, the small runway was a great place to come and think. My boots connected with rocks and soil as I walked back and forth, trying to gather my thoughts. For so long I'd gotten out of bed every morning with one goal in mind: the contest. Our team sailing across the clouds, the glittering Chicago skyline behind us. It was a constant picture in my head. Each moment out on the wing, every new trick invented, pushed me toward that vision. But what did we have now? An endless run of shows in places I only saw from hundreds of feet above the ground. Towns that were only pinpricks on a map.

As if on cue, the air filled with the buzz of an engine. A bright white Jenny shot overhead, signaling the beginning of the fair's early morning show. The plane's nose shot straight up into a loop that exposed the black star on the Jenny's tail —The Flying Finellis. They always put on a good, if predictable, show.

After two barrel rolls, the plane disappeared into a cloud blank. I sunk onto the rocky ground with nothing but the steady ache in my heart for company. How could I keep going if each day was a struggle to keep The Soaring Eagles afloat? Never knowing when the government might show up and use any excuse to ground us. At least with that Hollywood contract we had guaranteed work. Steady pay keeping us together, ensuring we had more days in the sky.

"Is this a private mourning or can I join in?" Nathan stood ten feet away. Like Uncle Warren he wore a haunted look that warned we were in trouble.

"Don't bother to sit if you're going to give me a lecture," I bit out.

"Do you need a lecture?" he chuckled.

I groaned as he sunk down, his long legs *thunk*ing against the dirt. Even though he drove me crazy, Nathan and I were a lot alike. Flying was in our blood. It was the common bond that tied us together. Made us get up every morning, eager to conquer whatever the elements threw at us that day. I never thought I'd meet anyone who loved the air as much as I did, until I met him.

He curved his hand over his eyes, searching the sky. "That white plane the Finellis?"

"Yes. They got the opening spot on the morning bill."

He bobbed his head and continued to stare at the deep-blue sky. A minute passed with nothing but the whistle of the wind and the squeaky bark of nearby prairie dogs to keep us company.

"Not sure if Daniel ever told you this story, but the day he and I met was one of the worst of my life." His long, thin fingers pulled the collar away from his throat. "I was in the mess hall eating lunch and some pilots spent the entire meal congratulating me on my first mid-air kill. Amid my pleas to stop, they kept patting my back and cheering that I'd put down another Kraut." His deep-brown eyes went dark with the memory. "When one of the fellas wouldn't give up, I took a swing at him, but Daniel caught my punch before it could connect. Without knowing who I was, he yanked me out the mess hall doors. When we got out of earshot I was grateful, because I'd already had a warning from my commander for fighting."

He pulled at the oil-stained cuffs of his shirt, his hands trembling. "I'd been flying a basic formation when a German pilot in a Fokker locked me in his sights. We exchanged gunfire for a long time until one of my shots sent the pilot down in a fiery ball of flame." He scrubbed his hands over his eyes like he wanted to erase the memory. "I was only days past my twenty-fourth birthday. Besides Daniel, I've never told anyone that story before."

In all the years I'd known Nathan, I'd never seen him so off-kilter.

"Why tell me now?" I asked. His legs stretched long past mine. The toes of his boots were covered in runway dust.

"I never thought I'd get past that day. When I landed people greeted me like a hero, but I felt like a killer. I'm sure that pilot had a family, people waiting for him to return from the war. Because of me, that would never happen."

He sighed and swiped a loose hair away from his eyes. "Daniel understood my grief, why I didn't want to celebrate. On the battle-field, he'd killed men and had friends die in his arms. He understood war was not something to celebrate. I suppose that's what built our friendship at first: a mutual disdain for the death we saw every single day. It's also why we decided we wanted to barnstorm. We wanted to use the planes to bring joy rather than death, although the deeper we get into it the more we both realize the dangers."

"I'm sorry, Nathan."

"I don't want your pity, Grace," he grumbled. "What I want you to remember is that even on the most difficult days, when we feel crushed and alone, we can move beyond it. It only takes time."

While I appreciated the sentiment, the contest was important and I wasn't letting it go.

He brushed a hand over his mouth, his eyes narrowing on a patch of clouds overhead. "Have you ever thought of what you'll do if the government shuts us down? Would you join another team? Perhaps find another job?"

"That'll never happen," I insisted. "We'll keep performing as always. The government is only putting on this show to prove they're acting on a few complaints."

"Even if we could get to Chicago, what makes you so sure we'd win? We'd be up against a lot of capable teams." He pointed at the plane zooming across the sky toward us again. "For example, those Flying Finellis are getting good, and I hear there's a team out of Bloomington called The Black Bombers that's doing an inverted double loop."

"We'll win because no one can fly like my uncle and you, Nathan." I nudged his arm but his mouth stayed in a grim line.

After flying among the clouds, I couldn't picture myself sitting behind a desk or waiting tables. The thought of being cooped up indoors all day shot goosebumps down my arms. "This life is what I live for, Nathan. As long as I have you and all The Soaring Eagles, I'll be happy."

I kicked at a patch of weeds near the toe of my boot. There was a question on the tip of my tongue I wanted to ask, but a part of me felt guilty for even thinking of it.

"What else is on your mind?" He turned to me, his steely gaze ordering me to confess what I was thinking.

"Do you think there's a reason why Henry waited so long before giving us the telegram?"

Nathan's spine stiffened. "I was wondering the same thing. Guess it makes sense he'd forget about it if he was busy, but if it was me, I'd have given it straight to your uncle." His shoulders went tight and he opened his mouth as if to say more, then snapped it shut. His gaze drifted to the outline of the Ferris wheel in the distance. "Perhaps we should head over to the fair. Eat popcorn. Play a few games."

"I'm not ten, Nathan." I clambered to my feet. "A few treats and some carnival rides are not going to change my mood."

"Grace, you have to let this go. We need to be smart about our money. Chicago isn't a realistic choice. If you'd take a moment to act like an adult, you'd understand—"

"Act like an adult?" I sputtered. "That's all I've done since I was thirteen. Don't you talk to me about acting like a grown-up. Every day I'm fighting to keep us together. Why can't you see that?"

He jumped up beside me. "I know you're still thinking up ways we can get to that contest. Why won't you listen?"

"Because unlike the rest of you, I won't give up. We've sacrificed so much over these past months. I've heard you and Daniel grumble about not having an extra dime for the picture show. I've dealt with Uncle Warren's complaints about not being able to buy a fancier brand of cigar. All those sacrifices were important because it allowed us to go after a bigger dream. Can't you see that?" Tears burned at the edges of my eyes but I refused to let them fall.

Nathan gnashed his teeth together. I'd pushed him to the edge, but I didn't care. It was time he stopped treating me like a ridiculous young girl.

He turned away and his shoulders lifted up and down like he was trying to regain control. The way his body drooped made him seem shorter than six foot six.

The Finellis did another barrel roll and then moved into a wide loop, leaving a trail of black exhaust in their wake. The wind blew at the black ring until it disappeared into a nearby cloudbank.

"I remember the day Daniel and I walked into the hangar looking for a job." Nathan had regained some of his composure, and he shaded his eyes to follow the plane as it zoomed toward the fairgrounds. "We'd heard about your uncle in Wichita and flew down to see if he was on the level. Lots of men claimed they were barnstormers, but you could tell the serious ones by how they cared for their planes and what their performances were like." He playfully poked my shoulder. "Some of our trip was out of curiosity, too. We'd heard about a young girl who could do death-defying stunts. You seemed more like a myth than a real person," he chuckled. "That was until we saw you up on the wing. Stiff and strong, doing a single-arm handstand like you didn't have a care in the world. But it wasn't until after that first show we worked together in Des Moines that I realized we had something special."

Des Moines. A trip forever etched into my mind.

I was only a few days past fifteen when October blew into Iowa like a bitter old woman—harsh and cruel. We worked the first show and shared the bill with a local team.

"The air was so cold that day I couldn't feel my hands or my face even though I was wrapped in three layers and a fleece-lined coat," I practically shivered, recalling the icy snap of the wind.

"I remember. It was hard to control the stick because my hands were stiff from the cold."

"The turbulence was bad that day as well," I said. "It knocked the plane up and down like it was a small toy, and even the easiest tricks were difficult to perform."

"Do you remember what happened when we landed?"

"How could I forget? I had to climb off the wing, but my frozen hands made it hard to grasp a strut. I lost my footing and did a nosedive onto the ground. Not my most shining moment."

He chuckled although the lines around his eyes stayed firm. "You fell straight onto that hard-packed dirt. The crowd held its breath waiting for you to wail or at least let out a whimper. Instead you climbed to your feet and gave a polite curtsy."

"Like Uncle Warren says, 'You gotta give 'em a good show.'"

"Your shoulder was separated in two places, Grace. Any man would have gone down and stayed down, but not you." He pulled at his whiskers. "Since that day in Iowa, I knew we would become family." He shook his head as if the memory was happy, yet painful, too.

A new plane soared overhead. My stomach tumbled as the slick, black body came into view. A Skyhawk shot across the sky and did a barrel roll, throttled forward, and then repeated the same roll. This time the pilot overcorrected, tilting his wings back to the right to regain control.

"That was sloppy," we said at the same time. Nathan nudged my shoulder. "We'll make a pilot out of you one of these days."

"Nope. My place is out on the wing."

My eyes remained on the sky. From now on I'd spend every waking hour figuring out how I'd get The Soaring Eagles to Chicago. We had to get there if we wanted to survive.

13
A Blank Canvas

Nathan dragged me across the field toward the fair that waited in the distance. Dozens of white tents covered the space of empty farmland. In the distance music filled the air as children selected their favorite horse on the carousel. I trailed behind Nathan while he swept past the hot dog vendors and carnival attendants challenging us to try our luck at the ring toss for a nickel.

"Let's try the Ferris wheel first. It'll take your mind off Chicago," he insisted.

"How much does it cost?"

He rolled his eyes. "It's free for performers today so there's no use fighting me. I already told Daniel and Henry we'd meet them, and you know your uncle won't let us back in the hangar today."

We were only yards from the contraption when Daniel, all lumbering arms and legs, plowed toward us. "That Ferris wheel is really something! I'm going up again. Nathan, you're with me." He looked back over his shoulder. "Grace, you go with Hen. . ." His brows jammed together. "Where did he go? He was here only moments ago."

"Aw, he'll be back. Let's get in line," Nathan said.

I scanned the masses, looking for Henry, but the bodies on the midway were packed shoulder-to-shoulder. We moved slowly toward the front. The swaying steel creaked beside us. Each groan and crack made the hairs on my arms stand at attention.

Henry appeared a few minutes later, slightly out of breath.

"Where've you been?" Nathan asked.

"Wanted to get the lay of the land, check out all the sights." He wiped a shirtsleeve across his forehead, tipping his cap to the back of his head. It was only ten o'clock, but the blazing sun promised a long, scorching day.

"Don't wander off again. It's almost our turn and Grace needs a riding partner." Daniel nudged my shoulder and heat raced across my cheeks. Sitting in close quarters with Henry was a dizzying thought, especially since the last time we were together I almost lost my head and kissed him.

"I think I'll sit this one out," I said.

"No way, darlin'," Daniel said, grabbing the sleeve of my blouse. "Take one trip around. It'll be a gas." His brown eyes pleaded for me to give it a go.

The wooden bench seats eased down toward us an inch at a time. Young couples whispered around us, their gazes fixed on the wheel's slow rotation. Laughing children darted through the line. A few wide-eyed farmers watched the ride move round and round.

A small steam engine behind us was turning the Ferris wheel. The ride resembled an oversized Tinkertoy creation, the parts locked together with only a few nuts and bolts. The wheel moaned like an irritable giant as the operator stopped and started the ride.

When we reached the front of the line, the operator ordered us to climb aboard. The top bench above us hung at least forty-five feet in the air. My feet remained in place even as Henry motioned me forward. A breath lodged in my throat as the wind made the ride sway.

Henry offered his hand to help me climb aboard. The ride continued to move to and fro as though it would topple over and burst into a pile of metal spokes and sharp nails any minute. What if we got to the top and the giant wheel was swept off its footing, crushing everything in its path?

Henry moved to my side. "Are you afraid of a carnival ride?"

"No," I said too quickly. "I just remembered I have something to do back at the hangar."

A gentle smile pulled at his mouth. "It may look a little rickety, but I've been checking her over while we've stood here. The steel is premium grade and the spokes are locked into place in several spots."

"I am *not* scared," I repeated, my voice a little too high.

"You going or not?" The operator barked.

The steam engine *clicked* and *whooshed*, beating in time with the frantic thrum of my heart. Two young boys behind us grumbled, anxious for their own turn. If they weren't afraid, then I couldn't be either. I swallowed hard and climbed up to the bench. We sat and it groaned under our weight. Instinctively I grabbed the side, hoping the shock of cold steel would calm my racing pulse.

Henry focused on my white knuckles. "At the highest point the operator will stop us so we can get a look at the wide-open plains." His voice was low and full of reassurance. I tried to block out every sound, but blood pounded in my ears. The wheel creaked toward the sky and the bench shifted. My hands flew out and grabbed the bar in front of us. Henry chuckled under his breath.

"How is it possible that you can soar through the heavens, but at forty-five feet you can barely catch your breath?"

"It's different up here." My fingers clenched the seat while we puttered farther up into the sky. "In the air I know where my body goes. How the plane will react. But here, that man operating the machine is in control." The spokes creaked beneath the bench and I did everything in my power to ignore how this tin can ride was rattling me. "And those metal bars are the only thing keeping us aloft. Not the force of an engine or the push and pull of the wind." My sentences came out in rough spurts, like I couldn't take in enough oxygen.

Henry reached for my shoulders and turned me toward him. "Take deep breaths. You're going to be fine." I closed my eyes. His fingers pressed against my thin blouse and heat shot through me. My head went light, but it wasn't because of the ride.

"Do you want me to signal the operator to bring us down?" Henry held me in place, and my body trembled under his touch.

"Look at me, Gracie." The tenderness in his voice encouraged me to open my eyes. "I'd never let anything happen to you. You're safe here with me." He slid my hand off the edge of the seat and curled his fingers through mine. "Let's get your mind off this ride. Tell me about your family. I overheard Warren say your father was a musician." Henry's smooth voice unwound the knots in my stomach.

No matter what I did, I couldn't hide from my memories. I tried to push them back. Force them out of my head when they became too much to bear. This life I was living with Uncle Warren wasn't what my parents would have wanted for me. They'd talked about how they wanted me to go to school to be a nurse or a secretary. To make my own way in the world. Hanging from an airplane hundreds of feet in the air was not what they had in mind for my future.

"I'm sorry." Henry gripped my fingers tighter. His pulse thrummed against my skin. "We don't have to talk at all. We can sit here and simply enjoy the beauty of the day."

"It's all right. I want to tell you." In Arkansas, he'd shared a part of his life. It was time to share mine.

"That little girl we met a while back, Ruby, she reminded me of my sister, Anna."

"You have a sister?"

"Had," I said quietly. His eyes dropped away from my face as if he sensed my loss. "In 1918, I lived in Chicago with my parents and younger sister. My father played trumpet in a jazz band, and my mother worked as a seamstress out of our home."

If I closed my eyes, I could see the twist of my father's special rag as he brought his beloved trumpet to a dazzling shine. How the sound of its beautiful high and low notes filled our small kitchen every morning while he practiced his scales. The way he hovered in the doorway of our apartment. The cut of his dark-blue suit clinging to his tall, thin body while Ma raised up on her tiptoes to give him a kiss before he went to play music in a club on the south side.

"One Sunday after church my father complained of a headache. The next day my mother and Anna couldn't get out of bed. When my father started coughing up blood, I went to our landlady for help." My voice wobbled but I continued. "When the police arrived, they swept me out of the apartment and took me right to the hospital. I cried for hours. I begged for my family and asked when I could go home."

I'd never spoken about what had happened to my family to anyone but Uncle Warren, but as soon as the words were out of my mouth the memories were as fresh as if the nightmare had happened yesterday.

"I can still smell the rotting stench of death that clung to every doctor who examined me." My throat was suddenly so dry it was difficult to swallow. "As much as I try to forget it, I can still hear the keening sound of patients crying out in pain. When a nurse finally came to talk to me days later, she explained my family had contracted the Spanish flu and had all succumbed to it."

Henry scooted closer, his shoulder brushing mine. "You can stop now, Gracie."

I shook my head. I needed to finish. "The state wouldn't let me go to the funeral. To keep the sickness from spreading, they stopped public gatherings of any kind. I stayed in the hospital for weeks after my family passed so they could monitor my temperature. Somehow I stayed healthy. Afterward, they put me on a train to Nebraska to live with my mother's brother, who up until that time I'd only known through pictures."

"You must have been frightened."

"Numb is more accurate," I managed to stutter out. "Poor Uncle Warren, he must have thought I was mute because I didn't say a word for days." The ride creaked and swayed below us in the slightest pitch of wind.

"You seem close now," Henry said.

"Close as a bachelor and an orphan could ever be, I suppose. He had to change everything about his life when I arrived. His tiny apartment was a mess. Dirty dishes filled the sink. Flies buzzed over bits of dried food glued to the kitchen table. I did my best to blend into the walls, not wanting to be a nuisance to my only living kin. After a while we moved into a routine, giving each other space. Uncle Warren let me do whatever I wanted except for when it came to his beloved airplane."

"Yes, his airplane. You seem to have won him over in that aspect."

"It's hard to ignore a thirteen-year-old who won't take no for an answer."

He leaned in, the heat from his body mingling with mine. "You said before that you thought I was brave, but after what happened to your family I believe you're the one who is truly brave."

"Let's not call it bravery. Perhaps we can think about it as pure survival."

"The will to live," he added quietly.

My breathing slowed as I sank back into the seat. In the distance I could make out the hangar. Around it, gentle clouds drifted past like soft, white blankets.

"Who knew the plains could be so gorgeous?" While I stared out at the Nebraska landscape, Henry watched me. He reached for a loose lock of my hair and swept it behind my ear. His touch blazed across my skin, leaving invisible scorch marks that only I could feel. Why was he looking at me like I was some gorgeous painting when I was more of a blank canvas?

"We're almost to the top," he whispered.

The ride moaned below us until we came to a complete stop at the highest point. Nebraska farmland spread out before us. Browns and greens were intertwined across a vast countryside. On the horizon, the faded, white paint of small farmhouses gleamed in the sun.

Henry shifted and leaned over the side of the bench, his eyes narrowing towards the ground below.

"Is something wrong? Did a part fall off? I knew this contraption was dangerous!"

I followed his line of sight and landed on two faces that twisted my gut: Rowland and Louis.

"That man and his goon are everywhere. Next time I see him he's going to get an earful about that Louis beating you up."

"He won't listen. When a man like that sets his mind to something he never gives up." Henry's shoulders tensed and his gaze focused on Louis. His ears turned red as if rage filled his entire body.

"But we can't let him get away with it."

Ignoring me, Henry inched closer and my mind swirled. "For now, let's forget about everything." I tried to look away, but he swept a hand under my chin and gently pulled my face back in his direction. The shouts of the crowd below and the faint tune of the calliope in the distance faded away. He filled all my senses. I could no longer think, taste, or feel without being immersed in his oil-and-soap scent. I was an idiot to think he would keep the telegram from us. He'd done nothing but prove to me time and time again that he wanted The Soaring Eagles to succeed.

A small smile ticked up the corner of his mouth and there was no denying what he wanted. He moved in and brushed a hand across my cheek. Today his eyes were a deep shade of emerald, and I thought I could lean in and meet him halfway. It was only a kiss—a man and woman pressing their mouths against one another—their bodies invading each other's intimate space. People did it all the time. Husbands and wives kissed hello. Mothers pressed soft lips to their children's forehead. It was simple. Or so it seemed until I imagined what would happen between Henry and me. Once our mouths found each other there would be no going back. No looking at each other and denying what had passed between us.

"What are you thinking?" he asked, sitting so close I felt the heat floating off his body.

How much I want to kiss you. Feel your body pressed to mine, even though I know it's wrong.

"Money," I managed to mumble.

He inched back, his eyes widening. "Money?"

"Yes, I mean how we're going to make our next dollar. We can still earn enough for Chicago if we try."

His lips thinned. "You heard your uncle. It's time to move on."

The ride jerked and shifted as we made our way down and then up again for the second revolution. This nonsense with Henry had to stop. While he still had his dream of the garage, mine was slowly slipping away. My focus had to be on the team and only the team. This wasn't the time to make foolish mistakes or wallow in self-pity. If we couldn't enter the contest, we had to make a name for The Soaring Eagles in other ways. I glanced in the direction of the hangar, a plan forming in my head.

Nathan greeted us as we stepped off the ride. "Wasn't that fun, Grace?"

"Should we get in line and go again?" Daniel asked.

"I forgot. I told Mary and Ethel I'd stop by during their break at the diner," I said. "You boys go and have fun. I'll see you tomorrow, bright and early."

Henry's eyes narrowed as if he could read my mind. "Maybe I should head back to the hangar. There's still work to be done on Nathan's landing gear."

"No sirree," Nathan said. "Warren made it clear none of us were to go back today. Let's go have a little fun."

Before Henry could protest, Nathan and Daniel pulled him deeper into the fair. A man in a crisp, white suit called to them through a megaphone heralding the "nonstop musical madness" of a barbershop quartet. Workers across the aisle waved them toward a game with empty milk bottles stacked shoulder-high in a pyramid. I waited until they were swallowed by the crowd and then dashed back across the field. All I needed was a few more quiet moments, and I knew I could make the Showstopper finally work.

The hangar was eerily quiet. I slipped off my boots and raced to the corner. I tugged on the mats to drag them under the Jenny. Once on the wing, I hoisted myself onto the top and pulled the spool of wire from my pocket. If we ever needed a surprise trick it was now.

A few minutes later the wire was secured around the top strut. Edging down to the end of the wing, I was about to toss the spool to the ground when two people rushed into the hangar. One was an older man dressed in overalls and a straw hat. The fella next to him wore a work shirt and faded, gray pants. His smooth face said he was at least a year away from needing a shave. Sweat covered both their brows liked they'd run from the center of town. Their heads swiveled back and forth until they spotted me.

"Do you know the man who owns this hangar?" the older man called.

Patches of mud covered his overalls. Strange. Why would a farmer be looking for Uncle Warren?

"Please, miss. Can you help us?" The young man raced toward me.

I pointed to the office just as Uncle Warren stepped out the door with Mr. Sorenson. My heart took off at lightning speed. What was he doing here? We hadn't broken any government rules. Lately.

"Axle on your plane is a little wobbly," Sorenson clucked his tongue. His eyes darted around the hangar like we were hiding something. "Got a few other teams to check out in these parts. I'll be back in a few weeks."

"Sir," the older farmer tore his hat from his head. "We must talk." Fear widened his eyes. "It's an urgent matter."

Uncle Warren ushered the men inside his office. The shouts started almost immediately, Uncle Warren's being the loudest. "Absolutely not," he bellowed through the thin walls. "I can't guarantee their safety." The other men mumbled a rebuttal I couldn't hear.

Their voices roared as Henry and the boys walked into the hangar.

"What's going on?" Nathan stopped just a few feet away from me.

"What are you doing here?" I asked, but my eyes never veered from the closed door.

"Same as you," he huffed. "Guess none of us can stay away."

"Who's in the office?" Henry asked.

"That man from the government, Mr. Sorenson, and an older farmer along with his son."

"Farmer?" Daniel lumbered toward the door but jumped back when the handle shook.

We scattered across the hangar and tried to look busy. The farmers scurried out first. Uncle Warren trailed behind them with Mr. Sorenson close at his side. They all approached the center of the hangar, their eyes shifting hesitantly around the Jennys.

Uncle Warren stopped when he saw us. "Well, can't say I'm surprised you're back. Saves me from tracking you all down."

"What's going on?" Nathan stepped around me like a protective shield against Sorenson's deadly stare. Daniel moved to his side and Henry quickly followed.

Uncle Warren rubbed a hand behind his neck. "We got a little issue we need to discuss." The tremor in his voice raised the hairs on the back of my neck. "These gentlemen are Gordon Prescott and his son, Arthur. Earlier this morning Mr. Prescott watched his other son, Joe, take off near his farm. His plane hit some debris on the runway and he's flying right now with one tire."

Nathan and Daniel swapped a measured look. Without two tires, the pilot had no other choice but to crash land. A situation that almost never turned out well.

"He's asked if one of you would go up and put a new tire on the landing gear. The only way to accomplish this would be to do a plane-to-plane transfer." The hangar stayed quiet. None of us had ever gone from plane-to-plane. We'd never even practiced it. "We need to make a decision quickly. The pilot's been in the air for some time and is low on fuel."

"Is this man a trained pilot?" Nathan asked. "For all we know he could kill us as soon as we step on the wing."

Mr. Prescott stepped forward. "My boy, Joe, was in the war and trained in one of those." He pointed to the Jennys.

"I've flown with him plenty of times," Arthur added. "You'd be safe with him."

His gaze darted between Nathan, Daniel, and Henry, but never once landed on me.

"I'll do it," I said, stepping out from behind the boys.

Uncle Warren's face turned white as he swapped a grim look with Mr. Sorenson. Mr. Prescott's lips trembled. He surveyed me for a long moment like he needed to decide whether he could trust me with his son's life.

"Gracie." Henry shook his head, pleading with me to say no.

The maneuver could be done. I ran through the flight in my head. If Joe was as good a pilot as his pa claimed, I could pull it off. All I needed was to be close enough to reach a strut on the other plane.

"How much time do we have?" I asked.

"No, Grace! It's too dangerous. No one's ever tried it before," Nathan said.

"I'll go!" Daniel insisted.

Uncle Warren's shoulders sank. "All the men weigh too much. You'd crack the axle. The only one who has a chance of pulling this off is Grace." He grabbed me by the shoulders. "In the end it's your choice." His voice wavered. "I'll be right there with you, keeping the plane steady, but I can't guarantee your safety with the other pilot."

Mr. Prescott approached me, his son hovering behind. His lower lip wobbled as he crumpled his hat between his fingers. "Please, miss. You can trust him. Go help my son."

The boys dropped their gazes to the floor in defeat. A fellow pilot was about to go down unless I did something to help. There wasn't time to argue about whether any of this made sense. I understood what I was risking. Every time I went up in a plane there was always a chance I wouldn't make it down alive.

14
For the Blink of an Eye

No one could decide where to put the tire. The men went round and round, arguing whether they should strap it to the wing or put it on the footboard at the front of my seat. The discussion rambled on until I reminded them the pilot was low on fuel.

Henry stood in a tight circle with the boys. Their voices grew louder with each passing moment. I searched the hangar, my eyes moving over Uncle Warren's Jenny and stopping at the junctions where the guide wires crossed from the top to bottom wing in an x-formation.

"Nathan," I called. "Hand me your belt."

His face twisted in confusion. "My belt? Why?"

"Give it to me and I'll explain."

With an aggravated huff, he yanked the brown leather belt from his waist and deposited it in my hand. After tucking it under my arm, I walked to a workbench and retrieved a spare tire. The men watched my every move as I weaved the belt through the spokes.

Henry broke away from the crowd and pulled the tire from my hand. "You never cease to amaze me." He spun me around until my back faced him. Once the tire was placed between my shoulder blades, he pulled the belt around to my front. "The wheel's no bigger than the one on a bicycle so it doesn't have much weight. But carrying it on your back means you can't sit during takeoff. You'll have to stand on the wing." He moved around me, checking the tire from all angles. "Don't try to detach the tire until you can get steady on the axle. When you're settled, untether it."

After he was convinced it was secure, he handed me a palm-sized wrench. "Make sure you bolt down both sides of the tire tightly before releasing it. If you don't, the tire could fall off mid-air and . . ." He didn't have to say the words. If I couldn't fix the tire, it was lights out for both me and the pilot. It was a possibility no one wanted to discuss, especially me. This had to be treated like any other trick, or fear would keep me from helping the man who was less than hour from crashing.

When he was convinced the tire was secure, Henry came around to face me again. He tried to hide it but the light behind his eyes was gone—he was as scared as I was. "No funny business. Do the job and get back down here in one piece so I can see those beautiful, blue eyes again."

I grasped his hand. If this was going to be the last moment between us what could I say? *Take care of the boys and my uncle. Be sure they stay safe.* If I spoke the words it would sound like a goodbye and that was the last thing I wanted.

Things between us were very confusing. One moment he was ordering me around. The next he was as gentle as a summer breeze, making me feel like the most special girl in the world. I couldn't help but admire his strength and the way he committed to his work with all his heart. The team would need that strength if I was gone.

"I'll be back in a flash, I promise."

He pulled my hand to his chest and settled it over his heart. The steady pump of it matched my own. "And you never break your promises, right?"

"Never."

His free hand reached up like he wanted to touch my face, but then his eyes swept around the hangar and landed on the boys who were standing only steps away.

Nathan's deep voice boomed through the air as he spun the propeller and yelled, "Contact!"

"I have to go." Henry nodded and gave me a tense smile before walking to the side of the hangar, standing near Mr. Prescott and his son. Mr. Sorenson stood only a few feet away, his piercing eyes warning we'd all be in trouble if I couldn't bring the pilot down safely.

Daniel waved his arms over his head, giving the all clear. Uncle Warren taxied out to the runway. When I reached Daniel he fell in step beside me. "Mind the struts if your uncle has to bank hard. And make sure you watch your foot placement. Don't want you tearing up that other pilot's wing." He shoved his hands into his pockets and took a deep swallow.

"This is going to be easy," I said, trying to ignore the way his voice cracked. "I'll attach the tire and be down in a jiffy."

He shook his head. "Things will never be right again if something happens to—"

"Trust me, Daniel. I'll only do the exchange if it feels right."

"I just don't get why you volunteered for this? The shows are one thing, but this transfer, it doesn't make sense."

"If it was you, or any other member of our team up there, I wouldn't hesitate. You're my family. You'd do the same for me."

Daniel looked at Mr. Prescott standing at the entrance to the hangar, his eyes searching the sky for his son. "I understand. Git now, and go do your thing."

When I reached the Jenny, Uncle Warren tugged down his goggles and signaled with a quick wave that he was ready.

Nathan walked up and looped his arm through mine. "I know I've been hard on you. When you try a new trick I'm always the first one to doubt you." He tugged on his beard, looking at me and then the plane. "Sometimes we make hard choices. Ones we're proud of and ones we regret." Pain flickered across his face.

I stopped in the middle of the runway, the noonday sun high in the sky. "I've thought this through. I can do it, Nathan."

Uncle Warren taxied toward us, bringing the Jenny around so we wouldn't have to fly straight into the headwind coming from the east. Nathan's hand thrummed at his side and I grabbed his fingers to force him to look at me.

"No more lectures," he said. "Back in one piece, that's all I ask." He grimaced, using my own words against me. Before they were only used to tease him, but now they had a deadly serious meaning.

Before I could say another word to reassure him he positioned his hands and boosted me onto the wing. The prop roared and Nathan tried to shout over the noise.

"Watch the wings on takeoff. With you standing on the frame it'll be hard for your uncle to get enough lift. Stay low until he can get level."

I inched across the frame and wound myself around a strut. We blazed down the airstrip. The landing gear rattled below me. The engine roared as Uncle Warren pushed for more power to get us off the ground. Air wound through the spokes of the tire and yanked me back as we climbed higher. When we reached 1,000 feet, Uncle Warren signaled to a plane bobbing and weaving toward us. A sudden weight pressed against my chest. I had to put my life in the hands of another pilot. An unknown pilot.

When Henry asked me about my first time in the air with Uncle Warren I'd left out the part about the days after. How I pleaded with him to take me up again and how he ignored me until my pleas became too much.

Back in the sky with him, the wind was like a calming breath. I don't know what made me do it, but I unlatched my safety belt and climbed out onto the wing. To this day I can still hear Uncle Warren's shouts as I hung onto the strut. My mind went empty of every thought except how much I wanted to stand out on that wing every day for the rest of my life.

After that flight, Uncle Warren gave me the silent treatment for another week. When the low grumbles and grunts got to be too much we had a showdown in the kitchen of the farmhouse one evening. Our screams shook the rafters. At a stalemate, and with the cuckoo clock in the sitting room chiming midnight, I went to bed defeated and without a voice.

The sun was just peeking through the curtains the next morning when my bed sagged under Uncle Warren's weight. Without a word, he beckoned me out to the car. An hour later we were in the sky, the beginning of The Soaring Eagles. That was close to five years ago. Now I had to trust someone else to keep me safe, someone who I only knew about through a brief conversation with his father. I was beginning to question my choices.

The yellow plane flew overhead and leveled off only feet above us. The force from the down draft made it difficult to take a full breath. I wrapped myself around the strut. If Joe's plane lost too much altitude, little bits of me would be scattered all over the Nebraska countryside.

Uncle Warren steadied the plane. Slowly he tapped his head twice. The deep crevices around his eyes filled with worry. I shot him a confident smile as Joe inched lower. If this was going to work, I had to believe I could do it.

Once I caught Joe's attention by waving my hands over my head, I pointed to the tire strapped to my back and then down to his landing gear. I did the motion over and over until he gave a nod.

The roar of his engine filled the air. What was I thinking? Was I strong enough to pull this off? Even if I could grab a strut, I wasn't sure I could get down to the landing gear. If the axle was too damaged, there'd be no hope of a solid landing.

The wind tore at my hair and clothes like an invisible demon. I took a steadying breath and focused on what I needed to do. This wasn't some performance to dazzle a crowd. It was saving a life, and I was determined to pull this stunt off. All I had to do was edge to the end of the wing and wait for a calm bit of air. I closed my eyes and saw Henry's encouraging smile. After one last glance at Joe's floundering plane, I tightened the strap on my lucky goggles and jumped.

For the blink of an eye I was airborne. The guttural chug of the engine filled my ears. Wind scratched at my face as my body collided with the frame. I slid across the wing and scrambled for a wire to slow my momentum. My shoulder jammed into a strut before my body ricocheted off a landing wire. When I finally got a steady hold on the wing's frame, I pressed my cheek against the worn, white fabric and waited for my heart to stop racing.

Joe knocked his hand against the wing over and over to get my attention. I stood and made my way toward him. When he saw me, his eyes went wide under his goggles. I shrugged. Girl or not, without me he was going to crash.

Once the shock vanished from his face, he jabbed at the flickering needle on the gas gauge. I nodded and walked back across the wing. Heat pulsed off the engine, filling the air with a burning tar scent. Hot oil sputtered out and singed the skin at my hairline. Hand over hand, I moved across the landing wires. Each step was hesitant. I didn't know this plane. One bobble and my foot would go straight through the material stretched over the frame.

At the edge of the wing, I slid onto my belly. My feet dangled in the air until my boots reached the axle. The wings pitched and the engine coughed out black exhaust: a sure sign we were dangerously low on gas. I clung to the landing gear until Joe leveled us out. When we were stable I sat down along the metal crossbar.

Below me farmland raced past in a muddy haze. Cows and livestock became out-of-focus stains against a brown landscape. Small farmhouses and aging barns were the only recognizable images as we tore across the sky.

With trembling hands, I unlatched the tire from the belt. A slight chop of turbulence shook the plane. The rubber skidded off my fingertips and banged against the bottom of the plane. I swung out my hand and caught the edge of a spoke before the tire plummeted to the ground. Adrenaline thrummed in my veins. If the tire was gone, so were we. No more mistakes. I had to fix this plane now.

The axle was bare but it looked like I could get the new tire bolted on. Carefully I lowered the tire with one hand, hanging on with the other, until it rested snug in place. I slid the small wrench from my pocket and tightened the bolts. After pulling on the tire to confirm it was secure, I leaned my head against the fuselage. The movement of the wind and hum of the engine soothed me. I stood on the crossbar and with all my strength heaved myself up onto the wing. With my hands gripped around a strut, I nodded at Joe. His once tense face relaxed. I gave a quick salute to Uncle Warren and he banked toward the landing strip.

The tire held, and we came to an easy stop. When my feet hit the ground, the boys surrounded me. Daniel and Nathan lifted me up, their whoops of joy filling the air.

Mr. Prescott smothered Joe in an embrace. The minute he released him, Mr. Sorenson started in with his questions about the debris the plane hit on takeoff. When he was satisfied with Joe's answers he cocked his head in my direction. "You might want to keep this quiet, considering *she* had to rescue you." Joe blanched as Sorenson snapped his notepad closed and stalked back in the direction of his car.

Arthur sidled up next to Joe and punched his arm. "Yeah, what would your pals say if they knew that little gal saved your hide today?"

Joe's once colorless cheeks flamed as he turned and stalked toward the boys. "Are you all a bunch of cowards? How dare you send a woman," he tore the white scarf from his neck, "a *girl* into the air to do a man's job? She could have been killed!"

What an ungrateful cad. I'd saved him from a certain death and his only concern was that I was a woman?

After setting me down, Nathan and Daniel stalked toward him, but Henry, even with his limp, got there first. Where did he come from? I'd looked for him when we landed, but didn't see him among the small crowd gathered around the landing strip.

"Listen here, fella, if it weren't for that 'girl' your father would be scavenging the countryside for pieces of your body right now." He grabbed Joe by the collar, balancing on his good leg. "Ever tried to look for parts of arms or legs in an open field? Taking small steps to make sure you don't tread on someone's severed hand or foot?"

Henry's voice faltered but he held on to Joe. "None of those men could save you because their weight woulda' cracked the axle. Grace risked her life for you today. That means you owe her an apology *and* a debt of gratitude." The men stayed rigid for a heartbeat. Neither flinched before Henry shoved him away.

Joe wobbled back. Arthur tried to drag him away, but Joe shoved him and barreled straight for Henry. He threw a punch that caught only air. Henry charged forward and slammed into Joe's gut. They rolled on the ground, fists flying as they each tried to land their own blows.

Nathan and Daniel broke them apart. Henry's face was that troubling ash-gray again. He'd gone several weeks without having an episode, but now he was muttering through his heaving breaths. I wanted to go to him, comfort him like I had after the diner, but Daniel reached him first. Henry's voice cracked several times as Daniel put a hand to his shoulder and squeezed. I inched in closer to hear brief murmurs from Daniel, and even Nathan, as they reassured Henry. Told him that his feet were firmly planted on American soil and that none of us were in danger.

Once Henry caught his breath, the boys released him and he hobbled toward me. A fresh drip of blood eased from the corner of his mouth.

I pressed my shirtsleeve to his lips. "You didn't have to fight him."

He flinched at my touch. "Yes, I most certainly did." He shot a dark glance in Joe's direction. "Most men, when faced with a life or death situation, will turn tail to save their own skin. But what you just did, risking your own life to save his, it was extraordinarily brave. I won't tolerate anyone saying different."

His protective words shot a surprising thrill through me. "Henry, I don't care what he thinks."

The edges of his beautiful, green eyes darkened as he focused on Joe, who was slow to get up from the ground. I placed a hand under his chin, urging him to look at me. "Are you okay?" A deep-blue welt was already forming underneath his right eye.

He clasped my hand. The light slowly inched back into his eyes. "I'm fine, Gracie."

"Can I get you some ice or raw steak for your eye? That will help with the swelling."

His eyes widened in surprise. "How do you know about that?"

I glanced at the Jenny, her shadow growing in the fading daylight. She'd been both a friend and adversary for years—but I loved her all the same. "I've spent quite a bit of time perfecting my tricks. There's been an occasion or two when I've knocked my head into a strut. Banged an elbow against the lower skid. Uncle Warren was always right there with a cold rag to relieve the swelling."

He shook his head as if he'd given up trying to understand me. "No, I'll be okay. I got worse in basic training."

"Come on, let me help. It's the least I can do. You did defend my honor, after all," I teased.

"What honor? You're as rough and tumble as they come," he joked, running a finger along my cheek. When I stood firm, hands on my hips, he relented. "Yes, ice would be great. But no steak. I only like 'em if they're on a plate and medium rare."

Even with his eye slowly disappearing into folds of swollen

skin, he was still more handsome than any man who dashed across the silver screen. He had his dark moments, but he'd proven he was a good man. Being around him was getting more difficult with each passing moment, and I wasn't sure how long I could stay away despite all the risks.

15
Trained Monkeys

Once the boys assured me they weren't going to allow Henry near Joe again, I hurried back in the direction of the fairgrounds to find the ice vendor. The barbershop quartet's rendition of "Let Me Call You Sweetheart" drifted across the field.

The mouth-watering scents of chocolate and popcorn from nearby vendors filled the air. My stomach growled, protesting that it was well past lunchtime and I hadn't had a crumb to eat. I dashed past the wooden booths toward a crudely written sign pointing in the direction of the ice tent. At the end of a very long aisle, past the lemonade stand and a vendor crowing about roasted peanuts, I found the tent.

Dripping hunks of ice lined every corner, dropping the temperature inside at least ten degrees. I called for the vendor but no one appeared. I thought about breaking off a piece on my own, but when I couldn't find an ice pick I gave up.

As I exited the tent, I bumped into a wall of muscle. The sharp lines in Louis' forehead reminded me of a villain I once saw in an old nickelodeon. All he needed was a black mustache to twirl.

"Excuse me," I said, angling around him. He snapped out his arm and grabbed the edge of my shirtsleeve.

"Where do you think you're going? Mr. Rowland wants a word."

I struggled to release myself from his grasp. "If you would like your hand to remain attached to your arm, I suggest you let me go, sir."

"You may get to run around when in the sky, but on the ground you should learn your place." He dug his fingers deeper into my skin.

"Enough!" Rowland appeared and rapped the tip of his umbrella against Louis's arm. "My sincere apologies, Miss Lafferty. Sometimes Louis takes matters a little too far." He waved his hand in the air to dismiss him.

"Yes, my team already knows that first hand." I smoothed down the sleeves of my dirty shirt, the press of Louis's fingers still throbbing along my skin. "Why are you here? I thought The Skyhawks were on the bill for the late afternoon show. Shouldn't you be out somewhere barking orders at your lemmings?"

"I wanted to check on you. I just learned of your little foray into the sky to help that pilot." A flicker of what looked like real concern moved across his face.

Well, I'll be. Did Alistair Rowland have a heart hidden somewhere beneath that expensive suit?

"It appears you are no worse for wear. It does concern me that your uncle would allow you to take such a gamble. Those farmers came to me first, but I'd never risk a plane for an infantile pilot who has no business in the sky."

And the small flicker of humanity I saw in him was gone.

"Can't say I'm surprised. You never make a move unless there's some benefit to you. That's why you and your team will always come in second. You can have skills and tip-top planes, but without heart your shows are nothing more than men behaving like trained monkeys at the circus."

"Trained monkeys who make a decent living." He smoothed down the lapels of his cream suit. The diamond in his tie pin glimmered in the late afternoon sun. "Let me ask you something. When you travel does your head rest at night on a real hotel pillow or the rough frame of a Jenny? Do you eat a steak dinner with all the accompaniments or cold beans out of a can?" He patted at the straw-blond hair that was perfectly clipped around his ears. "If you worked for me you'd always rest in a nice hotel and go to bed with a full stomach."

There was nothing about this life that was easy. It was those times, when we were shivering in a barn in the middle of nowhere, only a wool blanket protecting us from the cold, that proved how dedicated The Soaring Eagles were to the art of flying. "None of that makes for a successful team, sir."

"Perhaps not, but money does make a difference. Word is your little grounding put you in quite a pinch with funds." He made a small *tsk* under his breath. "The government seems to have taken an interest in your antics as well. There's a dark cloud following your every move. Not a positive outlook for a flier, is it?"

How did he know all the details of my life? The man seemed to have eyes and ears everywhere. We couldn't make a move these days without him showing up.

"The difficulties we've encountered only make us a better team. Stronger."

He slid his hands into his pockets and shook his head. I hated to admit it, but he did have a point. Traveling took money. Money we didn't have. My eyes moved to the gold pocket watch that hung from his vest. The inlay and ornate detail must have cost a fortune. That money alone could have gotten us to Chicago, paid for our entry fee and a top-notch dinner in one of those restaurants with fancy gold-trimmed plates and cloth napkins.

Rowland continued to stand too close. Men loved to use their height to try and intimidate me. It happened at shows across the nation. Whether they wanted an autograph, a photo, or just a chance to show their distaste for the life I'd chosen, it was a tactic that never worked. I battled rain, wind, and thunderstorms at 500 feet; men didn't frighten me.

"I know how desperate you are to get to Chicago to compete, but those pesky hangar fees are keeping you from attending."

"How do you know that?" I snapped.

"Barnstorming is a very small community." He waved his hand in the air as if everything about me was his business. "No matter.

I'm here to be a guardian angel who can get The Soaring Eagles to the World Aviation Expo. All it will take is a small agreement from you and your uncle."

Every bone inside of me urged not to encourage him, but desperation won out. "What small agreement?"

"The Skyhawks have a major show in St. Louis in two days. Unfortunately, one of my pilots and a performer must leave to attend to some family business. You and your uncle could fill in for them. In exchange, I will cover your hangar fees for the Expo."

Grace, keep quiet. The mantra rang over and over in my head, but curiosity won out. "What's the catch?"

A predatory smirk crossed his lips. "There are no other strings attached. One performance and then you can leave. Although, after you and your uncle see the plane we put you in, the costumes, and the size of the crowd, you may reconsider."

My heart knocked against my chest. Sixty dollars for one show. It would take us months and dozens of performances to earn that kind of money. St. Louis wasn't that far from Chicago. I'd sworn up and down I'd never fly for him but it was one routine. Fifteen minutes of stunts to achieve my dream. Keep my family together. I considered how I could talk Uncle Warren into the deal.

Month after month we toiled in the hot sun. More teams were crowding the skies, pushing us off our regular bills. Over the last few weeks no matter how hard we worked, the crowds were less and less impressed with our stunts. The worn hat we passed through the crowd that used to spill over with copper and silver coins now showed up half-full. The Flying Finellis and The Black Bombers matched our shows with their own car-to-plane transfers and double inverted loops. Besides performing the Showstopper, which wasn't quite ready, I wasn't sure what else we could do to earn more funds.

A push and pull snapped inside me like a rubber band. Was it worth it to give Rowland this one concession if it meant getting to the Expo? There was no doubt in my mind that once we competed that contract would be ours. So, did it matter if I took the money this one time?

"Your uncle has tried to give you a decent life." Rowland inched down the edge of his straw boater hat to keep the sun out of his eyes. "But without a shot at this competition, one day your team will be penniless. Mark my words, if you don't take this offer you'll spend the rest of your life regretting it."

The word penniless reverberated in my ears. I wanted to slap myself for even considering his deal. There was no way I'd ever be a Skyhawk, even if meant getting to Chicago. Agreeing to help Rowland was akin to selling my soul to the devil. He swore there were no strings attached, but the flyover, his goon beating up Henry, all of it proved he'd do and say anything to get what he wanted.

"Don't think so highly of yourself. I'd rather work at a diner than for you. At least there I'd know a rat when I saw one."

He brushed nonexistent dirt from his hands as if the conversation was suddenly distasteful. "Leave it to you to turn our little tête-à-tête ugly. Without my kind invitation to join The Skyhawks, your time in the air is dwindling. We both know it." The edges of his brows knitted together as he collected himself. "Despite what you hear or believe, I *am* an honest business man with good intentions."

I huffed out a laugh. When someone swore they had good intentions it usually meant the opposite. "The Soaring Eagles may be down, but never count us out."

"Louis!" Rowland called. The side of the tent ruffled and Louis appeared from the shadows. "Find the ice vendor. It appears in this heat Miss Lafferty has lost her wits."

"Yes, sir." Louis snapped his heels together and disappeared in search of the vendor.

It was hard not to roll my eyes. "You are *not* funny, sir."

"Do I look amused?" he chided. "One of these days someone will snap some sense into you, Grace." My name curled off his lips in a way that made my insides twist. "Let's hope it happens before it's too late."

Louis reappeared, holding the vendor by the scruff of the neck. He dropped the young man at Rowland's feet.

"See to it that this girl gets what she needs." Rowland pinched a dollar from his pocket. Before the boy could take it, I swiped it away.

"I don't need or want your money." I tossed the crumpled bill to his feet.

Rowland released a pitying sigh. "Louis, pick that up. I do believe we are finished here." He tucked the umbrella under his arm and strode away.

The young ice vendor was still flat on the ground. His eyes stayed wide as Rowland disappeared into the crowd. "Heavens, miss, I never heard a lady talk to a buttoned-up gentleman like that before. He must've really ruffled your feathers."

I rushed to help him up. "Never mind that. Can you please break me off a small chip?"

"Of course." He tapped away at a nearby block. Ice dust swirled into the air, dancing like snowflakes on a January day. A single piece the size of his hand broke off. He placed the thick chip into a white cloth and handed it to me. I slipped a coin out of my pocket but he refused it.

"Your money's no good here, Miss Lafferty."

"Why not? And how do you know my name?"

"Because everyone knows what you did to save Joe Prescott today." He watched me carefully. "Word spreads fast around here. The whole town thinks you're a hero."

I plastered a weak smile to my face. "Thank you for your kindness."

He bowed his head almost in deference. "My little sister thinks you're a real kick. She's talking about being a wing walker one day, too." He grabbed my hand and pumped it up and down. "Thanks for doing, well, what you do."

"You're welcome," I mumbled. "And thank you again for the ice."

"My pleasure."

I rushed out of the tent and past the lights of the midway. Not once, but twice, men tipped their hats in my direction and women gave me kind smiles. This time the pointed stares weren't in disgust, but filled with wonder, and to my surprise, respect. The wheels in my brain churned as I raced in the direction of the hangar. I needed to use the change in events to get us to Chicago. But how?

16
A Good Reminder

Lincoln, Nebraska
September 2, 1922
10 days until the World Aviation Expo

I snuck into the hangar every day before dawn to work on the new trick. The Showstopper still wasn't ready, but this new maneuver would wow the crowds and bring us the last-minute money we needed. We didn't need Rowland or his offer. I still cursed myself for even considering it.

After fine-tuning the stunt this morning, I decided it was time to present it to Uncle Warren. I paced back and forth in front of the hangar chewing on the skin around my thumb. My muddy boots clomped along the concrete floor. Every few minutes I glanced in the direction of his office.

The idea for the trick had come to me on our way home from Arkansas and I hadn't been able to shake it. I'd played with the maneuver in my head until I'd figured out how we could pull off a loop while I was standing on the top wing.

Convinced it was the only way to get us to Chicago, I swiped my sweaty palms against my linen pants and marched toward the office. My footsteps echoed through the hangar and I stopped short, trying to compose my thoughts. Just as I was finally ready, the door swung open unexpectedly.

"Grace? Did you need something?" Uncle Warren grumbled.

"Mind if we test a new trick today?"

He gave me a long look that warned he wasn't up for playing games. "What new trick?"

"There's a maneuver I think will add to our crowds. Let me show you."

After tucking back my curls and rolling my thin shirtsleeves to my elbows, I scrambled onto the frame of his Jenny. Uncle Warren hoisted himself up after me. Once up on the top wing, I secured two straps to the center struts. I moved my feet into position and explained my idea. How the force of gravity would keep me pinned to the wing during the double inverted loop. The way we could climb to a high enough altitude so the government couldn't complain. And more importantly, what the stunt would mean to the future of The Soaring Eagles.

His mouth gaped open like a fish hooked on a line. "Now I know you've lost your mind!"

His shout brought Henry around the side of the plane. "What's going on?"

"Another one of Grace's harebrained ideas." Uncle Warren jumped off the wing and headed back to his office.

I ignored Henry's stare and tried to keep Uncle Warren's focus on me. "Hear me out. Please!" While he was cautious, he was also a businessman. We needed to make more money, if not for the contest, than for the government's surprise inspections. I continued to talk until he grew tired of my pleas.

"I swear Grace, I don't know how I let you talk me into these things," he huffed. "We'll try it, but you'll wear a parachute. No arguments."

"Yes, sir!" I crowed. "You won't regret this. Wait and see."

Henry white-knuckled the edge of the wing. "Gracie, are you sure about this?"

"Yes, Henry. I'm sure."

He nodded. "Good enough, but give me an hour. I want to make sure the top wing is ready for your weight."

We landed successfully two hours later. An ear-to-ear smile covered Uncle Warren's face. When we added this maneuver, cities across the nation would be begging us to perform. Contest or no contest, The Soaring Eagles were going to be a name on everyone's lips by the end of the year.

~

The next day hordes of spectators jostled for a good view along the runway. Farmers, businessmen, and families filled the stands in anticipation of our show. The crowd was at least two times bigger than the week before. I winked at Uncle Warren as we walked to the plane.

"Don't get ahead of yourself, girlie—there's still a trick to perform." He yanked down his flying cap and climbed into the cockpit. I heard him whisper a short prayer for my safety and his sanity.

I tightened the goggles around my face, taking long, deep breaths. Once in the front passenger seat, wind lashed at my back as the Jenny nosed toward the heavens. At six hundred feet, Uncle Warren tapped his head and I slid out and across the lower wing. My boots inched heel-to-toe across the frame.

Uncle Warren banked the plane around the edge of the fairgrounds, gaining speed. The crowd became tiny dots scattered below. Placing my hand on the outer strut, I hoisted my body onto the upper wing. Air pressure knocked against my chest. If I lost my hold, the force of the wind would pull me straight to my death. While my heart pounded faster than it should, I pushed all fear from my mind. Like the car-to-plane transfer, this trick was all about timing, patience, and waiting for the right moment to thrill the crowd.

My feet slid into the straps attached to the wing. After balancing my weight, I stood and waved a hand in the air. The plane bulleted through the clouds. Mist fogged my goggles. I wiped away the moisture and focused forward like I'd practiced. My stomach rocked back and forth like a hammock. The nose of the plane lifted. I visualized the trick in my head. We started to invert and raw fear crushed me. I pushed it away, urging my body to float with the weightless motion. The force of gravity crushed my shoulders while the plane made an almost complete revolution. A dizzying rush of blood filled my head. The edges of my vision turned into an opaque blur. Instead of terror, my body hummed with a satisfying pulse of adrenaline. When the plane leveled out I screamed out a victory cheer. I squatted down and patted the frame. *Thanks girl, I knew you wouldn't let me down.*

Once my feet were firmly on the lower wing, I latched onto a strut. We streaked past the crowd, and I hung by one hand off the edge of the plane. My feet dangled above the teeming masses gathered around the edge of the fairgrounds. We darted down low. Men and women crushed their hands against their heads to keep the wind from plucking their hats away. The cheers crashed against my ears. A sense of joy brought a wide smile to my lips.

As soon as we landed, reporters swarmed the plane. Men elbowed each other out of the way as I climbed out of the seat. Two almost came to blows while jockeying for a better view. I backed away as they asked my name, age, and so many other questions that the sound of their combined voices exploded in my ears.

"Gracie," one voice rose above the shouts. Henry waved at me from the edge of the crowd. When I broke through the masses, Daniel, Nathan, and Henry stood next to a small, portly man I didn't know.

"That was an amazing performance, young lady." The man's handlebar mustache, waxed into perfect curlicues, hugged the lines around his wide smile.

"Thank you, Mr. . . ."

He yanked the black derby from his head and tucked it under his arm. "Knickerbocker. R.O. Knickerbocker." The name sounded familiar but I couldn't place it. "Is it true that was the first time you performed that inverted loop maneuver from the top wing?"

"Yes, sir." I glanced at the boys, trying to get an idea of who this man was. Wide smiles covered Daniel and Henry's faces. Nathan, as usual, looked like he'd swallowed a rancid prune.

"How did it feel to be so free up in the air?" The strange little man asked.

"Good, sir." I hesitated. "Excuse me, should I know you? Are you a reporter?"

Daniel popped a thick hand over his mouth to hide his snicker. What was going on? Were they playing some sort of trick?

"No, miss. I am not a reporter," he chuckled. "I happen to own a little business in California. Maybe you've heard of it. Palm Coast Studios?"

A knot the size of a nickel lodged in my throat. Palm Coast? The name on the telegram? I couldn't have heard him right. I yanked my goggles from my face and rubbed the dirt from my eyes. "Sir?" I started to mumble.

"I'm sorry I caught you off guard." He pulled a crisp, white handkerchief from his coat pocket and patted the moisture from his brow. "Perhaps we could head back to your hangar? Talk where things are a bit cooler?"

I must have nodded because he turned around and shuffled after the boys. Uncle Warren strode up beside me. "Who's the little fella in the dark suit?"

"R.O. Knickerbocker," I said.

He stopped in his tracks. "*The* R.O. Knickerbocker from Palm Coast Studios?"

He fumbled in his pocket and pulled out a worn piece of paper. He unfolded the piece of newsprint, its deep creases folding in at the edges. I sucked in a sharp breath. Like the paper currently nestled in my pocket, the details of the Chicago contest were spelled out across the page. The Palm Coast logo sat dead center.

"How long have you had that?" I gasped.

"Since the day we first saw it posted in the paper." He rubbed the faded edges between his calloused fingers before carefully folding it up and stowing it back in his pocket. "We may not be able to compete in the contest, but the paper is a good reminder of everything we can accomplish as a team. Just because we can't afford to go, doesn't mean we can't strive to be the best. Contest or no contest, I believe in us as much as you do, Grace. I just might not show it as much."

Since I'd come to live with him, Uncle Warren never talked about his dreams or aspirations for the team. His focus was always squarely on the next show—and getting me to act like a lady, of course.

"I may growl like a grouchy old bear, but my love and belief in you has never wavered." He chuffed my chin. "This life might not have been what your folks had planned for you, but I do believe they'd be mighty proud."

A sad smile pulled at his thin mouth. We'd never spoken much about my ma, but there'd been a time or two when I found him staring at a picture of her on the mantle—a tear hovering at the corner of his eye. He wasn't big on showing emotion, but in those moments I wanted to tell him I missed her, too.

His gaze moved to the boys and Mr. Knickerbocker. "Let's head back to the hangar. I'm curious why the studio mogul came all this way. And what it has to do with you."

17
Thirty Telegrams

Mr. Knickerbocker paced back and forth in front of Uncle Warren's old mahogany desk, his small legs shuffling under him. Tiny strips of brown hair flopped over his nearly bald head. The tops of his expensive leather wingtips were polished to such a high shine I was sure I would see my reflection.

"My secretary has been going batty. Over the last week my office has received thirty telegrams from this town. Fifteen alone in the last two days. All about one thing." He spun on his heel and pointed a sausage-like finger at me. "You, Miss Lafferty."

Nathan and Daniel stood behind me in the small, cramped space that barely passed as an office. Their shoulders pressed against the corners like they were trying to fade into the woodwork. Henry stood by my side. His fingers brushed along my back every time I shifted my feet.

"Why? Did I do something wrong?"

While Mr. Sorenson hadn't been pleased with my flight to help Joe Prescott, he'd left without grounding us. So why were people sending telegrams to a big shot Hollywood studio owner about me? It didn't make sense.

"Wrong?" he crowed. "Oh no. Quite the opposite, my dear." He fumbled in the pockets of his black suit. When he came up empty, he patted his coat, reaching inside and pulling out a telegram.

"I believe this may explain why I'm here," he handed the paper to me.

"Read it out loud, Grace." Nathan urged from the corner.

My eyes scanned the page. When I opened my mouth to speak no sound came out. I swallowed twice and tried again.

Lincoln NE August 25   450P
R.O. Knickerbocker
Care Palm Coast Studios, Los Angeles, California

Grace Lafferty risked life for Joseph Prescott after plane malfunction please reward Grace as hero and waive Chicago contest fee
Walter and Pearl Francis.

Everyone stood like they were frozen in place. The only sound piercing the silence was the monotone click of the clock on the wall. I stared at the telegram, reading the words over and over. There had to be a mistake. Why would complete strangers send a telegram trying to help me?

"Gracie, your cheeks are pale." Henry edged in closer. "Maybe you should sit down."

"Yes, please," I said in a small whisper.

Mr. Knickerbocker pulled a chair from Uncle Warren's desk and slid it under my wobbly legs. "There now. Can't have you fainting until you've heard the real reason I'm here." He patted my shoulder and his slate-gray eyes twinkled like he had a secret he was dying to share.

"Why are you here?" Uncle Warren grumbled. He and Mr. Knickerbocker had exchanged a brief greeting when we arrived at the office, and ever since, my uncle eyed him as if he was a fox circling the henhouse. "A telegram is nice and all, but how does this concern Grace?"

Mr. Knickerbocker twittered his hands in front of him. "I was about to get to that detail." He approached my chair, taking in the snarls in my dark hair. The layer of dirt caked around the edges of my eyes. The twitch in his mouth said it would take some work to make me a Hollywood beauty.

"When my associates at Palm Coast first approached me with the idea of an aerobatics contest I didn't give it much thought. To me it seemed more of a nuisance. Working with folks all the way across the country in Chicago. Spending money on advertising. Up until last week, I was still going over the numbers, trying to decide if I wanted to offer a cash prize instead of a one-year contract with the studio. Contracts can be messy things and our stunt actors have never been reliable."

He stalked around me like a cat, tapping his fingers along the back of my chair. "Then the telegrams about you, Miss Lafferty, started arriving. One after the other. Hour after hour. Intrigued, I had my secretary cull everything she could find on you. I was stunned at what she found. Only eighteen and already headlining this type of show? Quite impressive." He shook his head like the sight of me was a mirage—not flesh and blood. "The papers aren't always reliable though. They tend to make up headlines to generate more money. So I travelled here to see if you were the real deal."

"You bet she is," Daniel said. "There are other girls in the air, but none of them are like our Grace."

"I agree." Mr. Knickerbocker rubbed his chin. "I think she could be a real star."

Nathan stepped forward. His lanky frame towering over Knickerbocker. "That's all well and good, but we don't have funds to go to Chicago."

"I was getting to that." Mr. Knickerbocker gave a sharp nod in my direction. "Miss Lafferty is a hero. After what I saw today, she deserves a chance to perform in front of a big crowd. That's why we put the competition together, to find extraordinary talent. We have teams coming from New York, Boston, and St. Louis. Palm Coast wants Grace there to compete with the best of the best.

We'll cover her hangar fees and pay for lodging to help ease some of the cost."

Henry moved behind my chair and gave my shoulder a squeeze. Knickerbocker had only said my name. My hangar fees. That I was a hero. There was no doubt what he was offering was an incredible opportunity, but we went to Chicago as a team or we didn't go at all.

I jumped to my feet, almost knocking him down. Once I steadied, I said, "While I appreciate your gracious offer, I'm afraid I can't accept."

The lines around his mouth tightened. "Why not? This is an opportunity of a lifetime."

"Because I'm part of a team, sir." I swung my hand around the room. "Without these men and my uncle, I'm just a girl standing on a wing doing mindless tricks."

He slapped a hand to his mouth and shook his head. "Oh dear, I'm not explaining my intentions very well. The offer is for *all* The Soaring Eagles."

Uncle Warren stomped around to the side of his desk, tearing a stubby cigar from the corner of his mouth. "You're going to put all of us up in Chicago on the studio's dime? What do you expect in return?"

Mr. Knickerbocker's hands fluttered at his sides. "Why, nothing, sir." He nodded to the boys. "Consider this Palm Coast's way of saying thank you to the men for their military service. And to honor the selfless act you and Grace performed to aid that pilot in distress."

"Let me get this straight," Uncle Warren leaned in menacingly close to Mr. Knickerbocker, who didn't bat an eye. "There's no payback involved?"

"Only if you win. Then there's the signing of the contract. A few interviews and a photo for promotional purposes."

Uncle Warren popped the cigar back into his mouth. "Give us a minute to talk it over."

"Fine, but please make it quick. I told my driver to be here within the hour." Mr. Knickerbocker reached for my hand. "Whatever the outcome, it has been my pleasure, Miss Lafferty."

"Thank you, sir."

When he pulled away, grease covered his palm and the edge of his gold pinkie ring. A scowl pulled at his mouth. He reached for the handkerchief in his suit pocket and wiped at the grime. Once back to his pristine state, he tipped his hat to the rest of the room and disappeared through the hangar.

Uncle Warren closed the door with a slam. "Before you say a word. Let's talk about why this man is really here."

"Well, isn't it obvious?" Nathan blurted out. "He's slick like Rowland. He only wants to make a good name for the studio."

Uncle Warren crossed his arms over his chest. "I'm not sure what to make of any of this."

Henry cleared his throat. "I think we should go. Rowland believes we can't get to Chicago. He's sure he's already won. When we show up and beat him, it'll be proof we're the better team. And as far as that gent," he hitched his thumb out the door. "He seems harmless. It can only help us to have his support."

Daniel leaned in and whispered in Nathan's ear. They went back and forth until Daniel said, "We vote yes."

Uncle Warren hesitated for a minute before clearing his throat. "Grace, I know you want to go, but I can't say I'm sure this is the right thing. Knickerbocker seems like he's on the up and up, but . . ." His shoulders remained stiff, as if even the best news couldn't relieve his worry.

Daniel raised his hand slowly and Uncle Warren waved it away. "You don't need permission to speak, Daniel. Say your piece."

"In basic training we spent six weeks learning how to stay in formation, handle a Browning rifle, and dig trenches." Henry flinched like each of Daniel's words caused him pain. "We were forced to learn because we knew we were going into battle. Isn't the exact same thing going on here?"

"I'm not following," Uncle Warren said.

"We've spent hours in the air," Daniel continued in his calm, measured voice, "trying new tricks. Some were a success. Others complete failures. All of that training has built up to this moment, this contest." He looked at Nathan before training his gaze on me. "We've practically sacrificed our lives to make a living in the sky. It's time we take this chance and show the country what we can do."

He moved to my side and nudged his thick shoulder against mine. "Right, darlin'?"

"Right," I grinned back. My belief we could win the contest had never wavered. Not even when a loose wire shot back and sliced open my lip, or when a fist-sized goose egg appeared on my temple after I whacked my head on a strut during a rough patch of turbulence. In some small way, I knew deep down that what I was pushing them to do was crazy. Believing we could beat every other barnstorming team who entered the contest. Some of them had lots of money and fancy costumes, like The Skyhawks. Others, like The Flying Finellis, had skills and bravery. It was a risk, but Hollywood would give us the money and opportunities we needed to stick together.

"Well, it sounds like there's no more need for discussion." Uncle Warren swung open the door and called to Knickerbocker.

I didn't know anything about this man other than he was rich and powerful. Trusting him felt like trusting Rowland in many ways, but I had to get this team to Chicago. If that meant agreeing to Mr. Knickerbocker's offer, it was a risk I had to take.

18
No Arguments

The clock above the cash register at the diner chimed nine a.m. One hour until I boarded the train for Chicago.

The breakfast crowd was tapering off, but most chairs at the counter were still occupied. I surveyed the room and waved in Ethel's direction. After sliding two plates across a table full of husky farmers, she grabbed Mary's arm and scurried toward me.

"Are you excited for Chicago?" Ethel asked, wiping gravy off her hands.

"Nervous is more like it."

Mary placed a hand on my arm. "You'll do great. When you've got your eye on something it always seems to work out."

"Ladies, back to work," Archie barked out from behind the counter.

"Grace," Mary whispered to me, moving in closer. "We have a surprise for—"

The bell chimed over the door and the napkin Mary held in her hand fluttered to the floor.

Two men stood in the doorway. One was tall, had greasy, coal-black hair and looked to be close to the girls' age. The other was almost twenty years older, with a face worn down by the sun and decades of manual labor. Their clothes looked suitable for Sunday church, except for the stains on the knees and crumpled lapels which warned they hadn't slept in days.

"Mary, go into the kitchen. Now!" Ethel ordered.

Mary's feet stayed frozen to the ground as the two men approached, staring an angry hole through her.

"Grace, get her into the back. Grab her pocketbook on the coat rack outside the ladies' room and leave through the rear exit."

I wasn't sure who the men were, but when I heard the tone of Ethel's voice I reached for Mary's hand. She shook me off. Ethel released a low hiss and together we moved in front of Mary as if in battle formation.

The younger man tried to move around me, but I blocked his path. "Move outta the way. I gotta speak to Mary. Me and her pa here are gonna talk some sense into her and bring her home." He gritted a set of brown and broken teeth in her direction. This had to be the goon from Gering who hit her.

"Mary," her father barked. The scent of bathtub gin permeated the air around him. "We've been looking for you quite a long time now, girl. It's time to stop this nonsense and come on home. Settle down with Norman here and do what's right for our family."

Ethel reached and clutched Mary's free hand. "She's not going anywhere with you, so turn around now and head back to Gering. I'm sure there's plenty of women who can pretend Norman is a decent fella and marry him."

Norman lurched forward and grabbed Ethel's arm. She tried to wrench away from his touch but he dug his dirty, black fingernails into her skin.

"Let's not cause a scene," Mary's father stepped in closer. "Get your things and let's walk out the door."

"She's not going anywhere with you," I said. "Mary is an adult who can make her own choices."

He sneered down his nose at me. The scent of body odor and rancid alcohol made me gag. "I don't talk to women who dress like they want to be a man. Maybe you need a crack across the mouth to learn your place." He swung his hand back and Mary stepped in front of me.

"Stop!" With all of her ninety-five pounds Mary shoved her father away. When Norman tried to reach for her, she tugged a knife from her apron. "Step back. I'm not afraid to cut a hole the size of Texas in you, Norman."

Archie and a few cooks from the back swung out the kitchen door. "Mary! Ethel! What have you gotten yourself into now?"

"Quiet, Archie." Mary's voice was steady and filled with a confidence I'd never heard. "These men were just leaving." She tossed back her dark curls and pressed the tip of the knife against Norman's gut before swinging it in her father's direction. "I have a life in Lincoln, and soon Ethel and I are moving on to bigger and brighter things. There's nothing left in Gering for either of us. Head on home and tell everyone you can't find us, or I'll go to the police and report how the two of you are making illegal booze."

"You can't prove that," Norman growled.

"Of course I can," Mary stood ramrod straight, never flinching from his murderous gaze. "Besides the fact that the two of you reek of it, both your lips and palms have burns from the carbolic acid you're using to distill the wood alcohol. The coppers will recognize the signs of your bootlegging in a minute."

Norman and Mary's father swapped a measured look before glancing back at the knife clenched in Mary's hand. "What's more important to you?" Mary's voice grew louder. "Dragging me home, or the booze?" Neither man spoke. "Get out now or I'll let Archie and his men pull you outside and give you the once-over for disturbing their breakfast business. Then I'll call the police."

Although he was a rat and treated the girls like dirt, Archie stepped up then to join our battle line.

"Aw, she ain't worth the trouble," Norman muttered. They both slithered out of the diner.

Once the bell's chime fell silent, Mary's knife clattered to the ground. We caught her before she pooled to the floor and carried her to a nearby table.

"I'll get her some water," Archie spoke, showing he was indeed human. The cooks gave an approving nod to Mary before disappearing back into the kitchen.

"Mary, that sure was brave!" Ethel clutched her hand. "What got into you?"

A pink flush returned to her cheeks. "I'm tired of being scared. Or worried Norman could be around the next corner. I see how brave you and Grace are. How you hold your own with men. You don't let them bully you or knock you down." She fluffed her hair and took a deep breath, rolling back her shoulders. "I'm a modern woman now. I can vote. Go to the films on my own. And I can stand up to those brutes who have no business telling me how to live my life."

Archie rushed out of the kitchen and handed the water to Mary. She swallowed it in one gulp. I sagged against the back of a nearby booth, my ragged pulse still thrumming under my skin. Mary wiped a hand across her mouth and set the empty glass against the tabletop with a confident thud. It was like I was seeing her for the first time. As if she'd shed some uneasy shell that had weighed her down for too long. Ethel watched her from a few feet away. A smirk crossed her bright red lips, like she'd known Mary had that pool of strength inside her all along.

"Thank you, Archie," Mary said. "Now, Ethel and I are going to take a break because we have some business to attend to with Grace."

Without waiting for his response, Mary thrust her tiny hand around my arm and dragged me through the kitchen and toward the ladies room in the back of the restaurant.

"Grace, Ethel and I decided you can't go to Chicago dressed in that raggedy, old outfit." Mary's curls bounced against her pink cheeks as she shook her head at the state of my traveling clothes.

I skimmed a hand down the sleeves of my linen shirt. Sure,

the cuffs were a little grease-stained, and my trousers were worn through at the knees, but I was comfortable.

Ethel stood still, mouth wide open, completely shell-shocked by Mary's bossy tone.

"It's the big city. Don't you want to make an impression?" Mary went on.

"It's not like I have much choice, Mary. It's either this or my church dress, which is embarrassingly thread-bare," I said.

"Wait here." Mary deposited me next to the door. Ethel sidled up beside me, and while she remained oddly quiet, a mischievous grin I didn't like twisted her mouth.

After a few minutes the bathroom door opened and Ethel ushered me inside. Mary moved away from the sink and pressed a deep-red dress against my chest that made me look more like a quiff at the speakeasies than a barnstormer. She pursed her lips and shook her head. Moving back to a nearby coat rack, she grabbed a sapphire-blue walking suit. The jacket had a long torso with side-fastening buttons and a skirt with three tiers. The hem tapered slightly above the ankle. A cream, lace-trimmed blouse peeked out from underneath the jacket.

Mary *ooh*ed under her breath as Ethel held out a cloche hat with wide side brims and a short crown decorated in a matching deep-blue lace. When Ethel turned me to face the mirror, a breath caught in my chest. The person looking back at me was not some young girl but a true lady.

Ethel squeezed my shoulders. "We wanted to buy you a gift. It took us days to find the suit, but looking at you now it was the perfect choice."

"This is too much. I can't accept the suit *and* the hat," I sputtered.

Mary and Ethel shook their heads, mimicking one another. Ethel popped the hat off my head and motioned for me to start undressing. "We've been saving up for a while."

Mary pointed to my feet, insisting I kick off my muddy boots. "Yes, with all the soldiers settling here for work our tips have been rolling in like the rain in April. Now, with you heading off to Chicago, we insist you accept it."

Ethel waggled a finger in my direction. "No arguments."

The suit was a perfect fit. Mary and Ethel had me spin in a circle twice to see the way the hem kicked out when I moved.

"Oh, Grace. You look stunning," Mary said, pulling me into a hug.

A wave of sadness floated over me. I missed Anna every day, but Mary and Ethel's kindness mended a small part of my broken heart. Even amidst my protests, the girls always urged me to see myself as more than a barnstormer. And I had to admit that their constant pestering was making me rethink how I saw myself, especially with the bright blue suit now pressed against my frame. My only wish was that my mother and Anna were here to see it, too.

"Thank you. It's all too gorgeous for words."

"No," Mary replied. "You're too gorgeous for words."

Ethel wiped tears from her eyes with the edge of her gravy-stained apron and I wasn't sure if it was for me or for the changes in her lifelong friend.

Mary made me spin once more and then gasped when she looked at a nearby clock. "Look at the time. You better go."

The girls gave me a quick embrace and together they led me back through the kitchen, Archie ordering them to get back to work again. Both Mary and Ethel shooed a hand in his direction as we made our way to the front door.

"Be sure to have fun," Ethel said as she straightened out the line of my jacket.

"And take in all the sights. We want to hear about every bit when you return," Mary added.

"Thank you again," I said. "You girls are the best."

"You deserve it, honey," Ethel said.

Mary stepped back and clutched my hands. "I couldn't have stood up to those brutes today if you hadn't show me what real bravery looks like. Go now and show those men in Chicago who's the best barnstormer in the country."

The girls folded me into one last hug before shoving me out the door. Archie's grating voice ordering them back to work was the last sound I heard as I raced in the direction of the train station.

The last time I stood on the Lincoln station platform I was thirteen. The stiff, white dress the nurses had forced me to wear had clung to my skin and carried the smell of death and disinfectant. Thin and terribly afraid, I'd clutched a battered, brown suitcase that held the few belongings I owned.

Today, five years later, I stood in the same spot and my body still trembled. At thirteen, I'd been terrified of my new life. But now, I fretted over all the choices I'd made. Could I do this? Go to Chicago and perform in front of a huge crowd? Bring national attention to The Soaring Eagles?

The chaos of the train station surrounded me. Doors clacked open and closed as taxis unloaded their passengers. The conductor's boots snapped along the platform as he shouted out arrival and departure numbers. Cigarette smoke mixed with grease and train exhaust made my stomach tumble.

Just as I lost myself in the noise, a sharp whistle from an approaching train made me jump. I readjusted my hat and pulled at the tortoiseshell combs Mary and Ethel had insisted I wear in my hair.

"Exciting, isn't it?" Henry stepped beside me. The brim of his brown cap sat low over his brows. His starched, white shirt was a sharp contrast to his green eyes. With just one look, he made my heart race faster than the Jenny's engine at full power.

His eyes swept over my new clothes. "Blue is a good color on you. It brings out your eyes." While I wanted to reply, words lodged in my throat. "Do . . . do you not like blue?" he stuttered.

"No. No, of course I do," I mumbled. "Mary and Ethel insisted that a train ride to the big city required something other than my regular flying clothes." I brushed my hand over the skirt's silk fabric. "Think it's a bit too much?"

"I'd say it was perfect. I mean you look perfect." He scrubbed a hand behind his neck, pretending he'd found something fascinating on the ground.

Passengers jostled around us. Men scurried to the windows to buy tickets. Porters in black uniforms darted in and out of the waiting crowd, towing suitcases and steamer trunks to the edge of the platform. Even with the distraction, Henry's penetrating gaze never left my face.

Since the Ferris wheel, I'd tried not to think about how close we'd sat. How his strong arms held me in place like a protective barrier. Standing with him now, a strange peace settled over me. I'd argued with Uncle Warren that I could take the train trip alone. That Henry could fly along with the boys. But he wouldn't hear it. With Henry standing next to me now, the scent of the soap on his skin washing over me, I was glad he hadn't listened.

Passengers closed in tighter on the platform as everyone looked in the direction of the approaching train. The sharp *chug chug* of the engine filled the air. A thousand thoughts raced through my head as the frenetic pace of the train station picked up. I wanted to tell Henry about Mary's sudden strength. How she'd stood toe-to-toe with her rat of a father and not backed down. How I wished she and Ethel could be front and center when The Soaring Eagles wowed the big city crowd.

"All aboard for Chicago," the conductor called over the loud *whoosh* of white steam billowing out from under the rails.

"Are you ready?" Henry asked, offering his arm to escort me aboard.

My legs trembled. The inside of my throat felt like I'd swallowed a handful of Great Plains dirt.

Get it together, Grace. You challenge the wind and the clouds every day. Traveling to Chicago should be a piece of cake.

"Of course," I said a little too quickly.

Rolling back my shoulders, I grabbed the handle of my suitcase. Another sharp burst of the train's whistle sent me stumbling back. Henry caught me before I hit the ground. As a true gentleman he didn't say a word as he helped me up the train steps, but he did a poor job of hiding his smirk.

We moved through the body of the train. Wood paneling covered the walls and a scarlet-red carpet runner lined the narrow walkway. Inside our assigned car, an aisle separated two sets of pew-style seats. Henry selected a row at the back and settled in next to the window.

A long burst of the whistle and the wheels below us started to churn. The hiss of the releasing brakes punctured the air. I held on to the side of the seat while the train swayed back and forth on the rails. Even though I was heading in the direction of my dream, I couldn't help but think about the last time I'd ridden on a train. The curious looks from passengers as I rode all alone. How the conductor with the full, white beard bent down to take my ticket. The twitch of disapproval in his eyes when I declined his offer to take a piece of penny candy from his outstretched hand. It had been weeks since I'd spoken and I wasn't sure I even had a voice anymore.

"You're quiet," Henry tapped the spot next to him, urging me to sit.

I slid across the wooden bench. "Lost in my thoughts. Wondering how the boys and Uncle Warren are doing on their flight."

He popped off his hat and placed it on his lap. His skin still had a hint of tan from the summer sun. Around us children chased each other up and down the aisles. Once or twice their parents tried to capture them as they raced past, and the children's laughter filled the small car. The conductor swooped through the car and swiped the tickets from us before scurrying on.

"They'll be fine. I double checked both planes first thing this morning." Henry tapped at the window. "And that sky is the perfect shade of blue for flying."

"Thank you for keeping your word about making sure we're safe in the planes. When you first started with us it wasn't a secret how much I disliked you."

"No, you're not good at hiding your feelings. Especially where I'm concerned." He stopped mid-breath like he was searching for the right words. "I mean, well, before our truce." It was hard not to smile at the red splotches splashed across his cheeks.

"This trip is more than you signed on for," I said, the words refusing to come out the way I wanted. "I mean, I know you're only with us until you make enough money to buy a garage, but I appreciate you staying on to help. The contest means everything to me, and with you ensuring the planes are in top-notch condition we have a real shot at that contract."

"It's certainly exciting, and it's going to take quite a bit of time to raise the funds for a garage. Like I said before, I want to help The Soaring Eagles succeed." His hands drummed on the edge of his knee. They inched toward me and then a shift of the train on the rails had him pulling back.

A surge of disappointment shot through me. I wanted his skin against mine. To feel the thrum of his pulse against my hand. The thought froze me to the upholstered bench. I couldn't exactly place when things had shifted between us. Was it in Springfield after he tended to my hands? Or perhaps in Arkansas after he shared about his time in the war? All I knew was that from the beginning, my feelings for him were an odd mix of anger, fear, and attraction. With the planes, it was clear where my mind needed to be focused. But as soon as I got near Henry, my brain turned jumbled and fuzzy. In those moments I had to remind myself we were part of a team. My sole focus had to be on our next show, not on how his green eyes made my heart chug like a humming propeller.

Henry leaned his head against the window and closed his eyes. The landscape of small cities raced by the window until we broke away from the towns and headed in the direction of Illinois. Grateful for the silence, I took in a breath and allowed my body to relax. While Uncle Warren had insisted I take the train to have time to rest, I guessed it was more about having space away from me.

Since we'd agreed to Knickerbocker's offer, I'd been quietly pestering him about the Showstopper trick. As usual he told me I'd lost my mind until I'd shown him all my research. The mouthpiece I'd created and how the wire would bear my weight. When we took the Jenny up, his face contorted into an angry mask until I performed the trick flawlessly. In the moments after we landed, I swore him to secrecy. The trick was sure to bring objections from Nathan and Daniel, but they couldn't argue once I'd performed it to the cheers of the crowd.

I recognized a few familiar faces as they passed through our car. Some were pilots or wing walkers headed in the same direction as us. Others were newspaper photographers and reporters I'd met in various cities. The chorus of raised voices and thrum of excitement was palpable on the train.

Henry's eyes inched open and he focused on the line of men and women passing us. "I hope Rowland isn't on this train." He slowly stretched out his legs and arms. "I can't say I'd be real polite if I saw him and his goon."

I stayed quiet. When I returned from the ice tent the other day, I kept my conversation with Rowland to myself. The more I thought about it, the more I realized that considering his offer was a ridiculous idea.

"Whether he's here or not, The Skyhawks will not be happy

to discover our name on the contest lineup," I said. I attempted to pull off my gloves but the cotton fabric refused to slide from my clammy fingers. Rowland's offer still rang in my ears. How did he know we didn't have any money? It was unsettling how he seemed to know our every move. With one last yank, my gloves finally came free. I twisted them in my lap, balling the cotton into a tight fist. Henry reached over and pulled them away from me before setting them against the bench.

"I will admit that something about Rowland is bothering me." My voice wavered. "He always knows where I am. What's happening in my life. It troubles me that he can discover that kind of information so easily."

"I don't like it either." Henry rubbed his hands over the top of his legs, his gaze wandering out the window. After a few minutes, he stood and offered me his hand. "How about a change of scenery? Would you like something to eat?"

While food was the last thing I wanted, I couldn't sit still anymore—couldn't think about Rowland anymore. "Yes, a meal would be nice."

The train rocked below our feet as we made our way through two passenger cars and a sleeper compartment to the dining car. We weren't two steps inside when Henry stopped. Rowland sat at the largest table in the front of the long, narrow car. Louis and a few other Skyhawks filled the chairs at his table. When we locked eyes, Rowland's hungry stare made me feel like a turkey on Thanksgiving Day.

"We can leave," Henry whispered.

"Oh, no. We're going to stay and eat." I pointed to a small table near the window. Since the moment I'd met Alistair Rowland he'd tried to intimidate me, but I'd keep holding my ground no matter how much was on the line.

19

The Power of Unspoken Words

Henry escorted me to a table in the back of the dining car. Once we were seated, he removed his hat and set it against the starched, white tablecloth. An elderly couple exchanged quiet conversation behind us. To their left, a group of businessmen grew raucous as they argued over the looming pennant race. Two small children sat with their parents at the table in front of us, their faces pressed against the glass, eyes blinking at the ever-changing scenery.

Henry's voice rose to just above a whisper. "Let's make a pact. As long as we are in this dining car, we won't look in Rowland's direction."

I shot out a hand toward him. "Deal." His palm skimmed against mine. We stared into each other's eyes until a tuxedo-clad attendant stood before us. He spent his time rattling off the specials. While I looked at the prices, still worried about our money, my growling stomach announced it didn't care how much the roast beef cost. After taking our order cards, he scurried to another table.

The train continued to sway below us. We shot past the green countryside dotted with cattle, old barns, and the occasional windmill.

"Let's talk about the exposition. What are you looking forward to seeing most?" Henry asked.

"It's not so much a what, but a who." I straightened out the napkin in my lap one too many times.

He leaned forward and tented his hands on the table. "Now I'm intrigued."

My mouth went dry. Would he laugh? Think my interest in an aviation pioneer was childish? "I've heard whispers at shows about this new black female pilot named Bessie Coleman, who's just had her first performance in New York. They say her figure-eight is better than most aces."

His brows perked up in interest. "If you were fortunate enough to shake her hand, what would you say?" His warm smile made me curse myself for doubting him.

"You mean if I could actually form words?"

He shook his head in disbelief. "I can't imagine you *ever* being at a lack for words."

"That's true," I admitted reluctantly.

"But I imagine being in the presence of your heroine would make your brain a little fuzzy," he teased.

I tapped my fingers together before I spoke. "If I could get close to her, I'd ask how she deals with being a female leader in aviation. And of course, how she handles the crowds and the press. She's just twenty-five, you know." I took a dry gulp, trying to imagine what it would be like to stand next to her. "Honestly, I'm not sure I could form a complete sentence in front of her."

"Don't do that." The gleam in his eyes turned intense. "Don't fill your head with nonsense about her. She's human like you and me. She puts her pants on one leg at a time. And quite honestly, I think she'd be thrilled to be in your presence." His wide grin turned playful. "I'd bet that if you ever meet her, she'll be the one asking *you* for an autograph." The blush I was fighting slid up my neck and filled my cheeks with undeniable heat.

Instead of being a simple meal, this felt much more like a date. The idea sent a thrill through me. As much as I fought it, I found myself wanting to spend more time with Henry. But the feeling also terrified me. Allowing myself to get close to him made me vulnerable, and I wasn't sure I would know how to handle things graciously if he didn't have feelings for me, too. Thankfully, before I had to say another word, the waiter appeared and placed two steaming plates in front of us.

In between bites of roast beef I managed to find my voice again. "What about you? What would you do if you could gab with plane designer and pilot Glenn Curtiss?"

He took a long drink of water. His hand trembled against the glass. "I'd ask about his dreams of building his first plane. If he knew the JN-4 would become a trainer for the war." He shifted anxiously in his seat and I wanted to ask him again about the war. What he'd been through. Why the sound of a gunshot sent him to another place. But those were questions for another time and place. For now, I didn't want to pop a hole in our glorious and quiet bubble.

We continued to eat and he opened up about his sister and his family. He told me stories of playing hide and seek in the corn fields. How he worked on farm equipment late into the day with his father. The way his mother always appeared at the perfect time with cold lemonade. My chest went tight and it was hard not to wonder what my life would've been like if my parents hadn't died. Would I still be in school? The thought shot ice through my veins. I couldn't imagine my life being any different than it was today.

As I finished my last bite, Henry asked the waiter for our bill.

He nodded to Rowland's table. "It's been taken care of, sir."

"Oh, no. We won't owe that man a thing." He shoved back his chair, but I grabbed his arm.

"Let me handle this. Please." I approached the table where only Rowland and Louis remained.

"Miss Lafferty, a pleasure to see you. I just learned you will be competing in Chicago." Rowland swung out a hand to an open chair, expecting me to sit. "What a coincidence that we should be on the same train." He exchanged a look with Louis that told me there was nothing coincidental about it.

Henry came to my side. "The waiter says you paid for our meal." He shoved a hand into his pocket and pulled out a wad of tightly wound bills, and tossed several onto the table. "That will not be necessary." The dangerous look Henry swapped with Louis had me stepping in front of him.

A flash of anger touched Rowland's eyes before they returned to calm indifference. "I was only trying to be kind, sir." He shot out a hand in Henry's direction. "What was your name again?"

"Henry Patton. And we do not need your charity. Why don't you use that dough to teach your pilots some manners? Your goon here could learn a lesson, too."

Louis pushed to his feet, a low growl emanating from his lips. Rowland motioned for him to sit and he did so reluctantly. "What do you mean by that, Mr. Patton?"

Henry leaned in close to Rowland. "You *know* what I mean."

The dining car quieted as passengers glanced curiously in our direction. The wait staff hovered nearby. I reached for Henry's arm. "Leave the money and let's go. He's not worth your breath."

Henry blinked twice. He stepped back and clasped my hand. "You're right, Gracie." I waited for him to move, but he and Rowland exchanged another deadly look that made my skin go cold. The power of their unspoken words warned this was not the end of the discussion.

We brushed past tables where diners were watching the scene unfold. We were almost to the door when Rowland called to us.

"Good luck in the contest. I hope the skies are good to you and your performance is . . . uneventful."

Henry's mouth went hard again and he tried to turn back, but I pulled him close. "He wants to rattle our confidence. Please don't give him the satisfaction."

"I'll leave, but only for you," he growled.

Once we were out the door, I gave a final glance to Rowland. His confident grin unsettled me. He sat back in his chair, arms crossed over his chest as if he'd already won a battle we'd never had a chance to fight.

20
Facing the Elements

Chicago, Illinois
September 11, 1922
Day 1 of the World Aviation Expo

Even with its Tiffany lamps and expensive silk bedding, I spent most of the night pacing the floor of my hotel room. Though I'd tried to rest, worries about our performance swirled through my head and made sleep impossible. When the sun peeked over the top of the famous Chicago Water Tower, I dressed quickly in my blue suit, switching out the original blouse for one of my own linen shirts.

I raced down the hotel's grand staircase, unable to wait for the boys and my uncle to wake. After leaving a note for them at the desk, I headed outside. Cadillacs and Pierce-Arrows bounced down the already-busy streets. Their slick metal bodies glimmered in the rising sunlight. Along the sidewalks, glamorous women wrapped their fur-lined coats around themselves. Men slapped hands to their heads, securing their fedoras against the crisp wind roaring off Lake Michigan. The Wrigley Building stood like a looming sentry in the distance. Its sharp, white spire was a stark contrast to the bright blue sky.

Everything about Chicago spoke of speed and luxury. From the burgeoning skyscrapers that reached for the pinnacle of the heavens to the way people scurried down the streets. The city didn't whisper, but screamed excitement.

It was hard not to wonder how different my life would have been had I stayed here. Would I have walked these streets on my way to a job in one of those buildings that mingled with the clouds?

What would Anna be doing? Finishing school? I only allowed myself to linger on the image of my sister as a grown woman for a moment before I snapped back to reality.

At the edge of a busy corner, I hailed a taxi and instructed the driver to take me to the air field on the far side of the city. When we reached the exposition, silver-and-red banners lined the arched entrance, announcing, "Welcome to Checkerboard Field and The World's Greatest Aviation Spectacle."

I stepped through the gates and let out a gasp. Rows of shiny planes lined the dirt fields like tin soldiers readying for duty. Each had various symbols and letters painted along the tails, signifying which models were built for mail service or designed to train future military pilots. New planes taxied down a nearby runway. The manufacturers beamed with pride as their creations lifted off into a cloudless morning sky.

For over an hour, I wandered in and out of the rows, surveying new engine configurations and propellers. Many of the planes were covered in all-metal skins. Others had three engines and could transport up to thirteen passengers. Several of the planes had enclosed cockpits. The thought of being separated from the air made me shiver. One of the perks of the job was facing the elements. When the air was brisk and the wind scratched at your cheeks you never felt more alive.

As I walked from model to model, I had to remind myself that most of these were prototypes—each plane the potential future of aviation. It was tempting to climb inside and check out the new instruments, but the presence of a policeman at the end of each aisle kept my feet on the ground.

I was running my hand along one of the new metal-covered wings when two soft chuckles sounded behind me.

"Thinking about moving up in the world?" Nathan teased, his legs looking even longer than usual in his double-breasted, dark-blue suit. Daniel shook his head, but as usual he couldn't hide his smile.

"No, just admiring her beauty," I said. I moved to examine the plane's struts and landing gear. A recent storm had made the ground soggy, and the edges of my blue skirt were caked with mud. It was a good thing Mary and Ethel weren't here to see how quickly I'd made a mess of their gift.

Nathan moved his hand along the tail as he examined the plane's sleek lines. "Don't suppose we could convince the copper to let us take the old girl for a spin?"

"Old girl?" I said. "I think not. She's as beautiful as one of those Ziegfeld dames you're always drooling over."

"Hmmm. A Ziegfeld gal?" Nathan rubbed the dark whiskers at his chin. "No way. This baby looks much too tough to resemble a gal like that."

Daniel walked around until he could see inside the cockpit. His coppery-red hair gleamed in the early morning light while he examined the leather interior and pristine instrument panel. "Grace is right. She's too clean and nice." He tapped his foot and shook his head at Nathan. "You and I need dirty and durable. This darlin' wouldn't last two weeks with me scrambling across her wings."

We moved through the rows and I glanced down the aisles and over the tops of several planes.

Daniel caught my eye. "Looking for Henry?"

"Perhaps. I'm curious why he's not with you."

"He left the hotel early to check on the planes." Daniel said.

"We got word late last night at the hotel that we'll be performing fourth," Nathan said. "Daniel and I will go up first as usual and have time for a five-minute routine. You and Warren will follow. Once Henry heard the details, he was adamant about working this morning."

We continued to move between planes but the hairs raised

on the back of my neck when Daniel and Nathan kept stopping to whisper to one another.

I placed my hands on my hips and tried to give them a disapproving glare. "What are you two planning?"

Daniel pulled a brown box from inside his coat pocket and handed it to me. "Open it," he urged, tapping the top.

I pulled back the lid. Inside was a shiny new pair of aviator goggles.

A slight, knowing smile lifted Nathan's lips. "Your gear has seen better days."

"And you need you to have clear vision for the contest tomorrow," Daniel quickly added.

"This is too much. How did you pay for it? You've been saving just as much as me."

"Don't you worry about that," Daniel said. "Do you like them?"

"Of course," I gushed, pressing them to my eyes. It'd been a while since I'd worn goggles that didn't have a dozen gouges on the lenses. "Thank you!" I smacked both of their shoulders in the way I always did after a successful performance. Tears burned the corners of my eyes but I blinked them away. Daniel and Nathan, while huge thorns in my side, were also gifts I didn't acknowledge often enough.

"I'm lucky to have you both in my life, even if you do drive me nutty most days."

Nathan chuckled. Daniel picked me up and swung me in a wide circle, his shoulders shaking with laughter. "Ah, Grace, you'd be lost without us."

After setting me down, he and Nathan swapped a tense look I didn't like. "No more surprises today," I pleaded. "The goggles were enough."

Nathan blew out a rough breath. "We know about your secret trick." His accusing tone set my teeth on edge. I should have known the peace between us wouldn't last long.

"How do you know?" I asked.

"You've been going to the hangar early every morning because you think no one's there. You climb on the wing and measure out the wire you keep in your pocket," he practically spat out.

"Have you two been spying on me?" I stomped forward, hands braced on my hips. They could tousle my hair, hover over me like I was a child, but spying on me was unforgivable.

"What? No." Daniel sputtered. "We went to the hangar one morning looking for Henry. We wanted to talk to him about replacing a few wires and turnbuckles on Nathan's plane."

"We saw you up on the wing with the wire spool. The mouthpiece. It wasn't hard to figure out what you were planning," Nathan added.

"How did you talk your uncle into it, darlin'? It seems risky even for you," Daniel asked.

"The trick is called the Showstopper, because that's what it is," I huffed. "It was difficult to talk Uncle Warren into it, but all last week we tried the stunt in the morning before you boys got to the hangar. I figured if we weren't coming here, adding it to our shows would bring the team more notoriety, and in turn, more money. On our test runs everything went smoothly, so when Knickerbocker offered us this shot, my uncle agreed we could try it here."

"Grace! This isn't something you perform for the first time at a big event with hundreds of influential people in the crowd. Don't you get how dangerous this is?" Nathan started to pace. His boots pounded against the mounds of dirt surrounding the planes. "You're trusting your life to a mouthpiece and a thin length of cable Henry may have the Jennys in tip-top shape, but this is still too much of a risk. We need to talk about this as a team."

"You won't talk me out of it, and giving me a new pair of goggles isn't going to change my mind." My raised voice brought more than a few stares from the men and women circling the planes near us. "Please trust me," I said, trying to level out my tone. "If we want to win, we need to do this trick. The contest is about proving who's the best in the sky. We can show every judge that we deserve to win that contract by taking this risk."

"First it was the idiotic car-to-plane transfer," Nathan snapped. "Then the inverted loop from the top wing. Now you want to risk your life once again with a trick that not even the most seasoned wing walker has ever performed? It's like you won't be happy until you go out in a blaze of glory, and you'll take all of us with you!" Nathan jammed his cap on his head and stalked off in the direction of the grandstands, leaving Daniel and me behind.

"What has gotten into him? Last time I looked we were daredevils. Barnstormers who took risks. But now, he gripes over every trick."

Daniel slid his arm around me and guided us around the crowd of prying eyes. "Ever since we watched the Crazy Conroys go down in Coeur D'Alene he's been skittish about flying. I think it was a reminder of all he went through in the war. Give him some time. I'll bet by fall he'll back to his old self.

"I hope so. His constant lectures are getting tiresome."

We strolled from plane to plane, talking about the specifics of the new engines and frames, doing our best to avoid the topic of Nathan's growing temper. At one point, Daniel covered for me while I bent down and crawled along the grass. It wasn't very ladylike, but I was dying to examine the new landing gear. No more bicycle tires for wheels, but sturdy, thick treads guaranteed to grip any type of runway. When I hopped to my feet mud splashed against the corners of my suit jacket. At least I looked like a dirty matched set now.

Planes buzzed overhead like a descending flock of birds. A Barnhart Twin 15 tore through the clouds, followed by a Fairey Long Distance seaplane complete with a Rolls-Royce engine and oversized floats. Not far behind was a Bristol 10-seater I'd only read about in the paper. We *ooh*ed in amazement as its four-wheeled undercarriage cut through the clouds.

A horn blew in the distance. I reached for Daniel's watch to check the time. With only minutes before the show started, I hurried him toward the grandstand. Once we reached the bleachers, we located Nathan, who was still in a huff.

Daniel flipped through the pages of the program and read the details of the Powder Puff Air Derby out loud. "The female pilots travel for six days. They start on the California coast, making stops in over ten cities before crossing the finish line in Chicago."

We continued to pore over the program until Uncle Warren and Henry climbed the stairs toward us. Jumping to my feet, I stood and waved them in our direction. I accidentally bumped the gentleman beside me. He inched closer on the bench and a curious look darted across his face.

"Are you Grace Lafferty?" he asked.

I pulled down the angled brim of my hat and slid away from him, almost ending up in Daniel's lap. "Do I know you?"

"No." He reached into his pocket and pulled out a copy of the *Lincoln Star* with my picture on the front page. "You saved that pilot." A wide grin spread across his face. "May I shake your hand? You're one brave dame."

Well, this was a change from the usual staredown I got from men. I gave him a brief handshake and thanked him. When Henry reached our row he made a point of sitting between me and the man.

"Making friends, I see." He tipped his brown fedora at the man, who looked none too happy to be pushed down the row.

A loud voice boomed through the air as the master of ceremonies welcomed us to the opening day of the exposition. I let the surrounding noise drown out my thoughts about tomorrow's contest. We'd all worked long and hard to be here, and I wouldn't allow my worries to ruin the day.

The event began with rousing music from a marching band while a parade moved around the outskirts of the field. Chicago merchants big and small showed off their handmade floats crafted out of paint and colored tissue. Men and women strolled next to them, carrying giant-sized propellers fashioned out of old wood and metal. Schoolchildren dressed like their favorite aviators, complete with flying caps and goggles, marched in time with the raucous music. The joyous mood was infectious. It was impossible not to clap and cheer for my favorite displays.

The change in aviation since I'd started working with The Soaring Eagles was astonishing. Only a year ago people were calling for the grounding of barnstormers. Now major companies were building new planes and sponsoring teams.

Henry leaned in close. "I love to see your smile. What are you thinking about?"

"I haven't been this happy in a long time." I pointed to the planes as they made their approach. "This is all I've ever wanted. To be around planes. To be in the air. And now with things evolving so quickly it looks like aviation is here to stay."

"You deserve to be happy. I'm glad your dreams are coming true, Gracie."

I met his steady gaze and the light in his eyes told me he meant every word. Since the incident in the dining car, I couldn't stop thinking about the way Henry looked at me as he faced Rowland. It was as if we were a team fighting some menacing force. He wasn't asking me to step away, but face the trouble side by side. As a partner. An equal.

A horn bellowed across the field. The final derby competitors arrived and the winner, a young woman from Ohio, shook her hands above her head in victory. The announcer placed a crown of bright orange and red flowers atop her head and hung a similar wreath over the prop of her plane.

As the crowd filed out, Uncle Warren pulled me aside. "How

are you feeling? Being back in Chicago must bring back some memories."

"It's hard," I said, my voice wavering. "The ding of the trolley car. The smells of the city—all wet pavement and black exhaust—remind me of the walks I used to take with my mother. And it's hard not to think about the times my father took Anna and me to the park or for ice cream at the diner close to the apartment."

Uncle Warren gripped my shoulder. "When you go up tomorrow don't be afraid to think of them. Your pa was a real showman. I think he'd have my head for letting you be part of this life, but I also believe once he saw you up on that wing he'd be mighty proud."

"Especially when I perform the Showstopper," I added.

He rubbed a hand across his chin. "Maybe we should give that some more thought. Nathan thinks it's—"

"I know what he thinks, but this is my choice. You promised. It's the only way to ensure a win."

"Grace," he mumbled. "We could still win."

"With The Skyhawks doing everything in their power to beat us? No. We don't have a choice. We need to do the trick."

His shoulders dropped in defeat as he reached into his pocket. "This is for you." He slid a small box into my hand. "I've been keeping this for a special occasion. Your Ma would have wanted you to have it."

I tore away the brown paper to reveal a small, red-velvet box. As I inched open the hinge, a gasp lodged in my throat. Inside was a gold locket I recognized. The oval piece with the intricate, hand-etched cover and delicate gold chain used to be kept in my mother's bedside table. It was a beautiful piece she only wore on special occasions.

"The authorities sent it to me after they cleared out the apartment. I've kept it hidden until this day for you." He lifted the necklace from the box and motioned for me to turn. Setting it against my chest, he secured the clasp at my neck.

"Go on and open the locket," he urged. He yanked down his hat to hide the glint of tears in his eyes.

Once I unlatched the hinge, the images of two bright-eyed children stared back at me. Anna couldn't have been more than four in the picture. Brown curls covered her head in a soft halo. In the picture next to her, my eyes were as wide as my smile, even though I was missing my two front teeth. My mother cherished this small piece of jewelry, and now I would, too.

"Thank you," I whispered. "You'll never know how much this means to me."

Uncle Warren brushed a hand over my cheek. "You're a good girl, Grace, even if you do ruffle my feathers most of the time." I swiped away a tear tumbling down my face. He pulled me into a tight embrace. His jacket smelled exactly like the hangar—clove-tinged cigar smoke mixed with gasoline and motor oil.

"Everything all right over here?" Daniel asked.

"Yes, everything's fine," Uncle Warren chomped down on his cigar. He rolled his wrist and checked the time on his watch. "I'm off. Meeting an old pal for dinner." He pointed to Nathan and Daniel. "No funny business tonight. We need to be ready by seven o'clock sharp tomorrow morning."

He slid a wad of bills into my hand. "Go have a nice dinner. And no arguments about money."

"That's too much." I said, handing half the bills back to him.

"Order dessert. I mean it, Grace." He gave me one last smile before he turned and disappeared into the crowd.

"So, what are our plans for the evening?" Daniel asked.

"Well, I actually had plans for Gracie and myself," Henry started.

"Did I hear something about evening plans?" A high-pitched, almost tinny voice spoke behind us. A straw boater rested at the back of Mr. Knickerbocker's head. His starched brown suit was tailored perfectly to his small frame. His hands did that fluttery motion at his sides again. "I'm holding a small party tonight at a local establishment and you all must join me. There will be music and dancing. And . . ." He paused and surveyed the crowd around us. "Refreshments."

"Refreshments" these days was code for liquor. People may act all high and mighty, attending the local temperance meetings, but even the law couldn't keep people from their drinks—especially when music and dancing were involved.

Daniel and Nathan almost popped out of their shoes with excitement. Henry gave me a simple shrug.

"Perhaps I could sway you if I introduced you to a friend of mine," Mr. Knickerbocker said.

A woman stepped close to Mr. Knickerbocker and at the sight of her my mind went empty. My knees shook and I clasped my hands in front of me.

Bessie Coleman's knee-skimming dress was a brilliant shade of late-sunset orange that complimented her brown skin. The crown of her hat was covered in cream chenille and lace like I'd seen in the department store ads. The pictures in the papers didn't do her justice. Her black hair framed her small face, and her eyes were the color of honey. The casual observer would never know she was the first black female flying ace to ever earn a pilot's license.

She brushed past Mr. Knickerbocker, her hand stretched out toward me. "Miss Lafferty, it's a pleasure to make your acquaintance. Mr. Knickerbocker was kind enough to show me your newspaper article. You are quite the daredevil."

"Thank you, ma'am. But really, you're the marvel in the sky," I sputtered out.

Mr. Knickerbocker glanced between us. "About this evening, Miss Lafferty. I'm sure Miss Coleman would enjoy the pleasure of your company."

Uncle Warren's early call time rattled around in my head. Plus, I was confident that if I spent more than two minutes with my hero I'd spill a drink on myself or say something completely childish.

"Thank you sir, but—"

Nathan cut me off. "Grace, could I talk to you for a second?" He pulled me to the side. Daniel and Henry crowded around us.

"Please don't say no," Nathan begged. "It's the big city. None of us may ever get an opportunity like this again." For the first time in weeks there was joy in his eyes.

I turned to Henry. "What could it hurt?" he said. "We can go and still be home early."

Nathan gave me a pointed look. "One dance, Grace. We all deserve this. You deserve this."

Daniel, in his typical style, didn't say a word; but a hint of a smile gave me his answer. Henry shrugged. "It's up to you."

The chance to talk with my hero was a once-in-a-lifetime opportunity. What would it be like to sit with Miss Coleman and talk about her flight plans and next adventure? I looked between her and the boys.

"We accept your invitation," I said. "What time does the celebration begin?"

Mr. Knickerbocker clapped his hands in delight. "I'll send all the information to your hotel." He doffed his hat in my direction. "Until this evening, Miss Lafferty."

Mr. Knickerbocker gave a slight bow before popping his hat back on his head. Miss Coleman waved a quick goodbye and took Knickerbocker's arm, disappearing into the crowd.

"You won't regret this, Grace. I promise," Nathan said.

"I'd better not," I replied, shaking a finger at him.

Nathan and Daniel slapped one another on the back and took off toward the exhibition field. Henry swiped a hand across his mouth to hide a grin.

"So, are you going to join us?" I asked.

"Someone's got to keep those two out of trouble," Henry said. "I don't know how I feel about getting all dressed up though. Do you think Nathan can lend me a sharp suit?"

As soon as the words passed his lips, I wanted to part the crowd, hunt Mr. Knickerbocker down, and take back my answer —but it was too late. I had no choice but to keep my word. The thought of dressing up never crossed my mind. And with Ethel and Mary back in Lincoln, I didn't know what I was going to do. I could barely get a brush through my hair, much less choose a dress for a big party like tonight.

My face must have gone blank because Henry touched my shoulder. "Is something wrong?"

The press of his hand on my shoulder made my head swirl. "I'm fine. It's just been quite a day. I'm going to walk back to the hotel and clear my head."

"Can I walk with you?"

"No, I can get back on my own."

Disappointment flickered across his face. "See you tonight?"

"Yes, tonight."

I pushed through the mass of men and women who lingered near the planes from the Powder Puff Derby. Several women commented on how terrifying it must be up in the air. I chuckled to myself. The act itself was terrifying at certain moments, but it was nothing compared to the prospect of heading into downtown Chicago to find a suitable dress.

21
This Single Choice

Two flights of stairs. Sixteen long, steep steps. I'd never be able to get all the way down in these pointed-toe pumps. I still wasn't quite sure how I'd been talked into buying them. My visit to a local dress shop was a blur of satin gowns, long pearl strands, and a flurry of overeager shop girls who were more than willing to take the money lining my pocket. Each and every dollar I handed over felt like a pinch to the skin after saving for so long.

I placed a hand over my mother's locket and prayed I didn't end up in a heap at the bottom of the stairs. Clutching the mahogany banister, I made my descent. Gold fabric swished across my skin. The sequins covering the bodice shimmered in the lamplight. With each step, hairpins dug into the back of my head. The hairdresser had rolled my hair into what resembled a modern bob after I refused to cut it. The last thing I needed was loose hair getting stuck in a strut or flying into my eyes.

Women glided past me as if they were born in high heels, while I tottered down the final steps trying not to look like a cow on roller skates. On the final step, the edge of my dress caught on my shoe and I pitched forward. Before I smacked face-first into the plush, maroon carpet, a hand shot out to catch me.

"Careful, Miss Lafferty. You don't want to injure yourself before the competition tomorrow." Rowland stood front and center. As usual he wore a perfectly tailored black suit complete with shiny, silver cufflinks. The tie at his neck was looped into a perfect knot. He flashed his bright smile in my direction, almost blinding me.

"Thank you for your help, but I have no intention of giving

you the satisfaction of seeing me injure myself." I yanked my hand away from his, smoothing down the hem of my traitorous dress and hissing at the stupid heels.

"What are you doing here?"

A sly smile inched over Rowland's lips. "I'm a guest here."

Of course he was.

His gaze slid across my face and down the length of me. "I knew it," he murmured under his breath.

"Knew what?" I'm not sure why I bothered to reply at all. Alistair Rowland always spoke his mind whether you wanted to hear it or not.

"My instincts told me you'd shine up brighter than a new shilling with the right clothes. How does it feel to finally be dressed in a manner that suits you?" His admiring glance gave me the heebie-jeebies.

"It's a dress, sir. Nothing more."

"Ah, but that's just it. There *is* more. You deserve to wear nice, new clothes. To be treated like the fantastic performer you are."

He paused as if searching for the right words. "My father is quite the dodgy bloke back in England. My mum died when I was a lad. He batted me around for a bit until he got too caught up in his business. When I came of age, I traveled to America to separate myself from him. I wanted to build my own reputation here without his dark cloud following me everywhere." His chin dipped and he shook his head. "We're alike in many ways, Grace. Doing everything we can to make our way in this world. Fighting to keep our heads above water." He shoved his hands deep into his trousers. Arrogance seeped out of his proud face until I saw the first glimmer of honesty. "I *can* be trusted, Grace, if you'll give me a chance."

His voice cracked as if he actually had a beating heart somewhere in that cold body of his. Could it be possible that for the first time I was seeing the real Alistair Rowland? Not the blustery character he'd built in the world of barnstorming, but a true flesh-and-blood man?

"I know you have quite a past, too." He sighed, his eyes filling with the pity I hated seeing even as a child. "The tragedy that happened to your parents and younger sister is why the contest tomorrow is so important to you. It's a chance to keep your team together. Your family together."

My spine stiffened at his words. "How do you know about my family?" I snapped.

"Like I said before, barnstorming is a small world. People talk and I listen."

I gulped and tried to find the right response. He'd pushed me for so long and I'd pushed back, yet he'd still seen through me. My desperation. My need to hold onto the one thing death had stolen from me—my family.

He held my gaze for a long minute as if studying me, narrowing in on my single weakness. It wasn't honesty I had seen in his face, it was acting. Pretense to sway me into changing my mind. How dare he think he could use my family as a ploy to get his way? Offering up a sad story about his own past, which probably wasn't even true, all just another plan to woo me to his team. It was practically laughable the way he pretended he was some sort of white knight coming to my rescue.

Every inch of me wanted to slap him and scream that my past was none of his business, but we were in the lobby of a fancy hotel with dozens of eyes surrounding us. A few months ago, I wouldn't have cared. But now, I understood what was at stake. One misstep could take The Soaring Eagles down, and I would not give Alistair Rowland the pleasure of seeing me cause a scene.

A bellboy bumped into me as he swept up the stairs, his arms loaded down with several suitcases. Instead of wobbling about, I stood firm. Rowland eyed me for a long moment. A flicker behind his eyes warned he wasn't telling the whole truth. He too was unsure about the future of barnstorming. Even with all his money, he didn't know if he could make a go of his team. Men like Mr. Curtiss and promoter Ivan Gates were pushing aviation forward into new territory. Planes were changing, and without the Hollywood contract, the future of The Skyhawks—and every other barnstorming team—was uncertain. That explained his repeated offers of work. His quiet desperation. He was scared.

"Mr. Rowland, the car is waiting." The wall of muscle known as Louis appeared in front of us. He nodded to the entrance where a sleek, black Rolls Royce idled at the curb.

"Give us a minute," he barked.

"There's no need for you to stay, Alistair." His brows skyrocketed toward his snowy-white hairline as I used his first name to make my point. "For once and for all, we are done here."

I brushed past him, slipping into the throng of the lobby. Wild and vibrant voices filled the long, narrow space. Men in black evening clothes moved in and out of the lounge. Ladies dressed in gowns the color of sapphires and emeralds lit long cigarettes. Puffs of smoke danced and swirled toward the marbled ceiling. Attendants scurried behind the gold-plated arrivals desk, passing brass room keys into the hands of waiting families. A musician in the front corner of the room ran his fingers over the keys of a shiny piano, entertaining the crowd with a rousing rendition of "Ain't We Got Fun?"

I spotted Nathan and Daniel huddled near the entrance, staring at a group of women sitting at a banquette five feet away. I tip-toed up close behind them. "They'll never give you the time of day," I whispered in Nathan's ear.

He jumped and turned around, his top hat sliding to the back of his head. His mouth stayed open like a gaping fish while he scanned me from top to bottom. "Wowie, Grace," he whistled. "Don't you look ritzy tonight."

"You look beautiful," Daniel smoothed down his recently clipped hair.

"I could say the same about you two. New suits?"

They both stood a little straighter and thumbed the lapels of their tuxedos. "These are courtesy of Knickerbocker. That man doesn't miss a step," Nathan said.

I nodded but didn't say another word. The conversation with Rowland still pulsed through my head.

"Grace, are you all right?" Daniel reached for my gloved hand. "Your cheeks suddenly went pale."

"Did either of you say anything to Rowland about my family?"

They swapped a horrified look. "Absolutely not," Daniel insisted. "We'd never breathe a word to that snake."

"Why do you ask? Is he bothering you again?" Nathan searched the room as if hoping to find him. "We can track him down and give him a good talking to."

"Never mind," I said. "Tonight, I don't want to give that cad a second thought." I tugged down the hem of my gown. It still felt a little too short for polite company.

"That dress, darlin'," Daniel practically gushed. "You look brighter than the sun on a summer day."

I grabbed the clingy fabric that hugged my every bump and curve. "I don't look any different than usual except for this dress. Which by the by, pokes and pinches in places it shouldn't."

"Oh, I disagree. You most certainly look different." Henry's low voice was almost breathless. I turned and swallowed a gasp. His day-old stubble was gone. The once-tousled look of his hair was replaced with a slick cut trimmed above the ears. His own tuxedo was cut tight against his frame, accentuating his muscled shoulders.

All sound left the room. It was only the two of us in the lobby. Not the boys. Not Rowland. A strange power urged me to peel back my silk gloves and caress his smooth cheek. Run a finger down the scar etched into his chin. Our eyes stay locked until Nathan cleared his throat. "Shall we go? The invitation Mr. Knickerbocker delivered said nine o'clock sharp."

We moved in a group toward the exit. Henry bowed out his arm. I slid my arm through his, unable to hide the wide grin playing along my lips. Ethel and Mary weren't here to help me dress, but the admiring look on Henry's face said I'd done just fine.

Unlike Lincoln, Chicago was alive both day and night. Jazz tunes spilled out of hotels and restaurants. Laughter filled the air like the whole town was celebrating some great party.

Halfway down a dark alley a few blocks from the hotel Nathan started counting doors. When we reached a plain, black facade with the number four nailed into the wood he knocked out an odd signal.

One–two–three. One–two–three–four.

Metal fire escapes creaked behind us like dark monsters. As we waited for a response, heat creeped up my neck. We were standing in an alley like criminals waiting to go into an illegal club. Tomorrow our whole future was on the line and we were about to risk it all. I stepped back, words of protest already on my lips, when a cut-out in the door slid open and two almost-black, bloodshot eyes greeted us.

"Password?"

Nathan mumbled something like, "*Kaykeeter.*"

"Didn't hear ya'," the man growled.

"Cake-Eater," Nathan said, louder this time.

Daniel bent his chin down to hide a smile. Henry's eyebrows shot up.

The door opened with a groan. "Ladies man?" Daniel teased.

"It's just the password." Nathan rolled his eyes and slid the bouncer a few bills for his time.

My fancy shoes stayed glued to the dirty asphalt. The bouncer's thick frame hovered in the doorway. Henry came up behind me, his breath warming the skin on my neck. "It's one night, Gracie. Everything will be fine." He laid a hand on my back and urged me inside.

Candles lit the brick-lined hallway. The stench of mold and rot was overwhelming. When we reached a dead end another bouncer, this one short and squat with thinning hair, rapped a signal on the door. Nathan tapped a foot behind me. The beat kept time with my thrumming heart.

When the door finally swung open a wall of sound knocked me back. Horns bleated into the air. The deep timbre of a saxophone followed behind. Henry gave me a reassuring nod and led me into the smoke-filled room.

Round tables covered the open space and almost every seat was taken. A press of bodies lined the mahogany bar only steps inside the door. The combination of laughter and music made my head light. Henry's arm snaked around my waist. We shared a tentative look and I was thrilled I wasn't the only one overwhelmed by the raucous scene.

Nathan pointed to the far side of the room. Henry and I followed, while Daniel was quickly drawn away by a raven-haired beauty. We located Mr. Knickerbocker at the back of the room, sitting at a luxury table complete with champagne flutes and dinnerware decorated with gold trim.

As we approached, he shot out of his seat. "Miss Lafferty, I'm so glad you could make it."

"Thank you for the invitation."

He gave a slight bow. "It's my honor."

"This is quite a party," I said.

"It's a typical night in the great city of Chicago." He swept out a hand, urging us to sit next to a tall, thin man in the booth. "May I introduce Mr. David L. Behncke. He's the one kindly hosting the Expo this year at Checkerboard Field, which he owns and manages."

The man's name sounded familiar. "Didn't you win the Chicago Air Derby last year?" I asked.

A bright smile lit up his face. "Why, yes I did. Thank you for remembering that, young lady."

Henry's hand left my back and moved out toward Mr. Behncke. "I remember that from the papers. Didn't you go over fifty miles in forty-nine minutes?"

"It was fifty-five miles to be exact," he laughed.

Henry pumped his hand up and down. "Real nice to meet you, sir. You're a legend in aviation circles." He turned and nodded at Knickerbocker. "And thank you for including us tonight. This means a lot to Grace."

"I remember you from the hangar. Are you a barnstormer, too?"

"No sir, I'm the mechanic for The Soaring Eagles."

"Learn your skills in the war?" Mr. Behncke asked, smoothing his hand over the short brown mustache covering his top lip.

"Before and after," Henry said quickly.

"I joined up when I was nineteen. Had my wings by twenty," Mr. Behncke said.

"I had a nephew in an artillery company," Knickerbocker added. "He died in France. Damn shame. His mother was torn up for quite some time."

Henry simply bowed his head and shoved his hands into his pockets.

Mr. Knickerbocker motioned again to the empty spots at the table. "Please sit. Miss Coleman just went to the ladies' room but I know she's anxious to speak with you, Miss Lafferty."

The music raised to a feverous pitch and I took a deep swallow. Before I sat and talked to my hero, I needed to gather my thoughts. "Will you excuse me? I think I'll go and freshen up, too."

Henry shifted nervously on his feet, favoring his leg. I edged in closer to him. "Sit for a minute. I'll be right back."

Pressing through the crush of bodies on the dance floor, I

headed to the far corner of the room. I rushed past girls dressed in short skirts and glittering head wraps, selling cigars and chatting up eligible men. I dodged around several couples tangled in each other's arms. At a nearby table two men arm-wrestled. Their gals cheered them on between puffs on their cigarettes. Between the band and the patrons, the room practically vibrated with sound.

I climbed a small set of stairs. On the last step my high heel caught on the carpet and I tumbled right into the arms of Bessie Coleman.

"Whoa, honey. Be careful. Those heels can be more dangerous than losing an engine at a thousand feet."

"Miss Coleman, I'm sorry." I reached forward to straighten out the shoulders of her cream, beaded dress.

"Miss Lafferty, it's fine," she said, gently pushing my hands away. "Who are you here with?"

"My entire team. Well, except for my uncle."

She tapped at her chin. "Your team, huh?"

"Yes. Is that a problem?"

"No. I love that you have a group of men supporting you. Personally, I've always had to fight the men. In fact, I couldn't even get my pilot's license in the states so I had to go to France. You're a lucky woman."

"Thank you, Miss Coleman. Your flying is incredible. Do you know what your next challenge will be?"

She gave me a devious grin. "Please, call me Bessie. And actually, I was thinking about taking up wing walking."

A rough laugh left my mouth. If Bessie Coleman became a wing walker, I was doomed. She gave me a long, challenging look, and I stood ramrod straight, unable to form a sentence. I still couldn't believe I was in a big, fancy club speaking to the one-and-only Bessie Coleman.

Her laughter boomed through the room. "I'm pulling your leg, sweet girl. The only place I belong is in the pilot's seat, although the government is making that all kinds of difficult right now."

"You too?" I blew out a relieved breath. "Think they'll ever leave us alone?"

"Don't you worry. You keep doing your thing. Talent like yours is rare." She tightened her lips. "Can I give you some advice?"

"Of course."

"Be true to who you are. Men control the skies and they'll do and say anything to make you change into the woman they think you should be. Stick to what you think is right. I've seen lots of women get lost in this business when they forget who they are." She glanced over at Mr. Knickerbocker's table where he was deep in conversation with Mr. Behncke. "You comin' back to join us?"

"In a minute. I need to powder my nose."

She followed my line of sight to where Henry sat.

"I saw you with that fella earlier. You keen on him?"

"Yes," I said, unable to mask my smile.

"Like I said, remember who you are. But don't forget to have some fun along the way, too." She gave me a quick wink and swayed back to the table.

The loud scream of a trumpet pierced the air. A shiver crossed my skin. Was this the kind of spot where my pa spent his evenings? Did he play for a room of glittering, high-class folk like this?

A bass beat blended in with the trumpet, setting a new melody. Strings and piano followed. A statuesque woman with a white lily tucked behind her ear swayed toward the microphone. She opened her mouth and her voice was like an angel's—sweet and smooth. Before I could head for the ladies room, Henry stood and waved me toward the dance floor. When I reached him his fingers moved around my waist and pulled me toward the stage.

"Dance with me," he said. I hesitated, his story about the German soldier filling my head.

He stepped close, pressing his mouth to my ear. "Caroline

always told me to trust my instincts. You don't need to worry. Let me hold you and everything will be all right."

"But your leg." The words left my mouth and I instantly regretted them.

His eyes never left mine. I slid my arm around his waist. My hands turned clammy and I was afraid he'd walk away. Instead he pulled me to his chest. "Tonight, it's my turn to take a risk."

He walked me to the center of the floor and all sense left my body. His fingers traced down my arm before settling on my lower back. I closed my eyes and it was like my feet never touched the ground. The woman's voice was mesmerizing. Her lyrics about love and trust were sung like they were meant only for us. In the moment there wasn't the pressure of a show or a worry over where we'd sleep. For now we were only a guy and a gal caught up in the magic of the night.

Stepping back, Henry twirled me in a circle, the edges of my dress glittering in the light. He brought me back into his chest and the beat slowed. I pressed my head to his shoulder and closed my eyes. Images of my father filled my head again. I could almost picture his rail-thin body on the stage. His dark hair shimmering in the spotlight. The way his lips pursed before he pressed his mouth to his trumpet's mouthpiece.

"What's on your mind?" Henry whispered.

"This place brings up all sorts of questions. Did my father ever play here? Could he have stood on that stage and entertained a crowd of this size? Our apartment was only a dozen blocks from here."

"I forgot you lived here with your family. Does it bring back too many bad memories?"

"No." I shook my head, the hairpins digging into my scalp. "Being here comforts me. Makes me feel like I've had a chance to step into his world."

"Are you nervous about tomorrow?" he asked.

"I'd be lying if I said no. Every time I think about soaring up into that sky I tell myself it's just another performance, but the stammering of my heart warns it's so much more."

He leaned in and pressed his mouth to the edge of my ear. "You are the single most brilliant girl I've ever met. Let that shine tomorrow, and the contract is yours." His hand caressed my lower back as we swayed to the music. "Thank you for allowing me to be here. To experience this night with you. It's a moment I'll never forget."

I laid my hand against his cheek. He bowed his head, allowing himself to ease into my touch.

"It wouldn't be the same without you here," I managed to say. He wound me in closer. All the air in the room heated. Body-to-body I couldn't deny the way my heart raced every time I caught his eye. How my blood hummed under my skin at his touch. Our time together was fleeting. If we won the contract, The Soaring Eagles would be off to Hollywood. We'd never asked Henry if he'd come along, but he had his own dreams, and I could guess what his answer would be.

The final note of music faded away and in the silence a low pounding filled the room. The sound got louder until the main door to the club blasted open.

A dozen men with gold badges pinned to their jackets rushed inside. Several guests near the bar pulled guns from inside their coats and began shooting. One bullet clipped a chandelier. Shards of glass and metal spun out into the air. Several women screamed and bent down to shield their eyes.

My pulse pounded in my ears as I spun in a circle, looking for Nathan and Daniel. The agents swept amber bottles and glasses off the bar with the tips of their guns. Men and women stampeded for the nearest exit. Two young men raced past me and bumped my shoulder. I teetered on my heels. Henry caught me around the waist as gunfire cracked in the air. Bullets thudded into the walls and shattered glass. Henry wrenched me in tighter, his entire body shaking. His lips moved in their familiar low whisper.

"Henry, we need to get out of here." I shook him until his eyes flew open. He swiveled his head, watching the crowd scatter. I yanked on his hands, trying to drag him away from the gunfire, but his weight was too much for me.

Miss Coleman appeared at my arm. "Come this way. Mr. Behncke knows a secret exit."

I tugged on Henry's arm once more. He remained still. His body was frozen in place. I laid a hand against his cheek. "Henry, I need you to move," I yelled over the frenzy building around us.

Like a curtain being pulled back from a window, the light gradually returned to his eyes. "We need to follow Mr. Behncke." He gave a slow bob of his head and let me lead the way.

We rushed through the room as screams filled the air. Once we were past the bandstand, Mr. Behncke appeared with Mr. Knickerbocker glued to his side, his eyes wide beneath his wire spectacles. "This way," Mr. Behncke waved us to a small door hidden next to the stage.

"Grace!" Nathan and Daniel raced in our direction.

"Let's go." Henry's confident voice returned. He took my hand and urged me to follow our group.

We slid through the small door and down a flight of concrete stairs.

"This is how they load in the heavy instruments and liquor," Bessie whispered.

The rough sound of our combined breaths bounced off the narrow, brick corridor flickering with dim candlelight. Mr. Behncke skidded to a stop when we reached a dead end.

"We're trapped," I gasped.

A devilish smile crossed his lips. "Oh my dear, in places like this there's always a way out." He tapped at several spots on the wall until one tap made a hollow sound. With a gentle shove, he pushed on a brick and a panel swung open. He waved us through the secret door and out to an alley behind the club.

Rain poured from the sky in thick sheets. Miss Coleman, Mr. Knickerbocker, and Mr. Behncke scrambled toward the street, desperate to hail an available cab. Nathan and Daniel were pulled along with them. They had to stay safe and away from the police. If any of us went to jail, there'd be no contest tomorrow.

Henry pulled me away from the street and the approaching roar of sirens. We ran through several alleys, my dress clinging to me like a second skin. Sirens continued to wail in the distance. Oversized raindrops clouded my vision. A few blocks further down, we found shelter in a small doorway. Although we were finally out of the rain, Henry's body shook as fiercely as mine.

"Are you all right?" I asked.

"The gunfire," he said tightly. "I was back on the battlefield, like that night in the street."

"What brought you back?"

"You." His head dropped down. "I couldn't let you get hurt."

My teeth chattered as we held on to each other. The rain pounded against the asphalt. Its rough clink hammered like bullets against the steel fire escapes looming above our heads. Henry tensed at the sound.

I reached for his face and pulled his gaze toward mine. "You're safe."

His arms circled me and I shivered again. This time it wasn't from the cold. My fingers slid along his cheek and then over the fading black and blue shadow he'd earned courtesy of Joe Prescott's fist. I stood on tiptoe and gently pressed a kiss to the mark. A mark he got because of me.

The sensation of his skin against my lips sent a shock through me. I'd been fighting my attraction to him for so long. Every bone in my body ached for his touch. It was a risk, but one I was now desperate to take.

I pulled back and his eyes filled with hunger. "Are you sure?" he whispered above the din of the pounding rain.

I sunk into him, hoping the heat of my body would be enough of an answer. His arms formed a tight cage around my waist and then his mouth found mine. At first his kisses were slow and sweet. The movement of his lips a slight press against mine. Our hearts pounded in the same rhythm. His hands moved to the small of my back, tightening the fabric of my dress. His touch warmed every inch of my skin. Up until now, I'd believed that nothing could ever rival the thrill of wing walking, but with Henry's body molded to mine I realized I was wrong. His lips parting mine was more breathtaking than doing a loop-the-loop 500 feet above the earth.

I wanted him closer. My lips moved to the hollow of his throat. I was lost in his strength and my need for him. We stumbled back into the brick wall and melted into each other, each and every kiss not enough. He whispered my name. The sound was like fire curling in my veins. We clung to each other, not wanting to part even when a brigade of sirens wailed behind us.

Water drops cascaded off his hair and wandered over the dimple in his cheek before plunging off the edge of his chin. He wound a finger around a wet curl along my face. Even with the rain, I wasn't cold. Being wrapped in his touch was better than any blanket. He lit me from inside with a warmth I wanted to bask in all day. Live and breathe for every moment.

Another high-pitched siren shot through the streets. Lights flickered across the alley and raced toward us. Henry's mouth set in hard determination and he grabbed my hand.

"Run."

22
Somewhere Safe

We darted in and out of the shadows for several blocks, and the din of sirens faded. When we reached the hotel, the marbled entry, once alive with life, was now quiet as a church. We moved past empty banquettes before Henry checked the men's lounge for Nathan and Daniel. He was gone a few minutes and then reappeared with a tight mouth. No boys. I hoped they were somewhere safe.

Henry cocked his head toward the stairs. I followed, the soggy tail of my dress flopping along each carpeted step. Water dripped off the edges of my hair and streaked along my face. By the time we reached my room I was shivering.

"Best get inside and dry off." He ran his thumb along my lower lip. "You're turning blue."

I reached for his hand and pulled him in. His mouth was on mine again, uncoiling a need I never knew existed within me. An ache only his touch seemed to fix. We moved back against the door. I wound my arms around his neck.

"Maybe we should go inside," he whispered against my trembling lips.

He slid the clutch from my fingers and pulled out the key. While he fumbled with the door, my insides did a cartwheel. I'd never been alone with a man before. Was this right? Should I be doing this? The door swung open. Not knowing what else to do, I followed him inside.

With a flip of the switch, light ignited the room. He took off his jacket. His wet shirt hugged the lines of his chest.

"Come here," he said quietly.

My head buzzed. My body urged me closer, but my mind was afraid of doing something wrong. Saying something wrong. The thought held me in place.

"Gracie? What is it?" he whispered.

"I've never . . ." My words lodged in my throat. "Done this before."

A smile pulled at his mouth. "I know." He skimmed a finger along my cheek, sending a rush of blood through my body. "Let me stay a while and hold you. That's all I need."

His words poured over me, releasing all the fear gripping my heart. How could I have imagined he would be anything but a gentleman?

"Be right back." He returned a minute later with an armload of towels. "Let's get you dried off before you turn into a prune." I laughed and grabbed a towel from his outstretched hand.

I scrunched up my dripping hair as he scurried to grab his jacket from the bed. He reached behind the lapel. A large bunch of wilted dandelions sprouted from his hand.

"I thought you might want a few wishes before tomorrow." The stems were bent at an odd angle and some of the spindly, white fluff was missing.

"I can't blow on them here. It will make a mess."

He pulled the towel from my hand. "Forget the mess and make your wishes. You deserve each and every one."

I bent my head and closed my eyes. Before Henry I'd only wanted one thing. Now my mind buzzed with everything I wished for: not only for the team, but for the two of us.

With a deep breath, I blew every bit of fluff from each dande-lion. Henry placed a soft kiss to my forehead. "I hope every wish comes true."

Once my hair stopped dripping, I headed into the bathroom. I gasped when I saw my reflection in the mirror. Dark make-up coated the lines around my eyes. My mouth was stained red like a sideshow clown. I pulled off my dress and laid it in the bathtub to dry. After scrubbing my face, I took one last glance in the mirror. Although the make-up and clothes made me look older, it felt good to be the old Grace again.

Henry stood at the window, his black leather braces dangling at his sides. His shirt and coat hung in perfect alignment over the radiator. I pressed my hand to my lips, stifling a laugh.

"What is it?" He turned and focused on the thin slip covering my body.

"You always do that." I pointed to the arranged clothing, trying to ignore how his eyes burned with want. "Place things in a perfect organized line. Did the army teach you that?"

"No, my father did. He said in this life you need two things to be successful: organization and honesty." His voice trailed off on the last word. The beautiful dimple in his cheek disappeared along with his smile. I knew better than anyone how hard it was to think of your parents after they were gone. "Grace, we need to talk."

I took in the thin, wet undershirt that clung to the hard muscles along his chest. "Okay, but first, do you want to take that off? It must be giving you a chill," I said, avoiding the stern tone in his voice. He'd been thinking about his dreams, too. Where they'd take him. And tonight I couldn't bear the thought of letting him go.

"I wasn't sure you'd be comfortable with that."

I tossed the last dry towel at him. "It's your turn."

After the bathroom door closed, I shifted my eyes between the bed, the sofa, and the door. The good thing to do—no, the right thing to do—would be to ask him to leave. But when he came out of the bathroom, his brilliant green eyes focused on me, I couldn't turn him away.

He hovered in the doorway, the light from the moon outside casting his shadow along the floor. He looked at the door then the couch.

I laughed. Was he thinking the same thing I was?

He cocked his head. "What's so funny?"

"Nothing. It's nothing."

He sank down on the edge of the red velvet couch and patted the open spot beside him.

"I don't think I've ever said thank you for taking such good care of the planes. In the past we've had some real louses as mechanics. But you've kept your word to keep us safe."

I slid down beside him. A crack of lightning lit the dark room. Henry reached for my cheek with a trembling hand. He dropped his chin, fading back into his dark place again.

"Hey. Don't slip away on me," I pleaded.

A whisper of breath left his beautiful mouth as he reached for my mother's locket.

"That's pretty. Is it new?" His fingers moved down my bare arms. The soft caress made every element in my body snap to attention.

"Um, no," I stuttered. "It was my mother's."

"Then it must be precious to you," he said.

"It is," I said, touching the thin, delicate chain.

"You're still trembling," he said.

"Tonight frightened me." A deep need inside me wanted his skin against mine but I held back, still unsure with him sitting so close. "At first the club was new and glamorous. The band and the dancing. I never imagined I would step inside that world."

"Yes, the dancing was good." His grin made the fear in my heart slowly fade away.

"But when the raid happened . . . the gunshots. I was terrified. Not for myself, but for you."

He slid forward and placed his hands behind my head to pull out the hairpins at the nape of my neck. Curl by curl, my hair tumbled down along my shoulders. "It's been a long time since someone cared enough to worry about me," he said. The corners of his eyes grew tight. "I failed you tonight. You deserve a man who will protect you. Keep you from harm."

"Henry—"

His shoulders went stiff and he moved away to the window. "On the battlefield it was chaos every day. Two of my best friends and I were pinned down in the same spot for days. No food. No water. The stench of each other making it almost impossible to breathe. Artillery kept coming and one of my friends, William, started hallucinating. Dehydration I guess." He placed a finger to the glass and traced a descending raindrop. "He told me and our other pal, Sam, that God said we needed to stop fighting. We tried to calm him, but the next night he went crazy. We chased him out of the trench, but he tripped and fell into the barbed wire separating the two lines." His voice stuttered and he clenched his fists. "The shells were coming too fast and the wire sliced through him every time I tried to move him. His screams were deafening." His knees buckled under him.

I jumped from the couch and cradled him in my arms. My fingers found the taut lines around his lips and slowly traced them until his mouth relaxed. "We all have our demons, Henry. Your reaction at the club could have happened to anyone who lived through what you did. No one knows the evils of war more than the men who've faced them."

He shook his head. "But I couldn't move. That's not how a man should act."

I grabbed his chin, forcing him to look at me. "When it mattered, you were there for me." Pulling him into my arms, I let him catch his breath. When he was ready, I followed him back to the couch.

With a soft hand, he cupped my cheek. "I want to show you something." Reaching down, he rolled up his pant leg. In the dim light I could only make out a thin line of a scar that ran from the middle of his thigh down to the top of his heel. The scar puckered in places where he'd lost chunks of skin.

"I wanted you to see this. See all of me." His voice quivered.

Without hesitating, I ran the tip of my finger down the length of the scar. Henry closed his eyes and blew out a ragged breath. "You are a brave man, Henry Patton. Don't let anyone tell you different."

His eyes fluttered open. Gone was the haunted worry, replaced with the green warmth I loved. His arms moved to my waist and I held him tightly. We stayed silent, our heartbeats finding a steady rhythm together. In the darkness we found safety in each other's arms, and for tonight that was enough.

23
Quicker Than a Breath

September 12, 1922
Contest Day – World Aviation Expo

"No William! Don't!" Henry groaned in his sleep. His fingers gripped the edge of the couch. He thrashed and kicked the thin blanket from his body.

I jumped from the bed and smoothed back the damp hair on his forehead. "Shh. You're safe."

A stream of sunlight shot a path across the room. Dust specks swirled through the air in a perfectly choreographed dance. Henry's murmurs quieted. The smooth rise and fall of his chest mesmerized me. I ran my hand along the taut muscles in his arm, tracing each scar and freckle to convince myself this was real. That this beautiful man had taken me in his arms and kissed me last night.

Once I was sure he was back in a deep sleep, I pulled the blanket up to his chin. The strap of my slip slid down my shoulder. The thin cotton material smelled like him—soap and oil. I fought the urge to climb back into bed and shut out the rest of the world. Pretend Henry and I could stay in this moment forever.

The deep rattle of a car horn blared outside. It was a strange sound for so early in the morning. I slid Henry's pocket watch from the table in front of the couch. A yelp escaped my lips. Henry bolted upright. A tuft of wild hair ruffled against his temple.

I tossed the watch onto his chest. "Get up. It's eight o'clock. We're late!"

He jumped from the couch, the tail of his shirt bouncing behind him. Gathering his jacket and shoes in a huge pile, he raced toward me, planted a soft kiss on my cheek, and disappeared out the door.

We raced through the exhibition entrance, dashing around new planes and spectators making their way to the grandstands for the competition. Only feet from the hangar, Henry and I skidded to a stop in front of Uncle Warren, Nathan and Daniel. A beat of silence passed as they stared us down like two children caught stealing a piece of penny candy.

"Where in the blazes have you two been?" Uncle Warren stomped toward us, his cigar grinding between his rigid jaw. "Of all the days to be late."

"I overslept. When I got downstairs to the lobby Henry was there, too."

"Uh, yes sir. Seems we both lost track of time," he said sheepishly.

Uncle Warren pointed to the far side of the hangar. "Grace, get your gear. The nine other teams are already preparing for their performances." He jabbed a finger at Henry. "You, go do your job." He yanked the brown stub from his mouth. "And stay away from Grace. She doesn't need any more distractions."

I took two steps inside the hangar and stopped. The narrow building spanned what I guessed would be the length of fifteen Packard limousines parked bumper to bumper. Except for the metal walls, and a few tool benches scattered about, it was nothing more than a long tin can. They charged sixty dollars for this?

The sharp scents of gasoline and oil wafted over me as I raced past the other teams. The Flying Finellis circled their plane while arguing about the order of their routine. The brothers' Italian-tinged voices rose higher with each shout. On the opposite side of the hangar, one of the Black Bombers was flat on his back readjusting the right wheel on his plane's landing gear.

A man in a brown linen suit with a Panama hat pulled low over his eyes rushed from group to group. With a wooden clipboard clenched in his hand, he confirmed each team's flight order before scurrying outside to catch a bright yellow Jenny readying for takeoff.

An icy prickle climbed up the back of my neck as I strode across the hangar. When I turned, I locked eyes with Rowland. Today he was dressed in a bright white suit with a matching boater hat. A snicker left my lips. If he leaned anywhere close to a plane, those expensive rags would be covered in dirt and grease in a second. He tipped his hat in my direction and approached, waving off that goon Louis when he tried to follow.

"Glad to see the recent storms have passed. Quite a brilliant day for a contest, don't you think, Miss Lafferty?"

He was making a half-civil attempt to be polite. I supposed I could do the same. "Yes, it is." I reached a hand toward him. "May the best team win today."

He latched onto my handshake with a steady grip. "I do believe I owe you an apology about our conversation yesterday evening. There I was, insisting what a good chap I am, but then I crossed the line by mentioning your deceased family. In your eyes, I'm sure I'm nothing but a cad. I promise I only have your best interest at heart. No matter what happens today, I hope your dreams come true." He finally released my hand and cocked his head in Henry's direction. "Seems that bloke's turned out to be quite a help to your team. Perhaps I shouldn't have told him about your need for a mechanic after our run-in at the diner. But I'm glad it worked out." A hint of a sneer danced over his lips before he returned to his own swarm of planes.

Even with the summer heat blasting through the hangar, a chill raced across my skin. He told Henry about the job? That couldn't be right. Mary told him.

No. This was like the flyover. Rowland was trying to throw off my performance. Rattle me. His desperation was getting tiresome, but it would all be over when we won the contract today.

Uncle Warren continued to pace behind the tail of our Jenny. Nathan trailed on his heels, no doubt trying to convince him not to let me do the Showstopper. As soon as this show was over, he and I were going to have another talk about his constant hovering.

Henry moved around the struts and wires, doing a last-minute inspection. For the last few months, he'd done everything to keep us safe. Keep us in the sky. We were here, competing in this contest, a step closer to our dream because he'd spent night and day ensuring the Jennys were in tip-top shape.

I cursed myself for giving Rowland's words a second thought. There wasn't time for his nonsense. The Soaring Eagles had a contest to win.

All my gear sat piled in a far corner of the hangar near a long row of tool benches and a shoulder-high stack of canvas parachutes. I slid on my leather jacket and pulled down my aviator cap. My new goggles hung around my neck. I hesitated for a moment when I thought about the scratches and nicks that would soon come, but today was a new beginning for The Soaring Eagles. It was time to put away the old and welcome the new.

The thick spool of wire for the Showstopper weighed heavy in my pocket. I closed my eyes and pictured the mouthpiece settled behind my lips. The wire spinning out. The line snapping taught as my body soared through the sky like a bird. This performance would not only win us the contract, but I'd make history by being the first wing walker to perform the trick successfully.

Henry appeared by my side a few minutes later. His gaze darted over the rows of colorful biplanes and scrambling mechanics. "After that warning, I can't let your uncle see me."

"We shouldn't have been late," I said, a little too brusquely.

He slid his hands onto my shoulders giving them a gentle squeeze. "Put that out of your head. Focus on your routine. Get out there and show Knickerbocker how talented you are." He placed a gentle kiss on my forehead. When he gazed into my eyes all I saw was honesty.

The drone of nearby engines filled my ears. Henry was right. This performance should be my only concern. And did it really matter how he'd come to be a Soaring Eagle? Over the last months, he'd more than proved how invested he was in our team. In me.

"Nathan was waiting for me near your uncle's Jenny and gave me an earful. He told me to remind you about your parachute."

I hitched a thumb toward my back. "I don't want to wear it, but I promised Uncle Warren."

Henry inched in closer, talking over the roar filling the hangar as each plane taxied their way outside. "I'm sorry about being late, but not about last night," A small smile pulled at his lips.

We stood toe-to-toe. His hitching breath mirrored mine. All my worries, all my questions were washed away by the searing kiss he swept across my lips. He wound his hands around my waist. The chaotic sounds in the hangar faded away. I lost myself in his arms, his body warming me better than any summer sun. This was the man who held me in his arms last night and promised over the crash of thunder that he'd protect me with his life.

The man in the Panama hat appeared at the front of the hangar and called for The Soaring Eagles. Before I could take a step, Henry grabbed my hand. "Good luck. Although I know you don't need it."

I reveled in the heat of his hand and the thrum in my heart. The way his kiss still buzzed across my lips. It was the perfect start to a glorious day.

～

Uncle Warren stomped in front of me until we reached the wing of his Jenny. "Nice and easy today. Do what we practiced." He gripped my shoulder as we faced the bulging grandstands. Children waved red-and-white pennants above their heads. Men and women applauded The Black Bombers, who did an inverted loop against a cloudless sky. The announcer's voice blared across the open field announcing the team's final score—89 out of 100.

We could beat that.

Uncle Warren shielded his eyes from the sun. "The judges announced they're awarding points for technique, aerobatic control, and difficulty of stunts."

"With the Showstopper, it's in the bag." I patted my jacket pocket where I'd placed the wire cable and mouthpiece.

Uncle Warren sighed. He reached for my aviator cap and cinched down the neck strap with a little too much force. "Like I said, nice and easy, Grace."

Twenty feet away, Daniel waved Nathan's plane out of the hangar. Once they were settled on the runway, Daniel hefted his giant body onto the Jenny's frame.

"They'll do their regular aerobatics routine, ending with Daniel's freefall off the wing. Should earn us quite a few points."

Nathan soared across the sky. The plane did three consecutive barrel rolls, followed by two inverted loops, and a whip stall. After a few more stunts, Daniel climbed onto the wing. He did a single-arm dangle off the outer strut before climbing down to hang off the side of the lower wing. After he heaved himself back up, he readjusted the straps of his parachute. He moved to the edge of the plane's frame and leaned back. His body dropped through the sky like a rock. The hisses and moans in the grandstands shook the air. Beat after beat he fell and a woman screamed. A slight smirk raced across Uncle Warren's lips. Daniel's shadow continued to descend until his chute popped open. He sailed across the bright blue sky through the spectators' sighs of relief.

Uncle Warren tapped my shoulder. "Let's go show 'em how it's done." He pulled me into an awkward hug and then boosted me onto the wing, climbing up after me. We bumped down the runway, the silver-and-red banners fluttering to the west. Once we pulled up, Uncle Warren banked us to the east and throttled forward. He pushed us to fifty miles per hour and spun us in a set of consecutive barrel rolls. One . . . two . . . three until our wings were level again. He shot forward and then pointed our nose straight up into the air. Easing back on the power, we did a tail spiral. The plane plummeted toward the ground, making two full revolutions until he regained control. After soaring down low, the crowd showed their appreciation by shouting and clapping for more.

The plane climbed again. When we were level Uncle Warren tapped his head. Nothing was going to hold me back today. We'd fought hard to get here. This was our chance to show the country what The Soaring Eagles could do. This performance would be one the judges would never forget.

The shores of Lake Michigan glittered like gold in the distance. The white tip of the Water Tower pierced the stunning cobalt sky. Shifting to the end of the wing, I hung down in a single-leg maneuver. After a count of five, I scrambled up and moved into a headstand. Keeping the wings level, Uncle Warren piloted us down low. The crowd's roar filled my ears. Mist covered my cheeks in a thin sheen like a kiss from the heavens, and I greeted it with a wide smile.

After reveling in the quiet moment, I kicked down. Hand-over-hand I crossed past landing and guide wires, until I reached the opposite wing. With one arm curled around a strut, and the crowd now on their feet, I pulled out my compact and powdered my nose. Raucous cheers surrounded us as we skimmed so low the banners hanging against the grandstands fanned out in every direction. This was it. The moment we'd worked for over the last five years. Every late night and early morning. Days we went without meals and a proper bed. It all came down to this one perfect show.

When were back at 500 feet, Uncle Warren shot his fist into the air. Inching toward an outer strut, I leaned down and clipped the cable to the u-shaped metal skid below the lower wing. The mouthpiece slid easily into my mouth. I took a deep breath and waited for my body to go calm. Once I was ready, I threaded out the spool. The length of wire bit into my hand. With careful steps, I walked to the edge of the wing and started another count. Before I could get past two, the engine made an odd knocking noise that sounded like a pounding fist. A loud roar knocked me onto my back. The wings tilted left and right as Uncle Warren struggled for control. Grasping a landing wire, I spit out the mouthpiece and used all my strength to climb up the frame to the cockpit.

"What's happening?" I shouted above the grinding and moaning of the engine.

Uncle Warren shook his head frantically. "Don't know. Control stick will hardly move." He looked over the edge of the plane to the crowd below. "I'm taking her out as far to the east as I can." His face went blank. "You're going to have to jump."

"No. Take us down. There's miles of empty field. We can land."

He refused to look anywhere but straight ahead. "We won't make it that far. The only thing I can do is put her down where no one gets hurt. Make sure the straps on your parachute are tight before you jump"

"No, not unless you come, too."

He finally turned to look at me, and the pain in his eyes made all the blood in my body drain to my toes. The last time he'd looked that way was when he learned our entire family was gone.

"One of these days this was bound to happen. I only wish it wasn't here and now." He reached out and grabbed my hand from the back of his seat. "I love you, Grace. Since the day you showed up on my doorstep, all sunken eyes and skin and bones, I knew I'd protect you with everything I had. This is my last chance. Now please, use the damn parachute."

"No. Don't you do that," I shouted against the roar of the wind and sputtering engine. "Don't you dare say goodbye." Black exhaust filled the air, burning my nose and scalding the inside of my throat.

He looked at the instrument panel. "We're losing altitude. You need to go. Now."

"But . . ." A sob burst past my lips. I wanted to protest. Fight him. Tell him I was going down with him. But he'd never allow it, even if he had to climb out of the cockpit and shove me off the wing himself.

He pulled my hands off the back of the cockpit chair and gave me a gentle shove.

"You did my parents proud. You are an amazing pilot and"—I choked out the final word—"father. If anyone can set this Jenny down safely, it's you." Refusing to say goodbye, I reached for his hand. "I'll see you on the ground." A sad smile covered his lips and he let me go one finger at a time.

I wrenched down the straps of my parachute and moved to the edge of the wing. The engine continued to spew hot oil into the air and then, with a stiff sputter, it cut out completely. Uncle Warren tried to control the Jenny as we dropped quicker than a breath.

In the silence I took one last look at him, trying to commit to memory every line in his face. Remembering the moments of laughter, joy, and sorrow we shared. A last breath forced itself from my chest and I jumped.

Falling through the air was like a punch to the gut. All the wind rushed out of my lungs in one heavy gasp. The wind scratched at my clothes, hair, and face like it was trying to break my fall, but the weight of my body plummeting to the ground had too much speed. I was a stone dropped from a ten-story building with nothing but the hand of God and a thin parachute keeping me from hitting the earth.

I crashed through mist and clouds, my hand fumbling for the release cord. After a single hard yank, a loud BOOM shot through the air. My head snapped back while the parachute rocketed me away from the ground.

Sobs wracked my chest as I steered toward an open field with a small brown barn in the distance. A burst of wind shoved me east and I struggled to control my path. The ground became a muddy blur through my tears. The earth approached quicker than I anticipated. I didn't have time to get my feet under me. My body slammed into the hard-packed dirt, the left side taking most of the blow.

My head spun. I sat up and the ground shifted below me. Pain tore through my body and radiated down my arm. I struggled against the agony, determined to see Uncle Warren land. The Jenny disappeared behind a patch of trees at the edge of the field. I closed my eyes and prayed he'd keep the nose up and wings level when he touched down. The last thing I heard was a sharp crack before a wall of flames licked up into the bright morning sky.

24
Numb

Chicago, Illinois
September 13, 1922
1 day after the crash

The sound of Henry's voice filled my ears like a dream. His low whisper spoke a prayer I'd heard my mother recite when I was a child. My limbs felt lined with lead, as if a weight spanned the length of my body from my shoulders to my feet. Thick, heavy material scratched across my body. The acidic scent of disinfectant filled my nose.

No. I couldn't be back in the hospital. They'd sent me to live with Uncle Warren after telling me about my parents' death. Hour after hour I'd ridden on that train, frightened and alone.

"Grace, wake up." Henry's honey voice floated over me. It took every bit of strength I had to peel back my eyelids. When the bright light hit me, I double-blinked at my stark surroundings.

"Where am I?" I managed to choke out through a painful breath. The white walls and quiet murmurs gave me my answer, but I needed to be sure.

A warm hand slid over my forehead. "You're in the hospital, darlin'." A familiar southern-tinged voice filled the air. Daniel sat only inches away. His dark-copper hair was matted to his head like he hadn't seen a wash basin in days. Nathan sat beside him twisting something in his hands.

I took another painful swallow. My throat burned like it'd been pierced with a dozen shards of glass. "Are those my new goggles?"

Nathan tried to hide them behind his back.

"Show her," Daniel instructed.

He opened his hands. The left lens was cracked down the middle and the right strap was snapped in two.

They looked exactly like how I felt.

"How did I get here?" A panicked buzz rushed through me.

Black exhaust.

Spurting oil.

Bright red flames flickering against a blue sky.

"Where's my uncle? Is he . . ." The question faded on my lips. I wasn't sure I wanted to know the answer.

The scraping of chair legs moved through the room. Nathan, Daniel, and Henry leaned over my bedside. Each of their faces was as pale as the sheets covering my body. Their clothes were rumpled like they hadn't slept in years.

"He's alive," Nathan said, his voice trembling. "It was close, but he managed to get the second parachute on after he guided the plane toward an open field near the far edge of the lake."

The buzz in my head dulled to a low hum.

He was alive.

My family was still together.

"They're keeping him over in the next ward," Daniel said. "When he hit the ground, he got a bad bump on the head and his right leg is broken."

A slicing pain raced down the left side of my body when I tried to sit up. Henry reached forward to halt my movement. "Stay still. When you landed, your left side took the brunt of the collision. Both your collarbone and arm are broken."

My brain tried to comb through the cobwebs in my head. The routine had been perfect. The barrel rolls and inverted loops brought the crowd to their feet.

"Is the plane a loss?" The three of them swapped a broken look. This couldn't be happening. We'd needed this shot at a future. "Tell me the truth."

Nathan chewed on his lip. A flicker of darkness swept over his face as he attempted a weak smile. "Don't worry about it. Concentrate on getting better. The doc says you and your uncle can be outta here in a few days if you follow orders."

My hands wound into the bedsheets. "Tell me, Nathan."

His steely demeanor dissolved. The edges of his eyes went watery. "The plane went in nose-down. A few parts may be salvageable, but that's all."

The image of the shattered plane forced my eyes closed. "Who won the contract?" I managed to grind out through my teeth.

A quiet beat filled the room. The tick of the clock on the wall measured the unbearable silence.

"The Skyhawks took the prize," Henry said in a low, steady voice, as if somehow he could soften the blow.

Visions of Rowland and his team waving their arms in victory sent a nauseous twist through my stomach. I swallowed back the acid climbing up my throat. Memories of Rowland's attempt at an apology and the way he smirked and tipped his hat at me in the hangar yesterday shot an icy shock through my leaded bones.

"Grace," Nathan patted my hand. The creases around his eyes and mouth aged him at least ten years. "Can you tell us what happened? Did Warren lose control?"

Despite Henry's warning, and the agonizing pain, I pushed myself to a seated position. My head throbbed in time with my broken heart. "Everything was smooth at the beginning. Routine was going fine until I went to the edge of the plane to clip on my mouthpiece for the Showstopper.

"That trick. I knew it," Nathan growled.

"Quiet," Daniel said. "Let her finish."

"The Jenny." I hesitated, not wanting to relive the moment, but knew they had to hear every detail. "It started to shake and we lost altitude." I closed my eyes again, still hearing the grinding noise of the engine.

"Go on," Nathan urged.

I dragged open my lids and focused on Henry's steady green eyes. "There was a loud roar and the heat of spraying oil filled the air and singed my skin. I didn't want to jump without him, but Uncle Warren swore he could get the plane down in one piece." Tears pricked the corners of my eyes. I'd never forget his loving words and how he held my hand in those final moments. "He did everything he could, I swear."

Nathan jumped to his feet and began to pace. Daniel scooted in closer to the bed. He pulled a handkerchief from his pocket and dabbed at my eyes. "Sorenson and his men are going over every inch of the plane right now. They'll figure it out."

Nathan's boots hammered against the sterile white tile. The once-sagging line of his shoulders snapped into a tight line. "None of this makes sense. We've been careful with the Jennys. Parking them in the hangar at night. Keeping up maintenance. Buying new parts when needed. Unless . . ." His fingers curled into fists at his sides.

"Unless what?" Daniel prodded.

Nathan took two steps toward Henry. "Did you check the oil line in Warren's plane before we took off?"

An orderly in a stiff, white uniform stopped in the center of the narrow ward and stared in our direction. "Nathan, keep your voice down," Daniel whispered. "We don't need to cause a scene."

Even though pain lanced through me like a steel blade, I managed to sit up higher in the bed. "You can't believe Henry had anything to do with the crash. You've watched how he's cared for the planes. Over these last months, he's spent more time in the hangar than all of us combined. Nathan, you said it yourself. The planes have never flown better."

"Grace," Henry interrupted. "I can handle this." He stood and faced Nathan. "It was difficult with us being late, but I did my best to perform a pre-flight check. The only time I was away from the plane was when I spoke to Grace before takeoff."

"That doesn't mean a thing. No one checks your work anymore because you've lulled us all into believing you're this great mechanic. It would have been easy to tamper with the line before you spoke to Grace."

"Enough, Nathan." The words scratched against my throat. "You have no proof Henry did anything wrong."

He crossed his arms over his chest in a huff. "Think about it, Grace. Since the beginning, there's been something off about him. He shows up out of nowhere. Insists to Warren he's out of work and needs a job, yet weeks later he's got enough dough for fancy new tools." His mouth thinned into a tight line. "And didn't you say Rowland always knew where we performed? Knew how your family died? How would he know that information unless someone close to you told him? They're in cahoots. I'm sure of it."

I refused to believe it. From the beginning, Henry had promised he'd take care of the planes—and us. I tried to push Nathan's evidence out of my head, but I kept thinking about Rowland's revelation in the hangar.

"You want to point the finger at someone, but Henry wouldn't risk our lives for money." I said the words, trying to convince myself it was the truth. He wasn't like Martin and those other mechanics. But if he lied about how he'd found out about the job, what kept him from being dishonest about everything else?

"Really? How many times has he told us about his dream of owning a garage? You think he's going to earn that kind of money by working with us?" Nathan shook his head. "Rowland's been after you from the beginning. He's not the kind of fella who takes losing well. When we got to Chicago and he knew he couldn't woo you anymore, he decided to sabotage us . . . and he used Henry to do it." He stepped closer to Henry. "This was payback. Pure and simple."

Henry stood still. His eyes focused on the floor. Why didn't he defend himself?

"Grace, he forgot to tell us about the telegram, too," Daniel added hesitantly. "The only one who would benefit from us being out of the contest is Rowland. And the only one who touched Warren's plane was Henry."

The edges of my vision blurred, but I refused to give in to the pain until this was settled. "Henry, please tell me you didn't have anything to do with this."

He shifted on his feet and refused to meet my gaze. The room went colder. My body shivered under the paper-thin sheets.

In the silence, Nathan snickered. "Not a word outta him. Who are you going to believe, Grace?" He slapped a hand over Daniel's wide shoulder. "Your two closest friends? Or a guy you hardly know who ain't quite right in the head?"

Henry's head snapped up, his eyes darkened with a fury I hadn't seen since he punched Joe Prescott. "You've never liked me, Nathan, and now you're using any excuse to taint Grace's mind. I haven't said a word because Grace knows I'd never do this, and it's cruel to make her choose between us."

A nurse two beds away poked her head out of the privacy curtain and shushed us.

"I've explained about the tools and the telegram," Henry said, trying to keep his tone muted. "Rowland is a snake. I'd rather have my tongue cut out than spill a word to him. I believe in this team and would never hurt any of you." He turned to me, his deep-green gaze willing me to believe him.

"No," Nathan barked. "You're a lying cad who almost killed my team."

They stood frozen in place, swapping murderous stares. I wanted to go back in time. Check the plane. Prove Henry had nothing to do with the crash. But I had to face reality. The Jenny was a total loss. We'd never get to Hollywood. The thought settled over me like a heavy, wet sheet. How had we gotten here? We'd been so close to our dream, but now everything was in pieces. I tried not to let Nathan's and Daniel's accusations fill my head, but I kept coming back to Rowland's words that day in Springfield. His warning to be cautious about who I trusted.

"Henry, I think it's best if you leave," Daniel said.

"Not unless Grace asks me to." He moved to the bed and reached for my fingers.

My heart screamed to take his hand. To trust him. But I slid my fingers under the sheets. Nathan and Daniel were my teammates. My family. For years they'd looked out for me. Protected me from overzealous fans. Shielded me from prying eyes and the journalists' cameras. Together we'd built The Soaring Eagles from nothing into a recognized force in barnstorming, and now more than ever we had to stick together.

"Answer one question for me," I said. "How did you find out about the job with our team?"

The blood drained from Henry's once-heated cheeks. His body shifted to the right, favoring his leg, while he wound his cap between his fingers.

"Rowland told me outside the diner that day I met you," he breathed out.

"I knew it," Nathan hissed.

Henry ignored Nathan even as he hovered close enough to throw a punch. "Rowland told me about the job and offered me money to coerce you into joining The Skyhawks." He clutched his hat over his heart as if making a vow. "I told him I wanted nothing to do with his schemes and left. But I needed the job, so I showed up at the hangar. I couldn't tell you about the conversation because you would have never let Warren hire me. You have to believe me."

"No," Daniel growled at him.

"I wanted to tell you that night in Chicago, but I was too afraid of losing you."

He moved in and tried to touch me again but I inched farther back on the bed. In the still of the night, we'd shared the raw pieces of our lives. He'd whispered how he needed me. How I'd changed his life. Wrapped in his arms, I'd never felt more loved. It was hard to reconcile his promises with the fact that even though we'd shared our deepest secrets he remained quiet about Rowland.

"I don't know what to think any more. Right now, I need you to leave." Each word left my lips with an ache I was sure would never fade.

"Gracie, I care about you deeply. The last thing I want is to cause you more pain. I'll go," he locked eyes with Nathan, "but this isn't over."

Henry popped his cap onto his head and hobbled through the door without another word.

My bones cried out in anguish as I rolled to my side so the boys wouldn't see my tears. I'd trusted Henry's every promise, but now our moments in the hangar, on the train, in the hotel, all felt like one enormous lie.

Daniel and Nathan tried to whisper words of comfort but I refused to listen. The plane, our future, it was all gone. I couldn't help but wonder if the day I'd allowed Henry Patton into our lives was the moment I'd let it all slip away.

25
The Final Thread

Lincoln, Nebraska
September 30, 1922
18 days after the crash

Shadows crawled along the walls of the hangar as the first rays of morning light shot across the concrete floor. Every day since we returned from Chicago I sat in Uncle Warren's office trying to piece together a plan to keep The Soaring Eagles together. The doctors said Uncle Warren and I could go back to work in two weeks. Once we were ready, we could use Nathan's plane to perform again. We'd have to find another way to bring in additional income, but we could get back in the air if we tried.

When we stepped off the train, the thought of coming back here, seeing all the things Henry left behind, was like stabbing myself with a knife. Over time that pain turned into a dull, pulsing ache.

The day after the blow-up at the hospital, Daniel went in search of Henry, admitting he still couldn't believe he'd betray us. That's what I adored about Daniel. No matter the mountain of proof, he still believed in the goodness of people.

He wasn't truly convinced of Henry's guilt until he learned from a bellboy at the hotel that after Henry packed his bags, Rowland's car appeared to take him away.

We'd gone back and forth over the last week trying to figure out if we had enough evidence against them to go to the police. But after Sorenson provided a report that showed there was indeed an oil line break, but no definite proof of tampering, we had to let it go.

Out in the hangar Nathan and Daniel tried to stay quiet, but with only one plane sound bounced around the place like a penny in a tin cup.

"We need to give her more time, Nathan," Daniel said in an insistent voice.

I moved to the doorway and pressed against the threshold to listen.

"There's not a lot of money, and with only one plane I'm not sure how we'll get from place to place." Nathan let out a low, long breath. "You read that telegram from Sorenson. If the government is going to clear us for flight, we need over a hundred dollars to make all the repairs. It's time we thought about our future, Daniel. We've put it off for too long."

"What about Grace? Her future?" Daniel's deep voice cracked.

"She'll land on her feet. She always does."

"And what about Warren?" Daniel asked.

"He's been hinting at wanting to retire. This would be the perfect time."

"It's not right. There's got to be another way." Daniel said.

"Wake up, Daniel. This is our life now, and we gotta think about our next plan."

The sound of a wrench hitting the ground filled the air before the thud of Nathan's footsteps disappeared out the exit.

The agony of the crash was torturous, but it was nothing compared to listening to their hushed whispers. There had never been a doubt in my mind that The Soaring Eagles would continue, but the boys were obviously thinking beyond barnstorming. I had to do something to change their minds. It was true we only had one plane, but we could make it work. All we needed was a hundred dollars and a chance to prove ourselves again.

———

Ethel settled the strings of the gingham apron in her hands before tying them into a knot at my back. I shifted myself in front of the small bathroom mirror and patted down the starched, white collar pressing at my neck.

"The accident was just a few weeks ago. You're not supposed to be out of that sling. I can't believe you're doing this." Ethel huffed. "Come with Mary and me to California. We can pool our money and get a little place."

Mary appeared in the back doorway of the diner, an old, leather suitcase clutched in her hand. The line of her tiny shoulders now had a confident flair I loved.

"She's right. There's nothing left for you here. Well, except . . ." She shook her head and dropped her suitcase next to Ethel's.

When I told them about Henry, how he'd used them for one of his lies, Ethel wanted to gather a mob complete with flaming torches and pitchforks. Mary, always the voice of reason, tried to convince me he actually cared. Although, with her new spark, she admitted she wouldn't mind giving him one good slap across the kisser.

Their hearts were in the right place, but it was hard to ignore that everything Henry and I had shared started with a lie. If he hadn't been honest from the beginning, it left me to question every other word, every other promise he'd vowed to me.

I reached to straighten out the grosgrain ribbon on Ethel's green cloche. "You and Mary have been better to me than I could have ever asked, but I can't go. I need to stay and earn enough money to get Nathan's Jenny back in the air."

Ethel bit her lip and readjusted her hat so it sat at her ears. The edges of her blonde hair swooped up around the brim in perfect curlicues. "With your talent and notoriety, you could get a job in a snap in Los Angeles. Won't you change your mind?"

Even though they'd come to Lincoln looking for a better life, the girls had talked about Hollywood since the day I'd met them. It was their dream to be in pictures. To live that wild and fantastic life. After the pinches and gropes they'd endured at the diner, they deserved a fresh start. Hollywood had been a means to an end for me, a way to keep my family together. Now it was only a reminder of what I'd lost.

I forced a smile to my face. "I'll miss you girls. Make sure you send me a postcard of the Pacific Ocean."

The corners of Mary's eyes brimmed with tears. She launched herself into my arms and I stumbled back under the weight of her hug. The purple silk flower pinned to her suit crushed against my apron. "Promise if things don't get better, you'll come find us."

I returned her fierce embrace, the ache in my arm reminding me I wasn't totally healed.

"Mary's right. If you change your mind, you have a place with us. Even thousands of miles away, we're still your family."

Ethel's voice hitched as she nudged Mary out of the way to give me her own embrace. "I've been wrong all these years," she whispered. "You've never needed a man to secure your future. For so long I've seen you as this young, naïve girl; but you've grown beyond that, Grace. You are a brilliant woman with a boundless heart. There's no man in this world who can give you what you've already given yourself—freedom to live your life the way you choose."

A sob burst from my lips as I refused to let Ethel go. "A part of what you told me was true. It can't hurt to have love in my life. I just trusted my heart to the wrong man."

"Oh, Grace," she sighed.

"I'll be all right," I reassured her. "Have fun and stay safe. Take care of Mary."

A small hiccup escaped Ethel's lips. "After what happened with Norman, I think Mary can take care of herself now."

"How about you watch out for each other, then?" I reached for Mary and squeezed her gloved hand, her tiny fingers resting against my palm. "Make sure to get a good seat on the train. Take it all in so you can tell me about it in the postcard."

They both nodded, tears staining their rouged cheeks. With

suitcases clutched in their hands, they walked through the front of the diner and out the exit. The bell made a single, dull clank against the door. A crushing sadness filled my chest. I didn't want to admit it, but letting them leave was the final thread of my life unraveling.

26
In the Direction of a Bad Storm

Lincoln, Nebraska
October 7, 1922
25 days after the crash

The October sky remained dark over Lincoln, perfectly mirroring my mood. Black clouds formed into thick blankets of fog and forced cars to use their headlights even during the day. This morning the diner was filled with businessmen shouting out their orders in rough voices. Although I'd watched Mary and Ethel do this job for years, I hadn't realized how brutal it could be. It wasn't just the leers and gropes, but the back-aching task of serving heavy plates and clearing tables covered in dirty cutlery and half-drained coffee cups. Barnstorming was a walk in the park compared to this job.

I pushed away every single ache and pain. The money from my tips was piling up, and soon we'd have the last forty dollars we needed to get the Jenny back in the air. Nathan and Daniel had argued at every point over my plan, but promised to give me at least a full month to prove I could earn the money. They'd even agreed to take on odd jobs to add to our total.

I'd barely delivered my first order of the day when Walter, the new manager who I'd nicknamed Little Napoleon, bellowed at me from the back of the kitchen. He was a squat, roly-poly type who spent way too much time gazing at women's backsides and waxing his handlebar mustache. Next to him, Archie looked like a saint.

"Not sure what kinda nonsense that Archie tolerated, but I have strict rules about gents visiting waitresses during their shift." With a stubby finger, he pointed to the back of the restaurant where I spotted Daniel's copper hair. "He needs to order or get packing."

"Yes, sir." I scurried around the other waitresses until I reached the booth.

"Daniel?" He looked up and I gasped. His nose was shifted slightly to the left. A thin, one-inch gash sliced into the space above his right eye. Drops of blood colored his linen shirt and stained the edge of one of his brown leather braces. I didn't give a second thought to Little Napoleon, but slid across the booth. "What happened to you?"

He fiddled with his brown newsboy cap, turning it over and over on the white tabletop. "Doesn't matter. You need to come with me right now."

"I'm working, I can't leave."

His lips tightened and he flinched at the slight movement. "Nathan's in trouble."

"Why? What's going on?"

"He's in jail. There's no time to explain. Please, go grab your things."

Daniel's serious gaze said he wasn't moving without me. I rushed behind the counter and grabbed my pocketbook and coat. Clutching my sides, I complained of a stomachache. Little Napoleon gave me a sour look and waved at the door. "Get out. Don't need you getting the customers sick."

Daniel met me at the door and we raced out onto the sidewalk. I stayed on his heels, begging for more details. He wouldn't answer but his pained smile warned we were headed in the direction of a bad storm.

⁓

A group of men in heavy overcoats crowded the police station's small lobby. Their heads were bent low as they tried to shield their faces with their hats. Journalists pushed in from all sides. The loud boom of a photographer's flash shook the walls as he tried to capture the men's picture for the afternoon edition of the *Lincoln Star*.

"What's happening?" I asked.

"Bootleggers," Daniel replied. "Feds had a big raid last night, and the men don't want to show their mugs to the camera."

We walked past the suspects to a wide oak desk in the center of the room. A policeman with a pencil clenched between his teeth tapped at a typewriter. *Click. Click. Click.* He slowly jabbed at the keys, doing his best to ignore us.

We waited for another minute. The bootleggers pleaded their innocence, and the policemen's orders to "shut their traps" made the walls close in. Smoke filled the room in a suffocating, gray fog.

Losing his patience, Daniel tapped his thick hand on top of the desk. "Sir, could we trouble you for a minute?"

"Hold on," the officer mumbled. "Gotta finish this report." He continued to stab at the typewriter one finger at a time. When some minutes had passed, I stood on my tiptoes and looked at the scrawl on a nearby blotter, eyeing the last signature.

"Excuse me, Officer Wilcox." He started when I said his name. "We're looking for a friend of ours. He was brought in last night."

He swiveled in his battered, wooden chair and yanked the pencil from his mouth. "Name?"

"Nathan Whitaker," Daniel and I said at the same time.

The officer ran his fingers down the lines in the enormous book until he located him. "He's being questioned by one of our sergeants. Wait here."

He disappeared through an opaque door behind the desk. We waited for what felt like an eternity. One-by-one the bootleggers turned to each other, offering a light for their cigarettes.

Officer Wilcox finally reappeared. He pulled the collar back on his stiff, blue uniform, the rows of brass buttons glimmering in the light. "You wouldn't by any chance be Grace Lafferty?"

"Yes. Why?" I stuttered.

He shoved back the brim of his police cap and looked me over as if I suddenly warranted attention. "Follow me through the door, please."

"This is my friend, Daniel. He'll need to come, too," I insisted.

"Fine." He ushered us through the door and into an open room littered with a dozen desks. One wall was covered in a bank of call boxes. The shrill ring of several telephones filled the air. Two men sat in front of the boxes, their heads low as they jotted down messages. Other officers were scattered across the space, either bent over paperwork or tapping at typewriters.

Officer Wilcox pointed a finger toward a man at the back of the room. "Sergeant Mallory is waiting on you." He turned on his heel and disappeared back through the smoked-glass door.

Daniel and I walked side by side until we discovered Nathan and Henry on a wooden bench. They sat as far from each other as possible, each pretending the other wasn't there.

"Why is he here?" I focused my rage on Nathan, doing my best to ignore Henry's stare. Nathan's blue shirt had a rip in the collar and a small gash tore through his left eyebrow.

"Gracie, I can explain," Henry said quickly. His brown vest had a hole in the shoulder seam and his jaw was a deep purple. Did he think he could give me that stunning, intense look, the one that made my knees wobble, and suddenly I'd forgive him?

"Nathan, tell me why you're here or I'm leaving."

Nathan shoved his hands deep into his pockets but refused to say another word.

I turned to Daniel. "Please tell me what's going on here?"

"Henry came to me a week ago. He's been working over at McEntire's garage."

"It's a good job, Gracie." Henry interrupted.

I ignored his pleading gaze. "Daniel, finish the story, please."

"Henry said he overheard a customer talking about a man he'd met in a club who bragged about sabotaging a plane."

"I cornered the fella and made him tell me everything about the man," Henry interrupted again. "He sounded exactly like that goon who works for Rowland."

I continued to focus on Daniel. "Go on." Henry sank back onto the bench while Nathan curled into himself like he wanted to disappear from my brutal stare.

"Nathan swore it was another one of Henry's lies, but I dragged him to the club anyway. I had to know the truth." Daniel stared Nathan down like he wanted him to jump in, but Nathan stayed quiet. "Henry met us at the place. Sure enough, Louis was at the bar flapping his gums about how he knew how our plane went down." The lines around his eyes went tight. "That no-good louse laughed about it. Before I could confront him, Henry got to him first. That's why we look a mess. We broke a few glasses and smashed a window." His face flared red in embarrassment. "The coppers showed up a tick later. I managed to get away. Henry and Nathan weren't so lucky."

"Miss Lafferty?" A tall, broad-shouldered policeman with flecks of white in his shiny black hair waved me toward a desk.

I shot a dark look at the boys before moving toward him. A man was seated next to the desk. Even though blood covered his top lip and the space below his right eye, I'd know Louis anywhere. A navy suit jacket hung on the back of his chair. A matching fedora was crumpled in his lap underneath a set of raw knuckles. He shifted in the seat and hiccupped loudly. The pungent smell of booze and cigarette smoke wafted off his clothes and skin.

"Louis!" A sharp voice cut through the room.

Rowland tore in our direction with Officer Wilcox on his heels. When the officer caught Rowland's arm, the two struggled. Rowland's black fedora flew from his head and landed at my feet.

Two other officers raced to Officer Wilcox's side to help detain Rowland.

"Get your bloody mitts off me," Rowland ordered.

"No, sir. You can't push your way past the desk without permission," Officer Wilcox barked.

Sergeant Mallory looked up at the scene. "Wilcox, what's going on? Who is this man?"

Officer Wilcox continued to wrestle with Rowland. "This man says the suspect works for him."

"Let him go." Mallory waved Rowland forward. "Maybe with him here we can get this straightened out."

Rowland shrugged out of the officers' grasp and swiped a hand down to the floor to retrieve his hat. "You need to teach your men some manners." He popped his hat on his head but took a step back, his face pale, when he noticed me.

"Listen, pal," Mallory pointed a finger in Rowland's direction. "My patience is wearing thin this morning. Shut yer trap or you're going into lock-up with him." He nodded to Louis, who was now snoring louder than a freight train.

"Hey!" Sergeant Mallory kicked the legs of the chair. "Wake up. I've got some questions for you."

Louis's head lolled about like it was on a pulley, first dropping down and then snapping back. Mallory gave the chair another swift kick. Louis startled and opened his eyes wide. "What? Whass goin' on here?" His words slurred as they tumbled out of his mouth.

"Tell me what happened between you and those men at the club last evening." Louis swiveled his head to look at Nathan and Henry.

"I was alone, minding my own beeswax, when those two, plus him," he pointed a shaky finger at Daniel, "jumped me."

"Why would they attack you?" Rowland asked.

"Hey! I'll ask the questions here," Sergeant Mallory snapped.

Louis turned in his chair to face Rowland. "Sir, I can explain." He tried to get to his feet, wobbled a bit, and sank back down.

"Answer the question," Mallory demanded.

Louis took a breath and hitched a thumb at me. "We fought because of that broad."

Daniel clenched his fists like he wanted to knock Louis out. I wound an arm around his. I'd heard worse.

"What does Miss Lafferty have to do with the fight?" Mallory asked.

"Those men overheard a private conversation."

"What was the conversation about?" Mallory prodded.

Louis's eyes rolled back in his head like he was ready to pass out again. Mallory slammed a hand down on the desk. Louis's head reared up and he rubbed his eyes as if trying to remember exactly where he was.

"Since I followed Mr. Rowland to this foul-smelling town, he's talked non-stop about how we have to recruit her to his team. How he'll never be a success until she's a Skyhawk." He hiccupped again and swiped a bit of drool from the corner of his mouth.

I wanted to gag but inched closer, desperate to hear what he had to say.

"The only way that was gonna happen was from the inside. I got an idea and approached that man." He snapped his head toward the bench where Henry sat. "I convinced him that if he could get her to join the team, we'd be rewarded."

Fury burned in my chest as Louis continued to reveal all of Henry's secrets.

Mallory's eyes narrowed. "What kind of reward are we talking about?"

Louis scratched a hand through his oily, black hair. "Rowland said he'd give five hundred dollars to any fella who could lure her in. That gent told me he needed the money for some sorta big plan, so we agreed to partner up and split the dough. That kind a' scratch means a lot to a man like me who's been penniless his whole life."

He faced my direction and a sick smile crossed his lips. "You never knew we were spoiling your plans. Causing all sorts of trouble."

Nausea rolled through me as I stared at Henry.

"It was your pal's idea to contact that government goon to put on the heat," Louis went on. "Over the last few months, he's fed me details on where the team was performing. Even shared inside information that made her vulnerable. I'd mention it all to Mr. Rowland as barnstorming gossip." Louis smacked his lips together in pleasure. "He told me about that trick with her dangling by her teeth. We agreed she couldn't perform in Chicago and win that contest, so he tampered with the oil line. I didn't know the tinkering would cause the plane to crash."

An audible gasp left Rowland's mouth. Either he had no idea what Louis and Henry were up to or he was a better actor than Douglas Fairbanks.

Louis shrugged like it was all meaningless. He and Henry would pay for everything they'd taken from me, and being thrown in a jail cell wasn't enough. Before Louis could say another word, I was on him. With a closed fist, I pounded on his thick chest and landed a solid slap across his stubbled cheek.

"Do you know what you've done?" I screamed. "You've taken everything from me!" I raised my hand to give him another good smack when Daniel pulled me off.

"You stupid cow!" Louis bolted up. "It's your own fault for trusting one of your own team. All those years of working with you didn't matter to him. He only cared about getting enough dough to quit barnstorming."

Years of working together. Quit barnstorming.

A low buzzing started in my head. The sound of my racing heart blocked out every other sound in the room. I couldn't hear the shrill ring of the telephones, or loud chatter from the nearby desks, only the hollow sound of my life shattering before my eyes. All this time Louis hadn't been nodding at Henry . . . but at Nathan.

"No. No. It can't be true." All the wind *whooshed* out of me. My legs gave way and Daniel caught me before I hit the floor.

"It was you?" Henry's hand crashed against the side of Nathan's mouth. He went in for another punch but Sergeant Mallory pulled him away.

A slow trickle of blood raced down the corner of Nathan's mouth. "It was never supposed to happen like this, Grace. I never meant for anyone to get hurt. The oil line was supposed to go quickly. Warren was supposed to see it and bring you right down."

Sergeant Mallory nodded to Daniel, who moved to take Henry's arm and pull him away. "Tell us the whole story and we might see to it you don't spend the rest of your life in jail for attempted murder."

Nathan dropped his head into his hands. "First off, Daniel knew nothing about my plan. It was all me and Louis."

Daniel wrestled an agitated Henry onto the seat beside me. I tried to get Henry to look at me but his eyes faced forward, like the sight of me was too painful.

"Why would you do this to us?" Daniel stalked toward Nathan. "Since we've come back from the war, Grace and Warren have become our family. They trusted you. *I* trusted you." His words broke off and his shoulders crumpled. "I knew you wanted to leave barnstorming, but at the cost of Grace and Warren's lives?"

Daniel's wide shoulders shook. "Nathan, you more than anyone understand what I went through in France. How many friends I watched die. How could you ever think that betraying Grace, tampering with the plane, would be acceptable?"

Nathan opened and closed his mouth several times before words finally spilled out. "Since we watched the Conroys go down in Idaho, I can't stop thinking about their broken bodies. How the stench of death coated the air. Every night since, I wake up in a cold sweat, convinced we're next. I experienced enough of that terror during the war, Daniel, and I can't do it anymore. All I want is to get away from barnstorming. We could have our own postal delivery service, and the only way we can do that is with money. Rowland's money."

Daniel sank onto the bench next to him. "And what about Grace and Warren? You've taken everything from them."

"When I first met with Louis it seemed simple. I went to confront him about beating up Henry, and he mentioned watching me fly. How I hesitated before I got into the cockpit before every show. He could see I'd lost my interest in barnstorming and offered me a way out. He said all I had to do was convince Grace to work with Rowland, and I'd have the money I needed to be free."

Nathan's head snapped up, his gaze pinned on me. "I thought for sure when Sorenson threatened the team in Arkansas, you'd wilt. On the runway before the fair, I told you about my experience in the war, tried to convince you to back down, but you were determined to make The Soaring Eagles a success. In Chicago, I thought if I could only convince you how dangerous that Showstopper stunt could be you'd give up." His red-rimmed eyes flickered with pain. "I underestimated you, Grace. You may be grounded for a while, but with your drive, sooner or later you'll be back in the sky. Rowland was right about one thing. You are a star."

I would never be able to forgive him. No matter how much regret shined in his eyes. He'd used my dedication to the team, our family, to force me to make a terrible choice. Deep down he knew how I felt about Henry, but he didn't care. He needed to throw off suspicion and Henry was the perfect patsy.

I took two steps toward him, willing my voice to stay calm. "You risked our lives because you were too much of a coward to speak up and tell us what you needed. I'll never get over the way you've treated Henry. How you've worked with Louis for months and lied straight to our faces. You deserve to rot in a cell."

Tears burned the corner of my eyes but I refused to let them fall. "Sergeant Mallory, do you have everything you need to keep the two of them in jail?"

He gave a solid nod. "With that confession, and a few eyewitnesses from the bar, the case is solid."

"Thank you," I said.

"Grace. Please forgive me," Nathan pleaded.

His words stabbed through me, but I turned to Henry. "I'll never be able to apologize enough for what I said in the hospital."

"You should have trusted me." The acid in his voice shook my soul. "I promised you that day in Springfield I'd keep you and the planes safe."

"You're right. After all the time we spent together, I should have believed you'd never do anything to hurt me, but I was scared; and he,"—my lips trembled—"he was my family."

Henry dropped his elbows on top of his knees and shook his head. "It's in the past. We both should move on."

"Please, can't we try to work this out? I need you, Henry. The team needs you," I begged.

His beautiful green eyes flickered with conflict, pain, and regret. "I can't be with someone who won't take me at my word, who turns on me at the first sign of trouble."

He pushed himself up from the bench. His body pitched right and I stopped myself from reaching out to help him. He'd already proven he was capable of standing solidly on his feet. "Goodbye, Grace. I hope all your dandelion wishes come true."

He popped his fedora on his head and walked toward Daniel. They swapped a few words before Henry disappeared through the door.

Every inch of me ached. His parting words thrummed in my head. I didn't expect his response. He had every right to be upset, but I'd thought he'd be glad to have the air cleared. For me to know he was innocent. What I hadn't realized was how badly my betrayal had cut him to the core. Not trusting him had gotten me exactly what I deserved: a life without him.

Daniel guided me to the exit. We passed Rowland, who didn't utter a word. His head stayed low, as it should have been. Whether he wanted to admit it or not, he'd set all of this in motion by offering that money like a bounty on my head. He may have not given a direct order to cut our oil line, but to me he was as responsible for the crash as Louis and Nathan were.

Once we were outside, the fall air filled my lungs and cleared my head.

"Ready to head home?" Daniel asked. "It's been a rough day and it's hardly ten o'clock."

"No, I'm going to the hangar to check on things."

"Are you sure?"

"Yes. It's where I need to be right now."

"Can I walk you there?"

"No. Thank you. I need to be alone."

He took several steps forward and then stopped in his tracks. Spinning around, he tore his cap off his head, the edges of his wide shoulders trembling. For the first time since I'd known him, big, invincible Daniel looked small to me.

"He was my best friend and I had no idea what he was doing with Louis," he gasped. "I've known Nathan for years and he never let on he was troubled. Sure, we talked about what we'd do if we couldn't barnstorm anymore, but I never imagined he'd be that cruel or do something so dangerous." He took a deep gulp and swiped at his eyes. "I failed him."

I reached for his hand, my fingers dwarfed in his large palm. "Please, don't blame yourself. This life we've chosen is full of risk. Every day we go up into those clouds knowing there's a chance we may not come down alive. Some of us can put that fear aside, but Nathan, he couldn't."

"Maybe it's best if I think about another line of work. Without Nathan . . ." His voice broke.

I pulled him into a hug, his tree-trunk arms folding in around me. "Give me time to think. I'll sort out what we'll do next," I begged.

His body still shook, but he whispered, "Okay, darlin'." Without saying another word, he shuffled down the sidewalk.

There should have been solace in knowing the people responsible for our crash were behind bars, but the sight of Daniel's face, the defeat in his eyes, ripped a hole in my heart that not even time would heal. The reality of the moment hit me as if I'd slammed into the wing during a rough bit of turbulence. I'd not only lost a good friend in Nathan, but Henry—a man who I'd come to love—was gone, too.

27
In Charge of This Show

Lincoln, Nebraska
October 12, 1922
30 days after the crash

A warm northeast wind blew through the open hangar door while I worked. My arm protested as I cranked the cotter pin off the hubcap on the left wheel of Nathan's plane. It'd been painful at first to even look at it, but as Daniel reminded me, giving us the plane was the least Nathan could do after all the trouble and pain he'd caused.

It took a bit of work, but after an hour the wheels were off the Jenny. In his telegram, Mr. Sorenson said we had to replace all the landing gear, including the hubcaps and tires, if we wanted the plane in the air again.

I went through the entire inspection checklist. Examined the tension on every landing and guide wire. Inched across both wings, looking for holes and microscopic tears in the cotton fabric. Today, before working on the tires, I slid under the fuselage to ensure it was in good shape. An ache sliced through my chest as Henry's voice rang in my head, urging me to make sure all the nuts and bolts were secure but not too tight.

As I examined the lower skid, the hangar filled with the clatter of footsteps.

"Grace, you here?" Uncle Warren called.

"Maybe she's in the office," Daniel said, his heavy footsteps thundering across the hangar floor.

"I'm right here." I slid out from under the Jenny. Daniel and my uncle hovered near the wing, and Rowland and Mr. Knickerbocker stood a few feet from the hangar door.

"Ah, there she is," Mr. Knickerbocker tittered.

"What's going on, and why is he here?" I sneered at Rowland.

"Grace, I don't want him here either," Uncle Warren grumbled. "Especially after what happened with Nathan. But Mr. Knickerbocker has a proposition I want you to hear."

After I'd told him about Nathan's betrayal, Uncle Warren retreated to his room at the farmhouse for two full days. It was only in the last day or so that he could say Nathan's name without cursing under his breath.

"Fine, but this better not take long. I have work to do on our *only* plane." I shot an ugly glare at Rowland, who shifted uncomfortably in his fancy shoes.

Mr. Knickerbocker approached and offered a hand to help me up. I winced as a dull ache pulsed in my still-sore collarbone. Knickerbocker's happy smile plunged into a frown.

"Are you all right?"

"Yes, I'm fine," I said shrugging off the pain. "Please tell me why you've come all the way from California."

He let go of my hand and shifted back to look at Nathan's Jenny. With measured steps, he circled the plane, eyeing the oil-stained tarp covered with tools and hubcaps. "Over the last few days I've received several urgent messages from Rowland insisting I return to Lincoln. Apparently, he was anxious to speak about you."

"Me? Why?"

He and Rowland exchanged a quick look. Knickerbocker nodded as if giving him permission to speak. The act surprised me—but I was glad to see Knickerbocker was in charge of this show.

"Miss Lafferty," Rowland started. He scratched a hand behind his neck, his arrogant demeanor dissolving before my eyes. "My behavior regarding you has been unacceptable. I should have never encouraged that flyover or offered money as a way to draw you onto my team." His shoulders drooped and he shook his head. "All those things I told you in Chicago were true. I came to America to run an honest business, planning to stay on the straight and narrow, but I allowed ambition to get the better of me. Inevitably, I turned into everything my father is and I swore I'd never be."

He toed at an oil stain with his expensive wingtips, unable to look me in the eye. "This horrible incident with Nathan and Louis has shown me I've made some bloody awful choices and I want to make up for my indiscretions."

Rowland could deliver all the apologies he wanted, but it didn't change my life. He'd taken too many precious things from me. While he could continue with his team, start their new Hollywood contract in January, The Soaring Eagles were still scraping by—saving every nickel to get our only plane back in the air.

"What does this have to do with a proposition?" I turned to Mr. Knickerbocker, demanding an explanation.

"Rowland rescinded The Skyhawks' rights to the Hollywood contract. That means I need a new team to start next year."

"A new team? To work in Hollywood?" I said the words out loud to make sure I'd heard him correctly.

"It's true, Grace. And you need to know something else." Daniel nudged Rowland's shoulder. "If you insist you're such a changed man, prove it by telling her the whole truth."

In all my encounters with Rowland he was smooth. Confident. But today, moisture beaded his top lip while he hastily pulled at his tab collar.

"The day after the accident in Chicago, Mr. Patton came to my room and insisted we talk. He was sure I had something to do with the crash. After I vowed that it was not true, he pleaded with me to figure out a way to get you back in the air. In fact, he followed me down into the lobby and actually jumped into my moving car as I tried to speed away, all in an attempt to convince me to help you."

He shifted on his feet and Daniel poked his shoulder, urging him to continue.

"After the incident at the police station, Mr. Patton approached me again. He was rather forceful this time in his suggestion that I help you, considering my offer of a reward was the reason this mess began in the first place. That's when I decided to rescind the contract offer and help him contact the studio."

"My dear," Mr. Knickerbocker interrupted. He slid his hands over mine, ignoring the dirt and oil. "That Mr. Patton can be rather persistent. In the first incident with you it was thirty telegrams but in the last few days he has sent twice that number."

"None of that explains why you're here," I said, not wanting to think about Henry and the painful ache that coursed through my bones at the mention of his name.

Mr. Knickerbocker ran a gloved hand along the propeller that had been silent too long. "I'm here to offer your team a chance to perform again. Show me what you can do and the contract could be yours."

Uncle Warren leaned on the wooden cane he still needed to walk. His leg was healing, but slower than expected, so he'd need another week before he could fly. "Grace, what do you say?"

While I'd been working night and day the plane wasn't ready yet, and it felt like ages since I'd been on the wings. Another shot at the sky was not what I'd expected. I'd hoped and dreamed about it, but I wouldn't let myself get attached to the idea.

For so long I'd been determined to make The Soaring Eagles a success. But it was that same determination that drove Nathan to the edge. Pushed Henry out of my life. With this new opportunity, I couldn't help but wonder if I'd be doing the same thing—putting my wants and needs before those of everyone else.

Nathan was right. I had been acting like a little girl. Had I been a grown up, I would have recognized that my dream of a Hollywood contract wasn't what the other members of my team wanted.

For me there wasn't a choice. I was desperate to fly again. The same wasn't true for Daniel. He'd been helping to bring in extra money doing odd jobs, but I couldn't allow my own selfish wishes to overrule his plans. No matter how beaten down I felt over Nathan's betrayal, Daniel had always been there for me. Protected me. He'd shown me more kindness and patience than I ever deserved. The only thing that would make life right was seeing him happy.

"This is a surprise," I managed to say to Knickerbocker. "Could I have a moment with my team?"

"Of course. We did spring this on you rather suddenly." With a flick of his wrist, Mr. Knickerbocker ordered Rowland to follow him outside. It was nice to see Rowland cower behind a more powerful man. Perhaps he had learned a bit of humility.

Once the men disappeared from the hangar, Daniel pulled the rag from my pocket and dabbed at my oil-stained cheek. "This is quite the opportunity, darlin'."

"This is a second chance," Uncle Warren added. "Why didn't you say yes?"

I shoved my hands into the pocket of my coveralls. My pinky finger poked through a small hole that had been there since the day I shoved a screwdriver down a little too deep.

"I can't say yes," I said.

"Why not?" Daniel yelped. "This is your dream."

"That's just it. It's *my* dream—not yours. You don't need to worry about me. I've earned enough money at the diner to make my own plans."

Daniel shook his head. "What are you talking about?"

"On the sidewalk, after the police station, you said you weren't sure what you wanted to do. You said that working without Nathan was too difficult. It wasn't until now I realized how selfish I've been. This contract with Mr. Knickerbocker was *my* hope for the future. Uncle Warren was only going along because he loves me. But you have other choices."

Uncle Warren opened his mouth to protest but I talked over him. "You don't owe me anything, Daniel. You don't need to stay out of obligation or because you feel guilty that Nathan betrayed us. It's time you went after what your own heart wants."

"Oh Grace, you've got it all wrong," Daniel said. "Working with you in the hangar these last couple of days reminded me why I love barnstorming. It's not about the thrill of takeoff, or heaving myself off the wings in freefall before my parachute opens. The truth is, you and Warren are my family. This hangar is my home. I don't want to do anything else with my life but race across the sky with the two of you. That is, if you'll have me."

Daniel's wide smile was like the sun shining on us for the first time in weeks. I'd wanted to give him the opportunity to choose another life if he wanted it. Nathan had been unhappy for so long and I never noticed. The fact that he wanted to stay was the best news I'd heard in a long time. I flew into his arms and he spun me in a wide circle.

Once he set me down, Uncle Warren hobbled closer. "We're waiting on you. What do you say? Ready to get back in the sky?"

My mind raced as I surveyed Nathan's Jenny. It might take a few days, but she'd be ready. With the money I'd saved from the diner, we could rebuild the landing gear. Align the wings. Add new turnbuckles. This could work.

"We'll accept Mr. Knickerbocker's offer," I said.

Daniel crowed and shook his hand above his head in victory "We need to get working."

"Of course," I said. "Let's put together a list of what the three of us have to do to get the plane ready."

Uncle Warren and Daniel swapped a measured look that said I was missing something.

"We can't do this without help," Daniel said. "There's only one person who can make sure this plane is in tip-top shape."

"Grace," Uncle Warren propped a hand on my shoulder. "We need Henry if we're going to accept this offer."

Over the last few days, I'd convinced myself that my life could return to normal without Henry in it. But I'd walk past the movie theater, or the street where we'd heard the car backfire, and I could still remember the sensation of his hand squeezing my arm. The way his solid body deflated in in fear. He'd opened himself up to me in a way no one ever had before. Took a chance on trusting me when all I'd given him was grief. After the raid at the speak-easy, he could have run off to save himself, but he risked arrest to ensure I got away.

Even now, if I closed my eyes I could still hear his reassuring tone as he soothed me on the Ferris wheel. I woke up some nights thinking his leaving was a dream. That when I went to the hangar he'd be under the body of a plane cursing about how I'd wrenched a screw too tight, or didn't set the tools back in a perfect, organized line. But every morning when I went to work, there was nothing but brutal silence and the reality that he was never coming back.

I shook it all away. It was true that we needed him, but he'd never help, thanks to me. "I broke everything between us. He'll never agree to work with me again. Plus, nobody has seen him since the scene at the police station. How do you even know he's in town?"

Daniel's eyes lit up. "He's still working over at McEntire's garage. I think I can talk him into coming back."

Uncle Warren chomped on the edge of his cigar. "It'll be rough at first, but if you want to do this, Grace, you have to give Henry some space. He may not want to be near you or talk to you. It's the price you'll have to pay for his help."

The idea of having him back in the hangar was painful, but we couldn't fly without him. "Daniel, please go to the garage. Promise him whatever he wants. If he needs me out of the hangar while he works, I'll do it. It'll practically kill me, but for once I'm going to think about the good of this team instead of myself."

"I'll go right now." He took a few steps forward and then circled back. "This can't be easy for you, Grace. I'm so proud of the person you've become." He gave me a lung-crushing hug and headed out the hangar door.

Uncle Warren nodded toward where Knickerbocker and Mr. Rowland waited. "He's right. You've become a remarkable woman." He tapped his cane on the floor and gave me a reassuring smile. "I think it's time The Soaring Eagles started a new chapter. Why don't you go tell them what we've decided."

Knickerbocker clapped his hands joyfully when I gave him our answer. "This is outstanding news." He focused on the Jenny and furrowed his brow. "I'll give you until next Friday to fix your plane. Weather permitting, you can perform for me in the early morning so I can take the afternoon train back to the West Coast."

"My uncle should be ready to fly by then, but what about Mr. Sorenson from the government?" I asked. "He insisted we needed clearance before we took another flight."

Mr. Knickerbocker tapped his chin in thought. "Well, that is a problem."

"I know Sorenson personally," Rowland said. "The Soaring Eagles will be in the air in a week's time. I guarantee it."

"Well, that's wonderful," Mr. Knickerbocker gushed. "I expect to see great things from you, Miss Lafferty." With a quick flourish, he danced back to his waiting car.

Rowland turned to me. For the first time since he entered the hangar, I took a good look at him. His collar sat at an odd angle and his shirt twisted where he'd mismatched the line of his buttons.

All the bluster was gone from his once-confident demeanor. He ran a hand through his hair, messing up its perfectly combed style.

"I'd wish you the best of luck, but you've always had control of your own destiny. I was just too arrogant to see that." He gave a slight bow and popped his fedora back on his head. "May your skies always be cloudless and blue, Grace."

He strode toward the waiting car and slid inside. It sped down the runway and disappeared into a cloud of swirling dust, taking any trace of Alistair Rowland with it.

28

A Traitorous Leap

Lincoln, Nebraska
October 19, 1922
1 day until Knickerbocker performance

It took two full days for Daniel to track Henry down. He'd left McEntire's and moved out of the boardinghouse. On a hunch, Daniel waited near the Piccadilly Theater and happened to catch Henry on his way out of a matinee. He agreed to help, but as I expected, he demanded that I stay out of his way and keep our conversation to a minimum.

I did my best to stay invisible in the hangar, but in the final hours the night before the performance, when everyone was scurrying about, it was hard to avoid each other.

As Henry worked his strides grew uneven, the growing cold worsening his limp. His light-brown hair was longer now and grazed the tips of his ears. I cursed myself every time I caught sight of him in the hangar and my heart did a traitorous little leap.

The sun shifted to the west and shadows filled the hangar. Gasoline fumes and clouds of black exhaust wafted through the air as Daniel and Henry revved the motor, checking and rechecking the oil and water lines. My blood hummed in my veins at the sounds of the hangar coming back to life. I loved the clicks, whirs, and grinding cranks I was convinced I'd never hear again. To most people the chaotic noise would be jarring, but to me they were a sweet symphony I wanted to experience for the rest of my life.

When the last of the repairs were complete, Daniel and Uncle

Warren tried to encourage me to leave, but one landing wire was still giving me trouble.

"Grace, come in early tomorrow and we'll get it fixed," Daniel begged. "It's good that you quit the diner, but you still need to rest."

"Just a few more minutes," I said. "You two go on. I'll stay and close up the hangar."

They glanced toward the tail where Henry was still working. "Maybe we should stay," Uncle Warren said.

"Please go on. You need to be rested for tomorrow, too." I followed his stare to where it landed on Henry. "I promise I won't bother him."

They hesitated until I practically chased them out the door.

Henry didn't bother to look at me as he limped to the tool bench, stopping every few steps to rub his leg.

"Is the change in weather bothering you?"

And my promise went right out the window.

"I've gotten used to the constant throbbing now. Some days are better than others." The lines in his forehead deepened. "Things could be worse. A lot of men in my division lost limbs or were paralyzed. Others never came home."

His hand went back to working on his leg. His breath turned rapid as he kneaded the muscles along his calf.

"Maybe you should go home," I said.

"I can't. I still haven't gotten the tension right on the back drift wire." He grabbed a pair of pliers off the table and hobbled back to the tail.

The low grind of Henry's pliers and the small *snicks* of tightening wires were the only sounds that filled the hangar. I focused on my work, but the growing silence became too much for me to handle. We only had this final day. It was my last shot to make things right.

"You never did say how you were wounded in the war."

His uneven footsteps echoed through the hangar as he moved to the side of the plane. "No, I didn't," he said through gritted teeth.

"It's okay if you don't want to talk."

I expected him to turn and go back to the tail but instead he climbed up onto the wing. The lines of ropy muscle in his arms strained against his skin as he heaved himself up. He stood, bracing his arms on a strut. His chest heaved up and down like he might explode at any moment. I should have heeded my uncle's warning to stay quiet.

"The night of the raid, when I told you my friend Sam and I went after our pal William, it wasn't the complete truth. Sam ran out first. Instead of going after him, I froze the way I did that night at the speakeasy." He sank down onto the wing. The tight line of his shoulders deflated as if all the fight was flooding out of him.

"Mortar shells exploded all around us and I was terrified. Once I got over the shock of what was happening, my training kicked in, but it was too late. William was blown to pieces by the time I got to him. I took several bullets—one in the shoulder, two in the leg—before I could reach Sam. I crawled toward him, but a bullet went straight through his heart. He died in my arms."

He dropped his head in his hands. "The shooting stopped for only a minute," he whispered through his fingers. "I crawled across dirt, blood, and even body parts to get back to the trench. I wanted to live, Gracie. I needed to live."

His lips twitched and he took a deep swallow as he struggled to get the words out. "That day we saved the pilot, I was upset because he couldn't see what you'd risked. When his father asked for your help, you didn't think about yourself but how you could save his son. That's more than I'd done for my friend on the battlefield that day."

He sighed and shifted back across the wing. "Since I came home from the war my life has been a mess. I thought I could stay at the farm, but it held too many memories of my parents. Every time I looked at my sister I felt like a failure."

He rose slowly to his feet. "It wasn't until I came to Lincoln and met you that I found my way again. For so long I've been running from my memories. Daniel understood what I was going through. How the smallest things, like a car backfiring or a wrench hitting the floor, could bring back terrifying memories. Nathan had been teaching me how to calm down and deal with my episodes before the whole mess happened. It was the first time in years I've felt any sort of peace . . . until the crash."

He climbed down to the ground and approached the spot on the frame where I was standing. "Never for a moment did I suspect Nathan was behind all the things that went wrong."

It was sad how Nathan's betrayal cut us all to the core. How a series of lies could taint all our lives.

"Outside the tent in Springfield that day, Louis and I had words after he tried to convince me to accept Rowland's offer again. I paid for my refusal the next night when he roughed me up. For days after, Nathan stopped by my room at the boarding house to make sure I was all right. When he offered to go into town with me in Arkansas, I thought he was being a good friend. He fooled all of us, but somehow I feel like I let you down. Like I should have seen through his lies." He ran a hand slowly over his face. "I was angry at the police station because you accused me of sabotage, but I walked away because I understood Nathan's desperation."

He walked slowly back to the tool bench, then stopped suddenly and turned to face me like he needed to look into my eyes. "After that first time we met, when Rowland told me about the job and offered me that 500 dollars, I considered it."

"Why didn't you take it?"

"Because when you allowed me, a complete stranger, to take your hands and lay them in that icy water, you were the first person to look at me like I mattered. Like I wasn't some beaten-down soldier with obvious war wounds. You challenged me. You made me earn my place with The Soaring Eagles. That meant everything to me, and from that point on all I wanted to do was protect you from men like Rowland." He let out a rough laugh. "The whole time the real danger was under my nose and I never saw it."

"Henry, Nathan was the first man besides my uncle to fly me in a plane. While he was at the controls, I dangled 500 feet above the ground. I trusted him to drive forty-five miles an hour in an old roadster while I tried to latch on to a swirling rope ladder. Besides Daniel, no one thought they knew Nathan better than me. And I was wrong. We all were." I climbed down from the frame and moved toward him. My arms ached to touch him, but I stopped a few feet away when I saw the hesitation in his eyes.

"Maybe it's for the best that we didn't work out." He reached for a wrench, twirling it between his oil-stained fingers. "I could never be good enough for you. With my episodes, and my leg, I'll never be totally whole."

A sad smile lifted his beautiful lips. "And knowing all that, I still can't stay away from you. Since we've been apart I've worked my fingers to the bone, paced grooves into the floor of my room at the boardinghouse. I went to see the same film a dozen times, and I can still picture the way your lips purse when you blow the fluff off dandelions and how your hair curls up around your ears after you've been in the sky. You're a magnet pulling me in, and although I've fought it, I can't stay away from you a minute longer."

He dropped the wrench and closed the distance between us. "Tell me the truth, Grace. Can I ever be enough for you?"

Our lips hovered only inches apart. Our breaths synchronized in perfect time. "You already are." I wrapped my fingers through the ends of his hair and tugged him closer. He pressed his lips to mine. On instinct, my body leaned into the delicious curve of his arms. From the moment he'd appeared at the diner that day, I'd ignored the pull between us. When he showed up in the hangar, knocking the breath out of me, my irritation was really my fear of how my body reacted to him. His brash ways, and demands that I stay away from the planes, should have been enough to get me to hate him; but deep down my heart struggled with what I had always felt. In Chicago, I let go of my fears and I'd never felt more complete. Together we were the perfect example of turbulence: cold and hot air crashing into one another. It was harsh, and sometimes unexpected, but I'd chosen a life filled with risk, and I was willing to take this final leap if it meant being with Henry forever.

29
Beautiful Intensity

October 20, 1922
Day of Knickerbocker performance

The whistle of the wind in the open field outside the hangar calmed my racing heart. I didn't know if it was luck or Mother Nature taking pity on me, but the sky was a cloudless blue and the bright sun brought unseasonably warm weather to Lincoln.

Blue sky, perfect day to fly.

"You're quiet." Mr. Knickerbocker came up beside me and propped an elbow up onto the Jenny's wing.

I jumped at the sound of his voice, lost in my thoughts about the routine and the importance of performing the Showstopper flawlessly.

"My apologies." He patted at his mustache. "You looked sad there for a moment. Let me guess, thinking about the crash?"

"Yes, sir. It's my first time back up. And with what happened with Nathan . . ." I stopped. He was here to see a performance, not listen to me dribble on about my worries. "Never mind, sir. You expect a professional and that's what you'll get today."

He pushed his fine, black derby back on his head and readjusted the wire spectacles on the bridge of his nose. "In my business, people often get caught up in their roles, Miss Lafferty. There are certain days where I'll be discussing a contract with an actor and I'm not sure if I'm talking to the real man or someone playing a part. What I like about you is that you are truly yourself every single day. You may be a bit brash and outspoken," he chuckled, "but I've come to understand that only the strong make it in show business. You've proven yourself to be quite resilient."

R. O. Knickerbocker never ceased to amaze me. Here was a man who ran a major film studio. People vied for his time and attention, yet he wanted to encourage me. Perhaps he'd done it because he wanted to see a good performance, but the twinkle in his eye said he was much more than a business man. He cared about people, too. That fact made me want the contract even more. Our team had to be part of the Palm Coast Studios family, and I was going to do everything in my power to make that happen.

Knickerbocker waved a hand at his waiting Packard limousine that idled near the landing strip. The door swung open and two men climbed out.

"Hope you don't mind, but Rowland had a bit of trouble with Mr. Sorenson, so I reached out to a friend who has some pull in the aviation world to smooth things over."

I yanked the rag from the back pocket of my coveralls and knotted it in my hands. Mr. Behncke moved toward us with the cat-like grace of a true showman. His navy suit tugged against his wide shoulders as he walked. Mr. Sorenson wore his usual pinched expression as he lumbered behind him. Once they reached Knickerbocker and me, Mr. Behncke removed his khaki fedora and gave a smooth bow. "Miss Lafferty, excellent to see you again. I was sorry to hear about your crash, but you and your plane look to be in fine shape today."

"It's good to see you too, sir."

Mr. Sorenson didn't say a word, but his clenched jaw warned he was here under protest.

"Grace," Daniel called from inside the hangar.

"I better go see what he needs," I said in a wobbly voice. "We should be ready in a half hour."

"We'll wait in the car until you're ready." Knickerbocker looped an arm around Sorenson's shoulder like they were old friends and

265

Sorenson stiffened under his touch. Mr. Behncke stifled a laugh and offered me one last wish of good luck.

Inside the hangar, Henry walked through our final checklist. When everything seemed in order, Uncle Warren pointed to the office. "Grace, get your gear on."

"One last thing," I said. "Henry, did you check the lower skid again? That's where I'm going to attach the wire."

"Oh no!" Uncle Warren bellowed around the horrendous, brown stump hanging out of his mouth. "We're not doing that trick, especially with Sorenson here."

"Yes, we are, and Sorenson can't say a word. He's given us permission to fly and we are going to take advantage of this opportunity."

I understood my uncle's concern after what we'd been through, but today all our worries had to be put aside. This was the last time we'd get a shot at something as big as this contract, and we had to put on an unforgettable show—which meant including the Showstopper.

"You said the other day I was growing into a remarkable young woman. If you truly believe that, then I'm asking you to trust me. Let me perform this trick."

Uncle Warren's hands clenched at his sides. Sometimes he could be as stubborn as an old cow. "And what if I say no?"

Daniel reached for my uncle's shoulder. "It's time to let her go, Warren. Grace is her own woman now. If she says she can do the trick, you have to trust her."

Uncle Warren turned to Henry. "It's pretty obvious you love her. Do you think she should do this?"

Heat crept up Henry's cheeks and it was hard not to press a kiss to his lips. "Gracie is capable of anything. I think she's proved that to all of us. And yes, I do love her with all my heart." He'd said the words over and over yesterday as we watched the sunset fade into evening. I would never tire of the way his eyes bored into me with beautiful intensity when he said them.

"Fine, but you have to wear a parachute." Uncle Warren shoved his aviator cap down over his ears and slipped on his goggles. "Don't make me regret this, Grace."

I followed Henry as he limped to the corner near the office. He motioned for me to turn around. With a gentle touch, he slid one thick strap of the canvas pack over my left shoulder and then my right. His hand lingered along my collarbone, sending a shock of heat through me. I'd forgotten how my skin burned under his touch. The edges of his fingertips brushed the small patch of skin exposed below my jacket as he made sure the parachute was secured inside. He moved in close, his breath warming the back of my neck, while he notched the straps once more, making sure they wouldn't slip off mid-flight. The entire process was rudimentary but it ignited every element in my body.

"Good luck, Gracie." He reached out and slowly opened his palm, where a dandelion lay. "I want you to have this, but there's no need for a wish. You've already shown all of us how fearless you can be."

I braced my feet against the floorboard as the Jenny barreled down the runway. The wheels left the ground and my stomach did its regular tumble. When we reached 500 feet, an icy blast of wind burned my cheeks.

I yanked down my cap and adjusted my trusty old goggles. Scratches and nicks still covered the lenses. The straps remained thin and threadbare. Once I'd considered them lucky, but they took on a different meaning now. They were a shining example of how you could be worn down, beaten up by the elements, and still be strong enough to handle whatever the world threw at you.

A stiff east wind hummed in my ears. Uncle Warren called my

name. I swung around in my seat and he tapped his head twice. While I'd fought them earlier, the tears came easily now. I hadn't said a word, but Uncle Warren understood what I needed even before I did. This time back in the air couldn't be different than any other trip in the sky. The crash. Nathan. They had to be pushed far from my mind. The only thing that mattered was where I placed my feet on the frame. How I hung on to the struts and landing wires. When I decided to let go of the cable and fly free.

The nose of the plane shot up. We did a single loop, shot forward, and went into another loop. Before I could catch my breath, Uncle Warren moved the Jenny into a series of barrel rolls, spinning our wings across the bright blue sky. Once we were level, he banked us left and back in the direction of the hangar. Mr. Knickerbocker and the other men were merely black dots on the brown canvas of ground below.

Uncle Warren shot his finger in the air and brought it down slowly. I held on to the lap belt as we vaulted straight up. We started to descend, tail pointed down. Clouds swirled around us in an opaque mist as we plummeted to the ground in a whip stall. My head buzzed as we hurtled toward the earth. A quick breath burst from my mouth when Uncle Warren regained control and leveled the wings.

He patted the body of the plane to signal it was my turn. I climbed out of the seat. Pressure from the wind smacked at my shoulders and back. Each movement pulled at the straps of the parachute. The roar of the prop rattled my teeth, and it was oddly comforting. It was here I'd experienced my first real taste of life. Felt the sting of hot oil pulsing off the engine, reminding me that even though my family was gone, my heart was still beating. Uncle Warren, without knowing it, had given me the gift of being able to breathe and live again.

Once my hand circled a wooden strut, I sat down and wrapped my legs around the base. I inched toward the edge of the frame and dropped down head first. My body fluttered in the wind. Exhaust and gasoline fumes filled my nose in an acidic bouquet. After a count of ten, I pulled back up and did a series of spins off the edge of the wing. My arm still ached, but I ignored the pain. Whether I was a hundred percent or not, this performance had to be flawless.

We banked in a circle and flew down low. I kicked into a headstand and held on as we raced past the men. My uncle forced the plane up again and I scrambled to the top wing. Once my feet were secured in the straps, we shot into a loop, swapping the sky for the ground once and then twice in two full revolutions.

My head went light. Every inch of my skin pulsed with adrenaline and a shout of joy escaped my mouth. I'd been gone too long from the sky, but I was finally home. My parents and sister would never be able to witness my performances. Perhaps they would have thought I was crazy like the crowds who craned their necks to the sky. But a big part of me believed they would have been like Uncle Warren—resistant only until they saw how this life filled me with a joy that words could never describe.

I climbed down to the bottom wing and a sharp pulse of energy surged through me as I moved to hang by both arms from the lower skid. I dug into my pocket and pulled out the wire with the mouthpiece attached. It bobbled in my hand before I took control and clipped it to the u-shaped skid. The edge of the mouthpiece scraped against my tongue as I bit down. Below me miles of farmland flew by in a hazy, gray streak.

A slow countdown began in my head. At one there was no turning back. I clamped my jaw shut and let go. My body plummeted through the air. I struggled for a breath. The wind snapped at my body. I rushed toward the earth. Images of Henry, the boys, my uncle, and my family spun through my mind. I let go of it all: fear, pain, regret.

The wire continued to spool out. It shuddered once and then went taut, stopping my descent. I sailed through the sky hanging by my teeth. The force of the air knocked me back and forth like a pendulum. I fluttered my hands at my side, allowing the wind to take me. The roar of the engine filled my ears before the rope ladder appeared. It swung away and then raced toward me until a rung slammed against my hand. I grabbed hold, and the mouthpiece tumbled out of my mouth. I scrambled up the ladder with my heart lodged in my throat. It seemed like a dream, but I'd done it. I swung through the heavens and lived to tell the tale.

I found my way back to the passenger seat and strapped myself in. My uncle's cheers filled the air. We moved into two loop-the-loops and then banked back toward the hangar. When we were only a hundred feet above the ground he spun us in consecutive barrel rolls again.

No matter what happened when we landed, there was no possible way I could let go of this life. If Mr. Knickerbocker decided not to give us the contract, we'd find another way. We'd battled government interference, betrayal, and a fiery crash, but we were still here. Still flying.

30
Epilogue
Part of the Wind

"Courage is the price that life exacts for granting peace."—Amelia Earhart

Los Angeles, California
May 19, 1923
Palm Coast Studios Premiere Performance

A dozen sleek, black Rolls-Royce limousines lined the street in front of the theater. A growing crowd lined up along the sidewalk like ants marching toward a picnic. The Jenny buzzed past the theater and the roar of the prop rattled the windows. Men held onto their top hats while women clutched their pearls, eyes wide with excitement. The engine hummed and we soared back into the atmosphere. Uncle Warren shot us into a double loop-the-loop and the people below became nothing but a hazy kaleidoscope of color.

Mr. Knickerbocker had talked about this film premiere for weeks. When he visited the hangar he'd built especially for us, he went on and on about how the director was going to be the next big thing. How we needed to make a splash this afternoon by ending our performance with the Showstopper. After I performed it for him in October, the fear of dangling by my teeth was gone.

I yanked up the leather collar of my jacket. In my black wool pants, I skidded across the edge of the seat. Ever since Mr. Knickerbocker offered us the contract, I'd had to deal with what

Daniel liked to call "Silver Screen Saps"—men and women who worked at Palm Coast and told us how to act, what to wear, and proper etiquette for what they called "public interactions." This included performance costumes. While Daniel and my uncle could wear their typical flying clothes (aviator cap, goggles, fleece-lined coat) the Saps insisted I wear an outfit that made me look like a sideshow performer.

At first, they wanted me to wear a get-up that resembled a ballerina's tutu, complete with sequins, matching fuchsia head wrap, and ballet slippers. Ballet slippers? Did they want me to plummet to my death in front of the biggest stars of stage and screen?

The costume designer, Madame Renault, argued for weeks in her thick French accent about how the outfit was key to our performance. I finally had to go to Mr. Knickerbocker and explain that at 500 feet, even in summer, I'd still freeze my backside off in a tutu. After more than a few grumbles, he agreed to the pared-down costume I now wore.

The Jenny blew past the crowd again. The push and pull of the wind greeted me as I crossed to the edge of the wing. I let go and hung upside down. Roars of delight filled my ears as we raced low. Air pressure pushed against the edges of my goggles and tore at my short hair. Mary and Ethel had finally convinced me to cut it.

The California sky still didn't seem real, the way it glowed in swaths of tangerine, pink, and yellow at twilight. The air no longer smelled like manure, exhaust, and oil, but of salt and seawater from the Pacific Ocean only a few miles away.

We'd only been in Los Angeles a week when Mary and Ethel took us all to the beach. We all played in the surf, ignoring the way Uncle Warren scrutinized my and Henry's every move.

After we accepted the contract, Knickerbocker convinced Henry he needed to be part of The Soaring Eagles team. I'd left the decision up to Henry. He had his own dreams, and I'd learned over the past few months that what I wanted didn't matter. Every person had their own wishes for the future, and they had to decide for themselves what would make them happy. But when Henry agreed to travel to Hollywood I couldn't hide my excitement—much to Uncle Warren's dismay.

Henry now lived with Daniel in a bungalow four doors away from me. My uncle had made it clear that our relationship could never interfere with work. When we were in the hangar, Henry would sometimes reach for my hand and give it a quick squeeze. I caught my uncle watching us once and even though he acted like an overbearing parent, he couldn't hide his smile.

Henry still flinched when a falling set hit the ground, or a director screeched "Action!" through a megaphone. But with Daniel's help, the episodes happened less frequently as the months passed.

The Jenny nosed down and Uncle Warren bulleted us across the sky. The sun began to inch toward the horizon. We started another loop. Heaven and earth switched places for a quick breath. An electrical pulse zapped through my hands and feet. Sudden pressure filled my head while my arms and legs floated weightlessly in the air. No matter how many times we did this trick, I never got tired of the way my body became part of the wind and sky all at once.

We leveled out and tore through pillow-like clouds. I scrambled down to the skid below the lower wing. The wind clawed at my face and clothes. I placed the mouthpiece against my tongue. Shadows of buildings and cars flew past. With a quick snap, I clipped the wire to the skid. After tugging on the line to ensure it was secure, I took one last look at the Los Angeles skyline and let go. My body shot down. The wind twisted me in a circle. The line shook and then my descent quickly stopped with a jarring snap. Momentum pushed me back and forth. The steady, soothing movement reminded me why I loved this job.

Once our performance was over, we eased down to the landing strip behind the Palm Coast screening theater. Per studio protocol,

I had to wait for Uncle Warren to stop the Jenny and help me down like a proper lady.

Madame Renault rushed toward me. Her fingers glittered with an array of gemstone rings as she swirled a fur-lined cape around my shoulders. She urged me forward, whispering, "*Allez. Allez.*" Hurry. Hurry. Henry translated for me one day. The way she looked at me when she said it made me think it was something much worse.

"Smile, *s'il vous plait*. You're part of the show now." She dug her hands into my shoulders and thrust me toward the masses that waited behind a red velvet rope. Daniel and Uncle Warren were already busy shaking hands and posing for pictures. Before I could steady my breath, hands flew toward me asking for an autograph.

"Miss Lafferty," they screeched, "Will you sign here, please?"

The press of the crowd made my head light. I focused on the hand in front of me and scribbled my signature time and time again until it became a black stream of words linked together in a loopy scrawl. The act of signing my name felt ridiculous. I was still just a small-town girl from Lincoln, Nebraska—not a star in pictures. But to my surprise, people treated me like one. While Daniel enjoyed the glitz and glamour, as well as the admiring looks from the gals, it was going to take me some time to get used to all the noise and hoopla of Hollywood.

Mr. Knickerbocker tapped my shoulder. His wide smile was a beacon in the fading daylight. "One more and then we must go inside." He pulled a silver pocket watch from his black tuxedo and clucked his tongue. "The picture is about to start and there are people inside who are anxious to meet The Soaring Eagles."

I scribbled my name along the last bit of paper and turned to follow Daniel and Uncle Warren toward the theater. A cool ocean breeze blew against the nape of my neck. I tightened my cape and was almost to the theater entrance when a familiar voice called my name.

Henry stood ten feet away, shifting uneasily on his feet. As I approached him, he took off his top hat and swiped a hand over his brow. The black tuxedo Mr. Knickerbocker insisted all the men wear accentuated his broad shoulders. A white bowtie was in a perfect knot at his throat. If I hadn't known better, I would have sworn he was one of the stars of the picture we were about to see.

"That look suits you."

A flush filled his cheeks and he reached for my hand, giving it a delicious squeeze. I still couldn't get over the fact that we were in this paradise living our dream together.

"Aren't you supposed to be inside with Mary and Ethel?"

He nodded and tucked the hat under his arm. "They're all settled. In fact, I sat them next to some fellas who are also on contract with a studio. When I left they were swapping stories about scripts, blocking, and other sorts of nonsense I didn't understand."

Mary and Ethel had found roles in the pictures as contract players for West Colony Studios. The parts, although small, rolled in for them. Mary continued to be bold, speaking her mind with actors and directors alike. And while statuesque, beautiful Ethel still made men shake in their boots, she insisted she was perfectly happy to be on her own. They made me laugh, and pestered me endlessly about my hair and clothes, but my life was fuller with the two of them in it.

"That still doesn't explain why you're standing out here," I said.

He fidgeted and played with the button on his formal coat. The edge of his jaw twitched, and he took several deep swallows before he spoke again. "I wanted to share some news with you. Privately." He inched in closer like he didn't want anyone to hear what he had to say. "Yesterday, I received a job offer from West Colony. They need a man to take over their studio garage."

He continued to talk but I didn't hear a single word. A job offer. It shouldn't have surprised me. Henry was quickly earning a reputation in town for his skill. At our last two performances, studio heads had buzzed around him to ask various mechanical questions—much to Mr. Knickerbocker's dismay.

Now he was going to take a new job. The thought sent a sickening rumble through me. I turned and headed back toward the Jenny. He deserved this opportunity. For months, he'd been working quietly. Doing everything he could to help make the transition to this new crazy life easier. Never pushing me for more than I was ready to give.

Henry came to stand beside me with his hand on the wing. "I'd have total control over the maintenance of the stunt cars and motorcycles."

"Airplanes too?" I asked, my voice cracking with each word.

"No. No planes." He held me in a serious gaze. "That's one of the drawbacks."

"Drawbacks?"

"Yes. For one, I like working on planes."

"But don't you want to be your own boss one day? Own your own garage?"

"That's what makes this an amazing offer. I'd run it through the studio as a contract business but it would be *my* garage. Part of my salary would go toward paying for complete ownership."

It was an amazing offer. He could spend years working with us and not make enough money to fulfill that dream. But if he was on salary, the business could be his in a very short time. He had to take the job.

The late afternoon wind blew at my hair and pulled at the antique combs Mary and Ethel insisted I keep after Chicago. Henry continued to fidget with his formal coat. The lines in his forehead increased by the minute.

"This is an incredible opportunity. Why don't you look happy?" I asked.

"It is incredible, but . . ."

"But?" I echoed.

"It would mean I'd have to spend more time away from you. These last months have meant so much to me. I can't stand the thought of being apart from you. Not even for a minute."

His words sliced through me and I knew what he said was true. Once he left Palm Coast, he'd work night and day to make the business a success, and I'd be flying and performing.

"Henry, this is your dream," I started. "You can't worry about me." The words slid from my mouth like shards of glass.

He stepped closer and reached for my hand. "No, Gracie. *You* are my dream." He swiped a hand across my cheek, sending a warm shiver down my back. "Before I met you, I was wandering in the dark, desperate for a guiding light. Then there you were in that booth. All covered in dirt and grease, your hair twisted and tangled. People stared and whispered. Instead of cowering away, you held your head high. You pulled me into your glow that day and ever since I've craved its warmth."

He shook his head, the edges of his mouth curling into a smirk. "You were beautiful. And aggravating. And irritating. You're unlike any other person I've ever met in my life." He chuckled to himself. "That little girl in Arkansas, Ruby, saw my feelings for you before I even realized them. That day when she bent down and whispered in my ear, she told me I should kiss you. I guess it's true what they say, that children often see the truth before adults."

My face heated but I couldn't allow the compliments to color my reaction. "Henry, I insist you take this job. We can work out ways to see each other."

He cupped my cheek, the love in his eyes stealing the breath from my lungs. I'd always thought that by living this dangerous life I'd chosen to be alone. But since the day we'd performed for Knickerbocker, Henry's love for me had never wavered. Our first meeting felt like ages ago. So much had happened since then, but in these last months, working side by side amongst the new planes, we'd become closer than I ever imagined.

He pressed a finger to my lips. "The offer is simply leverage. Knickerbocker has already approached me about starting a full garage here. This is a chance to push him into actually doing it."

Slowly he pulled his finger away and replaced it with his lips. The kiss started out slow, but as my hands circled his waist I wanted more. Every single one of my senses wanted to be wrapped up in him. To be lost in his arms without having to worry about what came next. Another show. Another practice. For so long I'd been living for the future, but now all I needed was this moment with him.

He weaved his fingers through my hair. We stumbled back against the plane, a breathless tangle of arms and legs. I'd never get used to the way my heart knew how to speed up to keep time with his. How my arms found the perfect resting place around his neck.

"Miss Lafferty!" Mr. Knickerbocker's voice boomed across the field.

Henry broke away from me. I reached to pull him in again, not caring if Knickerbocker found us this way, but Henry, always the gentleman, stopped me. His eyes searched mine before glancing toward the cockpit. "How important is seeing that picture?"

I shrugged. "That fella Lon Chaney is supposed to be frightening in the film."

"What if I could promise you something more exciting?" His mouth twisted into a dangerous grin.

"What did you have in mind, Mr. Patton?"

The green edges of his eyes flared and his sweet dimple appeared. "There's a sliver of daylight left. With the lessons from your uncle, and my new pilot's license, we can be in the air any time we please. How's about we take a spin right now?"

"I don't think that's a good idea. Not with Knickerbocker headed straight for us."

"Please, Gracie. Do this for me," he pleaded. "I've been cooped up in the hangar for the last week making constant adjustments to the engine and fuel lines. Sitting in a theater right now would be suffocating." He bit the edge of his lip and nodded to the plane. "One little trip into the air?" He made a sliver of space between his thumb and pointer finger.

The last shadows of the theater-goers disappeared behind the door. If we were going to escape, we had to make it quick.

Without hesitating, I raced to the front of the Jenny. When I reached the prop, my hands ran along its curved edges. The bend of the wood was smooth under my touch and a smile lifted my lips. Henry. Daniel. My uncle and the girls. Even this plane. It was all home to me.

Henry followed behind me and leaned in, brushing a gentle kiss against my forehead. It was hard to ignore the way our bodies fit together in perfect symmetry. Like we were made for one another. The crash had taught me that time was precious. That every moment had to be cherished. We couldn't change the past or what Nathan had done to us.

Even Rowland had faded into the background. He hadn't stayed around for our performance for Knickerbocker or seen The Soaring Eagles sign our contract. Whispers in the barnstorming community said he fled back to England. His team disbanded. It would be easy to stay angry at him, but in the end Alistair Rowland had given us a shot at this amazing life.

With gentle hands, Henry caressed my back and deepened his kiss. Every dark thought that once filled my head drifted away. None of us could predict the future, whether we would continue to fly or if the government would shut us down. All we could do was sail into the heavens and hope they stayed open for us a little while longer.

Henry pulled back and nodded at the cockpit. "Gracie, I could kiss you all day, but we should get a move on before Knickerbocker stops us."

"Miss Lafferty!" Mr. Knickerbocker waved his hands toward the theater. "Hurry, the film is about to begin," he bellowed.

Failing to do one of my contracted duties would come at a price, but my body screamed for the feel of the wind. "Let's go."

Henry hoisted himself up into the cockpit. I gripped the prop and yelled, "Contact!"

"Contact," he repeated.

With a single, stiff push, the propeller spun to life. Its roar echoed across the field. I scrambled up onto the wing and latched myself into the seat. We throttled down the grassy strip and my lungs lifted with a joyous rush.

The flicker of twilight greeted us. We wouldn't be able to stay in the air for long, but the swell of wispy clouds encouraged us higher. The wind rocked us in her gentle hand. The cold metal of my mother's locket pressed against my chest. Since the day Uncle Warren had given it to me, I'd never taken it off. It was a reminder that no matter where I was, Nebraska or California, my family was always with me.

Once the wings were level, I turned in my seat. Henry blew me a kiss. It was a simple gesture but it felt like a lifelong promise.

Author's Note

It's true what they say about inspiration striking in odd places. In the early summer of 2013 I was visiting Chicago for my nephew's graduation, and a side trip to the Museum of Science and Industry started my journey with this book. Upon entering the museum, I noticed a biplane suspended from the ceiling. As I approached the exhibit, I came across a placard announcing the name "Ethel Dare" who was a wing walker during the barnstorming years immediately after World War I.

Barnstorming was a term I'd heard briefly during a history class in high school, but I honestly didn't know much about it until doing further research. After World War I, many pilots returned home with a craving to still fly. They purchased old military trainers, many of which were Curtiss JN-4s (known as "Jennys"). The pilots toured the U.S. in the "Jennys" performing aerobatic tricks in air shows and doing their best to try and make a living.

Part of the appeal of these shows, known as "Flying Circuses," were the female wing walkers who performed risky tricks on the wings of a biplane—most of the time without a parachute. Over the years, women like Mabel Cody (niece of Buffalo Bill Cody), Lillian Boyer, Ethel Dare, and Gladys Ingle of Hollywood's 13 Black Cats fame drew increasingly larger crowds.

The idea of a young female wing walker took hold of me in the museum that day, and I knew I needed to learn more. When I returned home to Arizona, I began my barnstorming research, and in particular, female wing walkers. Amazingly there are YouTube videos taken from old film reels of these women doing their stunts. If you think Grace's antics are crazy, watch one of Lillian Boyer's videos. At just nineteen-years-old she was truly fearless!

Further intrigued, I read up on the period trying to educate myself about the history of barnstorming. I picked up C.R. Roseberry's *Glenn Curtiss: Pioneer of Flight*. Curtiss built the JN-4s known as "Jennys." This research lead to other important aviation pioneers, including the first black female to secure a pilot's license, Bessie Coleman, who makes a cameo appearance in this book. Doris L. Rich's *Queen Bess: Daredevil Aviator* was enormously helpful in describing the time period and made it plausible that Bessie and Grace could have crossed paths in Chicago.

Over the next six months, I researched early twentieth century language, clothing, and aviation history to ensure I could do this story justice. Mr. Rowland's mention of Charles Lindbergh is factually accurate as Lindbergh applied for flight training at the Nebraska Aircraft Corp. in Lincoln in 1922. In the speakeasy scene, we also come across David L. Behncke who owned Chicago's Checkerboard Field at the time and did have an acquaintance with Bessie Coleman.

Henry's experiences in the trenches came from research I did with *B.H. Liddell Hart's World War I in Outline.* The intricacies of airplane maintenance and repair came from the U.S. Army Air Corps' *Information for Air Service Mechanics* (October 1919).

If you've got a keen eye for aviation history, you will note that there was no such thing as a 1922 World Aviation Expo. This was an event entirely of my own fictional making. The idea was pulled from the air derby that took place at Chicago's Checkerboard Field in late summer of 1922. I also took some fictional license with government involvement in barnstorming. No real laws were placed on flying until the Air Commerce Act of 1926. There were crashes during the early twenties, and the government did become increasingly concerned with public safety, but it wasn't until 1926 that laws were put into effect that essentially curtailed barnstorming. I also took a small liberty with the Powder Puff Air Derby. The first derby did not take place until 1929.

While I have done my best to thoroughly research the details of this book, mistakes and inaccuracies do happen. I hope that readers will grant me a small amount of leeway in bringing them Grace's story. The rest of the events such as performing without parachutes and entire teams perishing in crashes is all fact. These women lived an exhilarating, and risky, existence all in an attempt to bring entertainment to the war-weary masses. And while Grace Lafferty's story is pure fiction, the details of her life, and her unwavering courage, are meant to honor those brave women who soared in the skies after the war.

Acknowledgments

There will never be the right words to express my gratitude to my editor, McKelle George, for believing in this book and making my dream come true. Her words of support and amazing edits have made this story infinitely better. To Mari Kesselring, copy editor Sonnet Fitzgerald, Megan Naidl, cover designer Jake Nordby, and the rest of the team at Flux, thank you for believing in *Nothing But Sky*. It means everything to me.

This has been a long journey and there are so many people to thank. First and foremost, my family for standing by my side, allowing me quiet Sundays to write, and for being incredibly supportive. David, Olivia, and Ryan, love is not a strong enough word for what I feel for you!

For my siblings (Mark, Julie, Wendy, and Paul), thank you for always making me feel supported and loved. I'm convinced that's what allowed me to be brave enough to go after my dream of publishing a novel. My mother, Joan, for introducing me to the joys of the public library. Thank you for always allowing me to sneak a book or two beyond my lending limit. Also, much love and thanks to Jon and Camilla Grossklaus, and the entire Welch family for being supportive when I first told you I'd written a book.

When I came up with the idea of *Nothing But Sky* I knew I could never pull it off without help from someone who understood planes and aviation. As soon as the first draft was written, I put it in the capable hands of my brother-in-law, and retired Navy pilot, Gunnar. From that first draft, he enthusiastically jumped in to make sure I was describing everything correctly (from the plane parts to the aerobatic tricks). He has been one of my biggest supporters and thanks in these acknowledgements hardly seems enough after all he has done to help me. Also to Carol Pilon, a real-life wing walker, for her patience in answering all my questions, and Ron

Chadwick for meeting me at his hangar and sharing his wealth of aviation knowledge. A shout out to the gentlemen at the Arizona Commemorative Air Force Museum at Falcon Field for letting me take way too many pictures and ask a lot of questions.

To all my beta readers and critique partners (and there have been many at various stages): A.J. Pine, Jen Blackwood, Ami Allen-Vath, Eve Castellan, Michelle Mason, Chanel Cleeton, Katie French, Liz Fichera, and MarcyKate Connolly, and so many others who read opening pages or query drafts, thank you for your time and incredible feedback. Ashley Hearn, editor extraordinaire and shining light, thank you for convincing me not to give up on this book. A huge *merci* to Natalie Blitt for her help with French translations. To Roseanne Wells, who first believed in Grace and Henry's story. For my KICK-AZ girls who read those early chapters: Kelly deVos, Riki Cleveland, Tawney Bland, and Lisa Arnseth, thank you for your constant encouragement. And of course to the AZ YA/MG community, I'm a better writer because of all of you.

One last word of note: Over the past seven years I've made some incredible friends in the writing community. No matter where I was in my journey, these friends stuck beside me and would not let me give up. For all those writers still working on their first draft, toiling in the query trenches, or waiting on that elusive "yes" while on submission, hang in there. Keep fighting. Keep writing. I'm proof your dream can come true!

About the Author

Amy Trueblood grew up in California only ten minutes from Disneyland which sparked an early interest in storytelling. As the youngest of five, she spent most of her time trying to find a quiet place to curl up with her favorite books. After graduating from the University of Arizona with a degree in journalism, she worked in entertainment in Los Angeles before returning to work in Arizona. Fueled by good coffee, and an awesome Spotify playlist, you can often find Amy working on the next post for her blog, Chasing The Crazies. *Nothing But Sky* is her first novel.

a small brown barn in the distance. A burst of wind shoved me east and I struggled to control my path. The ground became a muddy blur through my tears. The earth approached quicker than I anticipated. I didn't have time to get my feet under me. My body slammed into the hard-packed dirt, the left side taking most of the blow.

My head spun. I sat up and the ground shifted below me. Pain tore through my body and radiated down my arm. I struggled against the agony, determined to see Uncle Warren land. The Jenny disappeared behind a patch of trees at the edge of the field. I closed my eyes and prayed he'd keep the nose up and wings level when he touched down. The last thing I heard was a sharp crack before a wall of flames licked up into the bright morning sky.

He looked at the instrument panel. "We're losing altitude. You need to go. Now."

"But . . ." A sob burst past my lips. I wanted to protest. Fight him. Tell him I was going down with him. But he'd never allow it, even if he had to climb out of the cockpit and shove me off the wing himself.

He pulled my hands off the back of the cockpit chair and gave me a gentle shove.

"You did my parents proud. You are an amazing pilot and"—I choked out the final word—"father. If anyone can set this Jenny down safely, it's you." Refusing to say goodbye, I reached for his hand. "I'll see you on the ground." A sad smile covered his lips and he let me go one finger at a time.

I wrenched down the straps of my parachute and moved to the edge of the wing. The engine continued to spew hot oil into the air and then, with a stiff sputter, it cut out completely. Uncle Warren tried to control the Jenny as we dropped quicker than a breath.

In the silence I took one last look at him, trying to commit to memory every line in his face. Remembering the moments of laughter, joy, and sorrow we shared. A last breath forced itself from my chest and I jumped.

Falling through the air was like a punch to the gut. All the wind rushed out of my lungs in one heavy gasp. The wind scratched at my clothes, hair, and face like it was trying to break my fall, but the weight of my body plummeting to the ground had too much speed. I was a stone dropped from a ten-story building with nothing but the hand of God and a thin parachute keeping me from hitting the earth.

I crashed through mist and clouds, my hand fumbling for the release cord. After a single hard yank, a loud BOOM shot through the air. My head snapped back while the parachute rocketed me away from the ground.

Sobs wracked my chest as I steered toward an open field with